"I SHOULD HAVE KILLED YOU
A LONG TIME AGO . . ."

. . . he said, pressing the knife point hard against Barbara's skin. Her scream sent a surge of triumph and sexual excitement through him, an adrenaline rush not unlike the one he'd felt when he'd cut off a cat's head. *"Don't you move, or I'll kill you."*

Barbara tried to stay calm, sure he would kill her if she didn't do as he said. She had begun to fear him when she'd heard the awful stories about him killing animals. When he'd told her them, she had cried, but he'd kept telling her more and more horrible things, talking dirty, enjoying her wide-eyed repulsion and fear.

Only now he wasn't just telling her . . . he was doing them to her!

REAL HORROR STORIES!
PINNACLE TRUE CRIME

SAVAGE VENGEANCE (0-7860-0251-4, $5.99)
By Gary C. King and Don Lasseter
On a sunny day in December, 1974, Charles Campbell attacked Renae Ahlers Wicklund, brutally raping her in her own home in front of her 16-month-old daughter. After Campbell was released from prison after only 8 years, he sought revenge. When Campbell was through, he left behind the most gruesome crime scene local investigators had ever encountered.

NO REMORSE (0-7860-0231-X, $5.99)
By Bob Stewart
Kenneth Allen McDuff was a career criminal by the time he was a teenager. Then, in Fort Worth, Texas in 1966, he upped the ante. Arrested for three brutal murders, McDuff was sentenced to death. In 1972, his sentence was commuted to life imprisonment. He was paroled after only 23 years behind bars. In 1991 McDuff struck again, carving a bloody rampage of torture and murder across Texas.

BROKEN SILENCE (0-7860-0343-X, $5.99)
The Truth About Lee Harvey Oswald, LBJ,
and the Assassination of JFK
By Ray "Tex" Brown with Don Lasseter
In 1963, two men approached Texas bounty hunter Ray "Tex" Brown. They needed someone to teach them how to shoot at a moving target—and they needed it fast. One of the men was Jack Ruby. The other was Lee Harvey Oswald. . . . Weeks later, after the assassination of JFK, Ray Brown was offered $5,000 to leave Ft. Worth and keep silent the rest of his life. The deal was arranged by none other than America's new president: Lyndon Baines Johnson.

BORN
BAD

BILL G. COX

PINNACLE BOOKS
KENSINGTON PUBLISHING CORP.

PINNACLE BOOKS are published by

Kensington Publishing Corp.
850 Third Avenue
New York, NY 10022

Pinnacle and the P logo Reg. U.S. Pat. & TM Off.

First Printing: June, 1996
10 9 8 7 6 5 4 3 2

Printed in the United States of America

For Nina, my wife,
and in memory of
Christina Benjamin and Brian King

My life: It's been about chasing girls, finding the one to rape and kill. Rape is not enough. I must have a body for the next day or two, to hold, talk to, and make love. Bones to talk with. Burial sites to remember, towns in fear.

—Jason Massey

One

In the heat of the day on Thursday, July 29, 1993, Kenneth Ray Jones, a thirty-five-year-old heavy equipment operator, was running a road grader along Cutoff Road. The narrow gravel road provides a shorter route to one of the highways. Jones was concentrating on finding an old brush-cluttered dirt road that ran through the dense woods.

Sweat ran down his dust-covered face in muddy rivulets. The temperature was well over 100 degrees and the humidity was high, turning the rural spot into a sauna.

Driving an old-model grader, Jones had to stand to see ahead. Approaching a wooden bridge that spans Smith Creek, he was looking to the left, squinting through the sweat that stung his eyes. The sand and gravel company had told him to clear the old road in the woods to give its trucks a shorter route to the highway than the county road. First, though, he had to find it.

He caught a glimpse of something white that looked out of place in the lush greenery. He drove on to the bridge, then backed up for another look.

When he moved past where he had seen something, he still wasn't sure, so he backed up the old grader again.

As he drove by this time, he was assailed by a bad stench. At that moment he realized a naked human body was lying in a bare spot amid the trees and heavy brush. The overpowering reek left no doubt. It was a smell he wouldn't forget.

Backing up at full throttle to where a fellow employee was working, Jones hollered, "There's a body out there in the woods!" The two men climbed over a barbed-wire fence and walked north toward the white form on the ground.

"Gawd A'mighty!" the other worker exclaimed, as both men came to a stop. They were close enough to see that the female body had had its head and hands cut off. They ran back to the road, and while his partner remained at the fence line, Jones jumped into a pickup and sped into the little town of Telico, only three miles away. He stopped at a feed store and called the Ellis County Sheriff's Department.

The sheriff's department dispatcher in Waxahachie, which is the Ellis county seat about thirty miles south of Dallas on I-45, logged in the call at 2:56 P.M.

She scribbled on a notepad as the excited caller gave explicit directions: "You go to state highway 34, then east on farm road 1181 to Telico, then four miles to Cutoff Road, then east for about one and a quarter miles." He said he would meet the officers there.

The dispatcher radioed a signal 45 (deceased person) to deputies Victor Kemp and T. Johnson, who were riding in a patrol unit in that part of the county. When they arrived, the road workers had already cut the top strands of the barbed-wire fence to give them easier access.

It had the makings of a lazy, hot afternoon, when you wanted to sit in the shade and drink lemonade or a cold brew. Lt. Royce Gothard, a tall, sturdy ex-Marine sergeant and commander of the six-man criminal investigation division of the sheriff's office, was about to gas up his car at the county pumps when he heard the signal 45. He called the office on his mobile phone and was told a road worker had found a body out near Telico.

Gothard told the dispatcher to notify investigator Johnny

Cruz, and the lieutenant headed to the location with patrol captain Ray Stewart riding with him.

Cruz and Dep. Clint Tims had gone in Tims's car to interview a theft suspect. Cruz had learned about the body after being paged.

Tims drove Cruz back to his own car and both lawmen headed separately to the site given by the dispatcher.

Also responding was investigator Brian Thompson, the CID's evidence technician, who had just left his dentist and heard the radio traffic on the body call. He contacted Gothard, who was en route to the scene, and learned he was needed there.

When the officers parked on the side of Cutoff Road and stepped from their air-conditioned units, the steamy heat struck them like a physical force. They lashed out at swarms of buzzing mosquitoes, slapping to keep them out of eyes, noses and mouths. Within seconds their shirts were sweat-soaked. The woods on both sides of the road seemed to hold the intense wet heat like a sponge.

The CID men climbed over the barbed-wire fence and walked along a narrow trail like a tunnel through the heavy brush and trees. They ducked or pushed aside overhanging tree limbs. Ahead in a partly shaded bare spot lay the nude remains of a woman.

"Damn, she was butchered," one investigator said. The terribly mutilated body was partially on its back. The head had been cut off at the base of the neck and the hands severed at the wrists. They were nowhere in sight.

Examining the neck, the detectives could see that an exceptionally sharp knife or perhaps an ax had been used to cut off the head. The same was true of the wrists, where the hands had been severed cleanly.

She had also been eviscerated, a long cut extending from the sternum down to the pubic area. The intestines were partly out of the opening. Multiple stab and slash wounds could be seen on the thighs and in the genital area.

Both nipples were missing.

Discoloration showed that decomposition was well advanced. Pink nail polish on the left big toe gleamed in the sunlight.

The body was covered with maggots and flies.

While Thompson took photographs and Dep. Kemp shot a video of the scene, other officers spread out to search for the missing head and hands and the victim's clothing and other evidence. Gothard speculated that animals might have carried off the body parts after they had been cut off. The smoothness of the severance line showed the body parts had not been torn away by wild animals.

It was Gothard's belief that the killer had carried the head and hands away to hide them to prevent identification of the victim.

Dep. Tims walked down Cutoff Road toward the wooden bridge, which had no side rails and spanned the creek some 16 feet below. The bridge was almost 200 feet east of where the decapitated body lay.

A loud shout from Tims startled the deputies. "There's another body down here on the side of the creek!" he yelled, gesturing for his colleagues to join him.

Tims had leaned forward to look over the north side of the plank bridge for the woman's missing body parts. He had discovered the body of a fully clothed young man sprawled facedown on the bank of the creek a few feet from the water. The body lay amid brush and vines.

There was no way to reach the body without a long ladder. They called the Telico Volunteer Fire Department. A few minutes later a truck arrived and a ladder was lowered and braced against the bridge. As Gothard and Cruz descended, a large copperhead slithered from near the body into deeper brush.

Heat, mosquitoes, poisonous snakes, impenetrable undergrowth—the place was a hellhole, Gothard thought. He felt like he was dehydrating by the minute.

* * *

Because of the body's condition, it was impossible to see how the youth had died, but the gaping wound in his face indicated he might have been shot. It was impossible to tell because insects had destroyed any possible wound outline.

He was wearing faded blue jeans, a black T-shirt, white socks, and black Reebok tennis shoes. The shirt was split up to the armpit area.

After a preliminary examination and photos, the body was secured to a litter and carried up the ladder to the bridge. Nothing was found on the creek bank that appeared to be connected to the dead youth. A long-abandoned rusty portable icebox was in the water a few feet away, but it obviously had been there much longer than the body.

Gothard and Cruz believed the young victim probably had been thrown or had fallen from the bridge. Searching the pockets of the jeans, Gothard pulled out a brown leather billfold. Inside was a library card from the public library in Terrell, a town in the adjacent Kaufman County.

The card belonged to one James B. King. An older man's photograph also was in the billfold. The investigators hoped that the library card might be a lead to the victim's identity.

Whether the two deaths were linked was unknown at this point, but it certainly was probable.

Gothard told Cruz, "The thing I can't figure is why, if the same person killed them, he cut off the woman's head and hands—if he was trying to keep her from being identified—and didn't do anything like that to the boy."

They reasoned if the boy had been shot and immediately fell from the bridge, before the killer could do anything to thwart identification, the killer wouldn't have been able to get to the body any easier than they had.

Robbery was not a logical motive, since the billfold seemed to be intact, even if there wasn't any money in it, and it wouldn't have been left in the victim's pocket.

* * *

One of the first ideas to run through the minds of CID investigators was that the two victims might be connected to Dallas drug traffic violence, since the metropolis was only thirty miles away. In recent months there'd been some dumping in nearby rural areas of drug-related murder victims—snitches or rip-off druggies who'd paid the price. Yet, the officers realized, this desolate spot would be unknown to anyone except local residents, unless it had been discovered accidentally while someone was looking for a disposal spot.

Most "dumpers," as such bodies were called by homicide cops, were dumped as quickly as possible, usually in areas near well-traveled highways.

Another theory, which was raised by the almost demonic mutilation of the woman, was that some kind of cult sacrifice was involved. There had been rumors of satanic cult activities in the Ellis County area in the past, prompted by the finding of dead animals that had been stabbed, slashed, beaten, shot to death, or mutilated. The officers recalled that one or two such incidents had been investigated by the police department in Ennis.

There also could be a sexual motive behind the savage death of the woman, since the body was nude, but Gothard and Cruz leaned more to a cult ritual than a sex-driven crime because of the atrocities committed on the victim. Other speculation was that it was a vengeance killing by someone with a deep hatred toward the woman.

One thing the lawmen were sure of: the manner in which the woman was killed, possibly tortured, mutilated, disemboweled, and beheaded, was going to deeply scare area residents. People are always quick to decide that a raving maniac is on the loose and preparing to strike again, and their fears are fueled by the newspapers.

* * *

While the search continued for the head and hands, Cruz and Thompson made measurements to pinpoint the location of the bodies. From the middle of Cutoff Road to the barbed-wire line was 14 feet, 7 inches; from the fence to the woman's feet was 99 feet, 6 inches. The male's body was 284 feet from the woman, 25 feet out from the 14-foot-wide bridge.

To Cruz, it was dismal out here, a place no one would come to for a picnic outing. In the dark of night the woods would look like a setting for a horror movie. Back the other direction and near the heavy woods there were large mounds of sand near pits from which gravel had been mined. The junglelike woods consisted of hackberry trees, willows, pecan trees, thorny vines, and bindweeds, an entanglement of brush and undergrowth that wrapped around and scratched the legs of searching officers.

Add to this environmental mess swampy areas created in low spots after rains. The stagnant water was ideal for breeding mosquitoes, and poisonous reptiles inhabited the area, along with spiders, ants, and other insect life.

In the opinion of Gothard, it was a damn tough place to make a search for anything, and he had known some bad terrain in his Marine days. The lawmen had to force their way through the dense growth.

A chain saw was used to clear the way so that the litter bearing the woman's body could be taken to the gravel road, where an ambulance from a local funeral home waited. After justice of the peace J. W. Grigsby, the acting coroner, officially released the bodies, they were placed in body bags and taken to the Dallas County Medical Examiner's Office in Dallas to be autopsied. Smaller towns in North Texas frequently relied on the Dallas M.E. A group of exceptionally trained and experienced forensic pathologists on the M.E.'s staff and forensic experts from the Southwest Institute of Forensic Science (SIFS) did their work with highly technical equipment that no small-town budget could begin to match.

* * *

Gothard and Cruz agreed that a crime scene was almost nonexistent. They found no signs of a struggle, no weapons, no clothing, nothing that would speak of the victims' having been killed at the location. Could the murders have been done elsewhere and the bodies then brought to the desolate location?

CID investigators Othel "Butch" Smith, John Goss, and Tommy Payton joined the investigation and search. Later, members of the primary directed response unit of the Waxahachie Police Department also helped in the search at the scene.

While going over the site foot by foot, the county detectives discovered what appeared to be strands of blond hair entangled in the barbed-wire fence. They believed that the victim's hair had caught on the wire when the killer either forced her to go into the woods or carried her unconscious, maybe lifeless, body from the gravel road.

There was another possibility: the hair could have snagged on the fence line when the killer carried the severed head away from the scene. The hair on the wire was photographed, then the wire strands were cut loose with the hair still in place for later analysis.

During the remaining hours of daylight, the search for the missing body parts continued. It was called off as dusk turned to night. Even in bright moonlight and with powerful flashlights, the deep darkness of the inner woods was no place to be walking. There was the danger of stepping on a snake or getting a tree limb in the eye. Dep. Tims recalled later of the dark woods, "It was a darned spooky place."

The search would be resumed at daylight.

Two

Gothard and Cruz drove to their office in the modern new Ellis County Detention Center in Waxahachie to confer. They wanted to follow up on the only lead to identifying at least one victim, the library card in the brown wallet. Though the card didn't give an address, it was presumed that James B. King had been a resident of Terrell.

Cruz placed a call to the police department in Terrell. The name didn't ring a bell with local officers, but they promised to check the records when the library opened the next morning.

Cruz then phoned the Kaufman County Sheriff's Department to see if anyone there recognized the name, but the results were the same.

It had been a long day that had left the officers exhausted from the hours spent combing the woods in the intense heat. Cruz had not been home long when Gothard called him from home.

"Johnny, something just dawned on me that I don't know why I didn't think of earlier. I just remembered a couple of reports that came across my desk this morning about two kids missing from Garrett." Garrett is a small community near Ennis.

The lieutenant had called the office dispatcher to look up the reports. The missing teenagers were James Brian King, fourteen, and Christina Ann Benjamin, thirteen.

"There's a good chance they may be our victims in the woods," Gothard said. "Meet me at the office right away."

It was about 10 P.M. when Cruz reached the office, Gothard

had pulled the reports. When he had glanced at them that morning in the office, the two reports from the pile on his desk had seemed fairly routine; the lieutenant knew, from years as an investigator, that most juvenile runaways return home before an investigation can even get started.

Gothard's responsibilities included reading and assigning to the six men in the CID the offense reports on all county crimes. The reports on the missing juveniles had not stood out among the twenty-five or more of all kinds he'd read that morning.

The reports had been filed the previous day, and, following routine procedure, a missing persons bulletin had been broadcast locally and relayed to the National Information Crime Center for both state and nationwide circulation. The next step was the report's assignment to a follow-up investigator.

"The female out there looked older than a teenager," Gothard said, as he studied the reports. "But that could have been due to the bloat and decomposition. Let's go to Garrett and talk to the kids' folks." He reached into a drawer and took out the brown wallet that had been found in the boy's pocket.

The parents of the missing youngsters lived together in a house along farm road 879, about a half mile from its intersection with interstate 45, which runs through Garrett. Anyone driving through on the interstate could miss Garrett easily. Only a few homes and a service station-food store were lighted up at the late hour.

Gothard pulled into the driveway of an old-fashioned house with a wooden front porch covered by a roof. A trailer and a boat were parked in the yard. It was a comfortable home, nothing fancy, and the lights were on inside.

Gothard knocked, and a heavy-set black-haired man opened the front door partway. Gothard recognized him as the man in the photograph in the slain boy's wallet. When the officers identified themselves, the man invited them in, saying he was James King, the father of Brian King. He introduced Donna Brown, the mother of Christina Benjamin.

From the earlier missing persons report Gothard knew the

couple were living in a common-law marriage relationship. Along with Brian and Christina, an eight-year-old sister of Christina's also lived there.

Bringing the tragic news of violent death to family members always had been the part of Gothard's job that he hated and felt inadequate doing. He never knew how to put it, except to get it over with. There was no good way to tell people news this bad.

"I'm sorry to tell you this, but we think that two bodies found near Telico this afternoon may be Brian and Christina," the lieutenant said. "We're not sure about the girl, but this wallet was in the boy's pocket." He handed it to James King, who blinked as tears came to his eyes. The girl's mother began crying.

"It's Brian's," the father said. "I gave it to him. That's my picture in it."

The two investigators silently waited for the parents to compose themselves before continuing.

"I'm sorry," Gothard said. "We haven't identified the girl for sure, but we're pretty certain it's her." He didn't want to explain that her head and hands had not been found; there'd be time enough later for the gruesome fact to come out. He explained that the bodies had been taken to the Dallas County Medical Examiner's Office and asked if there were any past injuries or marks that would help make a positive identification.

The crying mother remembered that Christina had received an ankle injury in May, when she'd come down wrong while jumping on a trampoline. She had been taken to the Ennis hospital and an X ray had been made.

The officers asked if Christina had a comb or brush that might contain samples of her hair. The teen's hairbrush was turned over to the detectives.

Gothard and Cruz did not want to press the questioning of the grieving parents at this late hour. From reading the initial missing reports, they knew that James King had last seen his son sometime after midnight on Tuesday, July 27, when a car's honking twice had awakened him. He'd looked out his bedroom window and seen a car's taillights passing by.

A few minutes later, when he looked out again, a car was about even with his mailbox. Its headlights were off, its parking lights on. He'd gone to the front door and stood watching the small four-door light-colored car in his driveway.

Brian, who had been sleeping in a hammock outside, was leaning over and talking to someone in the car. James King had been able to see someone in the back seat who had "long, fuzzy" blond hair. The father had left the door to go to the bathroom. As he'd walked back to his bedroom, he'd heard a car take off as if the driver was in a big hurry. Glancing out the dining room window, he'd seen the taillights leaving. He'd gone outside to speak to Brian, but he wasn't there. *Probably went for a short ride with friends,* he'd thought, not all that unusual for a boy on a hot summer night. He had wished Brian hadn't gone, but he probably would be back shortly. He never stayed out long at night.

King had had no reason to check on Christina, who he'd known was asleep in her bedroom with her little sister. It was the next morning before they'd found that Christina was gone and Brian had not returned.

There wasn't much to go on. It was nearing 3 A.M. when Gothard and Cruz left the parents, mentioning they would be back for a more detailed interview later that day. The two officers knew there would be little sleep for them the rest of the night.

Three

Only a few pickups were angle-parked on Waxahachie's town square at 6:30 A.M. when Johnny Cruz drove along Main Street toward his office in the detention center. The Townhouse, a restaurant across from the historic courthouse, was getting its first coffee and breakfast customers. Already the morning was hot.

Cruz figured the square would be overflowing soon with people wanting to hear the latest on the murders, including an influx of newspaper and television newspeople from Dallas. It was the biggest story to break in Waxahachie since the hullabaloo when Waxahachie was chosen for the site of the superconducting supercollider and the later refusal by Congress to provide funds for the project.

Now the shocking double murder case was drawing wide attention fast, and there wasn't much to tell the district attorney's office, much less reporters. Cruz knew one thing for sure: it was the kind of case that would have people on edge and start all sorts of wild rumors. Especially since in past weeks there had been talk about possible satanic cult rituals and animal mutilations in the county.

Cruz and the rest of the CID investigators were accustomed to the relative quiet of small-town law enforcement. Murders were not completely unknown, and they had occasional drunken brawls or family fights, but never a freakish homicide of this magnitude.

***

Gothard came in early and made arrangements by phone for a special team with trained cadaver dogs to help with the hunt for body parts. He instructed Brian Thompson to pick up the medical records and the X ray of Christina's injured ankle from Baylor Medical Hospital in Ennis and deliver them to the Dallas Medical Examiner's Office, where a comparison X ray would be taken in hopes of making a positive identification. The hairs from Christina's brush would be submitted for laboratory analysis and comparison with the hair found on the barbed-wire fence.

Before going to the woods to join the renewed search, Gothard and Cruz talked again with the teenagers' parents.

James King and Donna Brown looked as if they hadn't slept at all, which was understandable. Recounting events on the night the teenagers had vanished, the distraught couple said they had delayed making the missing persons report until Wednesday evening, the day before the bodies were discovered.

Brian and Christina had been well-behaved kids. They'd never run away before. King and Brown had wanted to give them time to return, which they kept thinking would happen at any moment, before they set off a full-scale police search.

The girl's mother said that before she went to bed that night she'd looked into the girls' bedroom.

"I sent Christina to bed at 10 P.M. I checked on them before I went to bed at ten-thirty, and they were both sound asleep."

The next morning, when they'd learned that Christina and Brian were not at home, the mother had been in a dilemma. She was worried, but like James King, she thought the kids would be back that morning.

"I was trying to get to work, and I took my other daughter to a friend's house to watch her and I went to work," she said. "When I came back at lunchtime, they still weren't there, and I went looking for both of them. I looked until dark."

Then she had gone to the Ennis Police Department to make

a missing persons report. A sheriff's deputy happened to be there, so she filled out two reports, one for the Ennis police and one for the sheriff's department, and the teenagers' pictures were faxed out.

The mother and father looked every place they could think of in Ennis and in Palmer, calling or personally contacting friends of the pair. Brian and Christina frequently would walk down the road to the One-Stop store and service station to get a soft drink. The store was a hangout for kids of the tiny community, about the only place they had to get together during summer vacation. None of the clerks remembered seeing them on the night of July 26-27, or since.

Christina's little sister remembered that Brian had come into the girls' bedroom and awakened Christina. He'd told her, "Come on and let's go, before somebody wakes up," the child said.

Her eyes were shut at the time and she had not seen what Christina was wearing when she left; she had been sleeping in a large white T-shirt and white shorts.

Christina was described as 5 feet, 7 inches tall, 140 pounds, pretty, with blond hair and blue eyes. Brian King was wearing denim shorts, dark tennis shoes, and no shirt when last seen by his dad. The boy was 5 feet, 9 inches, weighed 145 pounds, and had brown hair and brown eyes.

Cruz noticed that the shorts were not what Brian was wearing when he was found. The boy must have changed into regular jeans at some point before leaving the house.

James King recalled that the car he'd seen leave had headed in the direction of the tiny town of Bristol. Brian was known to have friends there and in Palmer. King mentioned Stephen Baker, a school pal of Brian's. He and Donna Brown gave the names of several other youths who either Brian or Christina knew, but they could think of no person or any incident in the lives of the teenagers that might be linked to their slayings.

* * *

Christina's father was Chris Allen Benjamin, a 6'4" man. Her mother Donna had met and married him while living in her native state of New York. Chrissy, as she was called by her relatives and friends, was born on August 30, 1979, at Auburn Memorial Hospital in Auburn, New York. She was a pretty, smiling baby and remained a happy, active girl throughout her short life.

Her parents separated when Christina was about five. In 1985, she went with her mother to live in Texas. A year later, Donna called her mother, Jeane Bellows, and asked if Chrissy could visit her New York grandparents during Easter. The Bellowses were more than eager to have her visit. She flew to New York by herself, a sweet little kid who won the hearts of the flight attendants watching over her.

Her grandmother recalled how Chrissy enjoyed playing in the snow that still was on the ground at Easter, something rare that time of year in Texas. Jeane Bellows had many memories of Christina as a baby in New York and had talked with her by phone after the move to Texas.

Chrissy was ten when she, her mother, and her younger sister and brother had visited the Bellowses at a campground they had purchased on a lake in New York. Christina went for a visit again in 1992.

"I was amazed at the change," Mrs. Bellows said. "I couldn't believe the difference. She was twelve, and in that two years she had absolutely grown up."

She was being called Christina now, not Chrissy.

That was her last visit with her grandparents. Only a year later the Bellowses would go to Texas for the funeral of the girl they loved so much.

Chrissy was buried in the family plot in New York, only about a half mile from where her parents had been living when she was a baby. One side of the grave marker carries the inscription *Christina Ann Benjamin, 1979-1993,* and a color photograph of her, and on the other side are the words "Granddaughter of Fred and Jeane Bellows."

* * *

In the summer of 1993 Christina was looking forward with schoolgirl excitement to her freshman year at Ennis High School, beginning in September. She would have been in the ninth grade, a freshman. Christina was energetic and eager in all school activities,

She played a flute in the school band at Ennis Junior High School. She was a member of the Ennis Lady Lions basketball and volleyball teams. In junior high she participated in track. She liked to run. Those who knew her from the time she was a small child said that Christina never walked anywhere—she ran. She was a highly popular girl who made friends easily, and an excellent student who received top marks.

During that last summer of Christina's life her mother was working and Christina spent much of her time babysitting her younger sister. Occasionally she would spend a night at a girlfriend's house.

Lately Brian King had been saying he was bored, with nothing much to do. He seemed to be in the late-summer doldrums, with the beginning of the new school term and his fifteenth birthday only a few days away. He was getting anxious for the fall term to begin.

Brian had been living with his dad at Garrett for three weeks. Before that, he had been with his mother, Patricia King, in Terrell for five years. His birthplace was nearby Dallas, where he'd been born on September 3, 1978.

Brian enjoyed outdoor activities: camping, fishing, and riding his bicycle in the open country. He had artistic talent and spent time sketching, everything from outdoor scenes to people and animals. He and his dad had camped out when they could, and at present they were working together getting a boat in good shape.

Everyone enjoyed Brian's company. The skinny, fair-complected teen was cheerful and fun to be around. He wanted to be a comedian when he grew up. His folks joked that he was always trying his routine on them. He was good with imitations of celebrities.

He was a good student, well liked by his teachers and school-mates, active in school organizations and civic groups. He had been chief ruler of the Terrell Junior Odd Fellows, which was affiliated with the adult organization and he had helped with fund-raising drives.

It was totally unexpected that either Brian or Christina would leave the house at a late hour with someone in a car, which was apparently what they had done on that fateful night. The two youngsters had become close friends, almost like brother and sister, which most people thought they were. They liked to walk together to the nearby One-Stop for a Coke or a snack, to laugh together, and to talk about serious things together.

They died together at the hands of a brutal and obviously depraved killer on a lonely rural road on a bright moonlit night in the springtime of their lives.

Four

Most of the members of the criminal investigation division of the Ellis County Sheriff's Department had been born and reared not far from where they now served. They liked their jobs and worked well together as a unit.

The CID office is in the modern Ellis County Detention Center, built in 1990 to replace the old, outdated jail. Like the jail inmates, the criminal investigators work behind locked doors, admitted only after clearing the dispatcher in a glassed-in cubicle in the lobby.

Despite their proximity to Dallas, the CID men in Waxahachie have retained small-town friendliness and casual working manners, and the usual give-and-take war humor of any homicide squad room. However on this Friday, the atmosphere was one of dead seriousness and ringing phones. At a press conference Gothard had made an appeal to the public for any information that might help solve the murders of the two teenagers. Many of the tips were far out, but a number of them had to be checked fully. CID was getting many more tips than it had personnel.

The search that blanketed the woods and side roads and old abandoned buildings with the cadaver dogs and their trainers had yielded nothing, neither the missing body parts nor new clues.

Gothard had hopes the autopsies would produce some leads. The forensic people in Dallas had made a positive identification of the girl using the ankle X ray taken in May. Forensic anthropologists' identification of a victim through the study of bone structure is as positive as fingerprints are.

Tentatively, the crime scientists had also microscopically matched hair from Christina's hairbrush with the blond hair strands caught on the barbed-wire fence.

Gothard knew the investigation would take an around-the-clock effort to come up with the killer. He was the most experienced investigator in the office. Born in the little farm community of Palmer, Texas, in 1937, he returned to Ellis County after a four-year hitch in the Marines.

He had worked for the local police in Waxahachie and Midlothian and the federal inspector general's office before joining the Ellis County Sheriff's Department in 1988. He was promoted to lieutenant and placed in charge of the CID in 1991.

Although he had seen some bad homicide cases over the years, nothing matched the savageness and depravity of this case.

Gothard had confidence in the growing abilities of Johnny Cruz, a pleasant young man with a penchant for detail. He assigned Cruz as the lead investigator in the murders.

Cruz was also a native of the county and had never worked outside county borders. Born in 1956 in Bardwell, he'd had to drop out of high school to help support the family when his father had fallen ill with cancer.

After he married, he obtained his G.E.D. and became a reserve officer on the Ferris Police Department before joining the Ellis County Sheriff's Department. He was assigned to the CID as an investigator in 1991, and he felt he had found his niche. His easy manner helped when he questioned a suspect, and, as Gothard had noticed, he was a born stickler for investigative details.

The CID investigators had known from the time they'd first viewed the girl's decapitated and sexually mutilated corpse that they were seeking a twisted kind of killer none of the agents had encountered before. In fact, with the exception of the more experienced Gothard, none had ever been involved in a major homicide probe.

Dr. Sheila Spotswood, a pathologist in the Dallas Medical Examiner's Office, did the autopsies. In her written report, the impact of the gruesome pathological details was lessened somewhat by the medical language. The report pointed to a killer with extremely aberrant drives and appetites unusual in most sexual slayings, if sex was indeed a motive. The savage butchering of the girl was more indicative of vengeance and extreme hatred.

Because of the deterioration of tissues resulting from the girl's body having been exposed to the severe summer temperatures for two or three days, it was impossible to establish if she had been subjected to forced sexual intercourse or sodomized. Vaginal and anal swabs were no help.

Her head and neck had been severed at the base of the neck through the lower half of the thyroid cartilage. The skin edges had some sharp jags, indicating a sawing component to the decapitation. The wrists had been severed through the joint spaces, leaving smooth margins of skin and not cutting through any bones. It would have taken some force to slice through the wrists, the report said. One wrist also bore discolorations that could have been caused by handcuffs, the pathologist believed.

There also was a bruise on her right breast measuring three inches long and a half inch wide. Both of the nipples had been slashed off deeply, and there was a smaller incised wound on the left breast and smaller cuts toward the front of the breast. A few cuts were scattered over the left upper part of the chest, one on the left shoulder, and there was a cluster of stab wounds six inches deep.

The abdomen had been opened with three long, deep cuts through the abdominal wall, the largest a vertical line resembling a surgical incision extending from the lower chest down the front of the body to the lower abdomen. There was a deep eleven-inch gash on the lower left abdomen, parallel to the upper end of the vertical midline incision, and the upper abdomen had a three-inch-long incision exposing the intestines. Extending in multiple directions were smaller and more superficial cuts. The pathologist found six stabs wounds into organs inside the stomach, apparently made by reaching through the larger stomach opening. The stab wounds perforated the liver and went through all the way to the back wall of the chest.

Numerous knife or "sharp object" wounds were found on the girl's inner thighs, pubic, genital, and posterior areas. Six cuts had penetrated about one and one-half inches deep into the muscles of both thighs. There was a two-inch-long, one-inch-deep cut in the genital area adjacent to the right labia of the vagina, but neither the labia nor the vagina were cut.

Another shallow cut extended from the front of the left hip all the way down the side of the hip to the ankle. "She had some bruises probably inflicted while she was alive," said the doctor. "There was a one-inch bruise on the left leg eight inches from the bottom of the hip."

There was a bullet wound, not much more than a flesh wound, in Christina's upper right back, and a slug, thought to be .22 caliber, was recovered in the muscle.

Any number of the knife wounds, aside from the decapitation, could have been fatal, according to the pathological findings. But it was believed that several of the more serious wounds were inflicted after death.

The autopsy on Brian King's body revealed that he had died from two gunshot wounds to the head.

One slug entered the left scalp four inches from the top of his head and slightly above and behind the left ear. The range from which the bullet had been fired could not be determined because of lack of gunshot residue. The other gunshot was to the youth's left face. No exact entrance wound was visible because of a large, irregular gap caused by insect larvae activity. Two large fragments of one broken small-caliber copper-wash bullet—also thought to be .22 caliber—were recovered. There were no other injuries on Brian's body.

It was Charles Lynch's day off when he was summoned to the pathology lab where the autopsies were being done. Lynch is a trace evidence analyst for the SIFS. He knew his role would be important in this case because the body probably had been dumped where it was found and evidence to link the killing to the killer would be negligible.

When Lynch arrived at the lab, the first thing he asked for were the shoes of the victims. Christina's had never been found, but he took Brian King's shoes into a nearby operating room and looked at them first with his naked eyes under the bright surgical light. He spotted a tiny fiber barely attached to the side of the right shoe at the junction of the sole. It was very loosely in place within a crack on the side of the shoe. If the wearer of the shoe had taken only one or two steps, the fiber would have come off.

The boy had taken few if any steps after the fiber had adhered to his shoe; the evidence technician was sure of that. After all the activity in recovering the body and placing it in an ambulance and bringing it to Dallas, it was a miracle that the fiber was still on the shoe.

He carefully removed the fiber with tweezers, put it on a piece of tape, and transferred it to a glass slide for examination beneath a powerful microscope. Lynch knows a whole lot about all types of fibers from the hundreds of possible sources that exist. It is one of his specialities and he has made detailed studies, at times under the tutoring of FBI crime scientists.

Almost immediately he decided that he was looking at a carpet fiber, and it was not nylon, which he was used to seeing in carpet fibers. In his opinion, its origin probably had been a tan-colored carpet; one possibility was that it had come from a Japanese-manufactured vehicle. He had seen this type fiber, though infrequently, on the carpets in Japanese cars.

He made arrangements for enlargement photos to be taken of the fiber that would show its color and texture in full detail. Unknowingly, Lynch had just wrapped up what was perhaps to be the most vital piece of trace evidence linking the killer to the crime.

Five

It seemed like the summer heat wave would never break. Johnny Cruz hoped the same wasn't true of the murder case that was now occupying all his waking hours and keeping him from getting much sleep. He was thankful that his wife was a reserve officer herself and understood the hours a cop puts in.

Cruz drove to Palmer to talk to one of the kids whose name had been given by the parents of the slain teenagers. He rang the front doorbell of a modern, brick home and a woman came to the door. He asked to speak to Stephen Baker. The woman was the boy's mother and she asked, "Is there some kind of problem?"

Johnny told her he only wanted to talk to Stephen, since he'd been a friend of Brian King's, to see if he knew anything that might help with the case. Kids often share their problems with their pals when they won't tell anyone else.

Stephen wasn't home, but his mother promised to have him get in touch with Cruz as soon as possible. He told her Stephen could call him or come to the sheriff's office.

Later, when the youth showed up at the CID office, Cruz asked if he was a friend of Brian King and Christina Benjamin. Stephen said he knew Christina, but he was more familiar with Brian.

"We spent a lot of time together, me and Brian," the boy said sadly. "I don't know anything about what happened to him, but I'm sure sorry it happened." The youth said he had been shocked by news of the murders, but he had no idea who might have done it, or why. Brian never did anything to make anyone mad at him, Stephen said. He just could not believe he had been killed, and Christina, too.

"Do you know any other friends of Brian's?" the detective asked. He said he didn't know who else Brian and Christina might have run with. Cruz thanked him for coming in and told him to be sure and call if he thought of anything or heard anything.

As Stephen got up to leave, he paused. "I don't know if this would have anything to do with it or not, but Brian and I gave a statement to the Palmer Police Department about a burglary that we had information on. We didn't have anything to do with it, but we heard some stuff we thought the police ought to know."

Later, Cruz dropped by the police station in Palmer and talked to the officer who had taken the boys' statements.

It turned out to be a minor burglary, nothing that would have brought retaliation against Brian for talking to the police, Cruz felt.

On Saturday, Johnny Cruz was relaxing at home before going back to work. The Ennis dispatcher, Norma Robertson, phoned to tell him an anonymous male caller had said, "The one you're looking for that killed those kids is Jason Massey. He's the guy you need to investigate. He lives in Canton." Then he hung up.

Cruz had intended to drive to Ennis to locate the other youths who had been mentioned when he and Gothard had talked to the parents. "I'll drive over and talk to you," he told the dispatcher. He doubted there was much more the dispatcher could tell him, but then again, somebody in the Ennis P.D. might have an idea.

Cruz talked to the dispatcher and to Det. Ron Roark about the murders in the woods. "I need to find a couple of boys who live here," Cruz said. "Do you know a kid named Mark Gentry?"

"Yeah, I know him," Roark said. "He was arrested for un-authorized use of an automobile. He's in jail now."

Roark had Gentry brought to an interrogation room. The eighteen-year-old had been in previous trouble—nothing seri-ous, but he was in the system. Cruz saw that he had blond hair. He was sullen, but he answered Cruz's questions.

He said he knew Brian King and Christina Benjamin.

"Do you have any idea who might have done this?" Cruz asked.

Gentry looked down, then up. "No, not really."

"What's that mean?"

"Well, I know this guy that's kind of strange—Jason Massey. He's always talking about killing women, and he cuts off cat and dog heads." Gentry half smiled. "I remember one time he was talking to this dead cat in a plastic bag he had in his car, like it was alive." He said he had run around with Massey when Jason had lived in Ennis. He thought he was living in Canton, Texas, now.

After asking some more questions, Cruz asked Gentry if he would give a statement. He agreed. The statement read:

"On or about July 17, 1993, I was at home talking to Chris Nowlin [another buddy] about this guy (he mentioned the name Ron) cutting me on my left arm and the left side of my chest. Then Nowlin started talking about how Massey and himself was supposed to go to Christina Benjamin's residence on July 16, 1993, approximately midnight, and honk the horn twice. Christina was to meet them at the service station on state 879 and I-45.

"Chris Nowlin told me that Jason Massey was talking about he wanted to take Christina Benjamin out and kill her. Chris said he told Jason he wanted no part of that because he was dating Christina.

"One time when I was riding around with Jason Massey through back roads drinking beer, Jason kept pointing out places and saying, 'Those would be good places to hide a dead body.' I also know Jason Massey would cut the heads off cats and dogs.

Jason called these animal heads his 'trophies.' Jason had all animal heads stored in a red rusty metal cooler. On or about July 18, 1993, while at Lake Bardwell, Jason Massey told me if I hear about a serial killer around the Ennis area, not to worry about anything because it would be him."

It was a weird story. Cruz wondered if Gentry was just spouting off, trying to get somebody he didn't like in trouble. Massey sounded weird enough to be the type of killer they were hunting, but arrests aren't made on the word of a subject in jail and charged with a crime himself. He needed to talk to Chris Nowlin, whose address he had gotten from Gentry.

Roark accompanied Cruz and they found Nowlin at home. Cruz told him he was interested in learning more about Jason Massey, and Nowlin agreed to accompany the officers to the police station and tell what he knew.

Nowlin said he was not dating Christina Benjamin but had known her for some time. "She was just a friend. She used to write me when I was away from home, you know."

He had gotten into some juvenile trouble and was confined for a while by the Texas Youth Commission in a halfway house in Dallas. When he returned to Ennis, he and Christina would see each other, but it was not a "boyfriend-girlfriend" relationship; they were just friends.

On July 15, only about two weeks before, Nowlin and Jason Massey had been riding around most of the day. They had been drinking and smoking some weed, he continued.

"Most of the people we knew were not at home, so I said we could go see Christina. It was about 8 P.M. We parked in front of her house. Jason was driving, and she and her brother came out to the car and talked to us. On the way over there, Jason asked me how old she was and I told him about fourteen. Sitting there in the car, he asked her how old she was, and she said something like, 'How old do I look?', and he said eighteen, nineteen, or twenty, and was flirting with her, you know. They decided she was going to sneak out later with Jason and me. He was going to honk the horn twice and she was going to go to the old Fina station down the road to meet us. We was going to go by and pick her and her brother up and cruise around and go riding."

But they'd never kept the rendezvous. After leaving Christina's, they had gone over to Gentry's house.

"Everything was cool and set up, and that night Mark got cut. We had been smoking primos (marijuana laced with cocaine) and doing lots of coke at this dude's house, then we went to Mark's. I was sick, puking and stuff, and I passed out before we got to Mark's house. I kinda remember. Jason tried to take me out of the front seat and put me in the back . . . couldn't do it. Jason and Mark were going to cruise around. Mark went to the side of his house to use the rest room, take a leak, you know, and someone grabbed him from behind and cut him across his chest. Then he fell and they cut him across his arm. Mark had to go to the hospital."

According to Nowlin, as they'd driven away earlier from Christina's place, Massey had said that Christina was cute. "He said he would like to fuck her, kill her, cut her pussy lips off, fry them, and eat them. I didn't pay much attention to it then, you know; it was weird.

"Jason always was saying some way-out stuff. Jason talks a lot about killing women. I always figured he was just blowing air. We was usually drinking or doing coke or something at the time, and riding around. You know how guys do."

Nowlin agreed to make a signed statement.

After dropping Nowlin back at his home, Cruz and Roark discussed Jason Massey. Roark was familiar with him, as well as Gentry and Nowlin. None of them had a good background.

Ennis police officers had handled Massey for minor incidents in the past, including driving under the influence, and once he'd been questioned about the killing and mutilation of a calf. Before that, when Massey was younger, he had been investigated about stalking and harassing a young schoolgirl over a long period of time. He was a juvenile then and there wasn't much they could do legally, other than give him a good talking to. They had also notified juvenile authorities in Dallas, where Massey had been living when some of the harassment had taken place.

Massey had been placed on probation after pleading guilty in the driving under the influence case.

Roark pulled the incident reports concerning Massey's run-ins with the Ennis police. The most recent had occurred not many days before the murders.

Officer Thompson Hart had stopped the driver of a tan Subaru on suspicion of drunken driving after police had received several calls on the car. Jason Massey was the driver. After he was asked to step from the car, Hart spotted what appeared to be a small amount of marijuana on the driver's seat. On the floorboard he saw a white Persian cat with a rope around its neck; the cat was alive. A three-pronged knife lay on the floorboard on the passenger's side.

Patrolman Esidro Lopez pulled up at the scene to assist Hart. The officers got Massey's permission to search the vehicle more thoroughly. Inside the trunk they discovered what Hart described as a "book, diary type, with different people's names in it, and check marks, stars of some type, by the names."

The patrolmen also examined "a small black book." Inside this "satanic bible" was a list of girls' names, at least one of whom was recognized by the officers as a young Ennis girl.

The car trunk also contained a three-bladed ax, another ax, a hatchet, a claw hammer, and a large knife. Massey didn't try to explain the cat with the rope around its neck. None of the items in the car was illegal except the marijuana, which eventually proved not to be a strong enough case to file.

Massey was booked for suspicion of intoxication.

Patrolman Hart had another call in which Jason Massey was questioned. The dispatcher had put out a call near 4 A.M. that someone was reporting a man in a closed McDonald's. When Hart arrived at the scene, he and the other officers responding spotted a white male wearing a black jumpsuit with a hood over his head running east from the restaurant. The man got away.

Searching in the area in an easterly direction, the officers came upon a dead and mutilated calf. The patrolmen found a bloody bracelet with the name "Jason" on it and a short-sleeved white T-shirt. Nearby was a beige-colored four-door Subaru registered to Jason Massey.

According to Patrolman Hart, Massey went to the police station with his mother later that morning. No charges were filed in the incident, with the exception of the intoxication charge, because of insufficient evidence.

Roark also gave Cruz the name and address of the schoolgirl who had been terrorized for several years by Massey.

Cruz thanked Roark for all the help and headed back to fill in Gothard on what he had learned. Gentry and Nowlin would need further checking and could not be discounted at this time, but Jason Massey had become the leading suspect.

As Cruz followed up on the dispatcher's anonymous caller's tip, Lt. Royce Gothard returned alone to the crime scene that Saturday. He wanted to go over the spot once more, to be satisfied that some small clue had not been overlooked during the bush-beating search operations of the past two days.

Nothing had changed. The heat and humidity still were like a blast of hot steam when he stepped from the coolness of his car. He felt a slight tightening in his chest, but it only lasted seconds. He guessed he was beginning to feel the long hours in the heat, and the lack of sleep.

Gothard made his way to the spot where the decapitated girl had been found. It was a lonely, sour-smelling place; the closeness of the underbrush and woods seemed to make it hard to breathe.

He could hear some passing vehicles behind him on the road—curious sightseers, drawn by the murders, had increased the traffic along Cutoff Road.

Gothard knelt down, took out his pocketknife, and began digging in the ground where the girl's head would have been before the decapitation. He thought there was a strong possibility that the killer had fired other shots besides the one that hit the girl in the back. If he'd shot her the first time as she was running away, it followed he might shoot her again, maybe a coup de grâce, as she lay wounded on the ground. Gothard hoped to find a slug or shell embedded in the damp earth.

He dug up a clod, then saw it looked like a lock of blond hair attached to a small chunk of clotted blood. The discovery convinced Gothard that the girl's head had been cut off at that exact spot, as she'd lain on the ground. She could already have been dead. He hoped to God she was.

When he returned to his car a few minutes later, he placed the clotted hair in an envelope and drove to the CID office. The hair would be delivered to the forensic lab in Dallas for comparison with the hair from the barbed-wire fence and from Christina Benjamin's hairbrush.

Six

Monday morning was always a busy time at the Ellis County Courthouse. It was the day everybody played catch-up from the weekend. The red granite and sandstone structure was built almost a hundred years before and loomed like a Romanesque castle in the center of the Waxahachie town square.

Among those preparing for a busy day was Clay Strange, assistant prosecutor in the 40th Judicial District Attorney's Office on the third floor. Today, the district attorney's staff was conducting a class on Texas's ever-changing juvenile laws for county juvenile officers and others from police agencies in the area who worked juvenile cases.

The forty-six-year-old Strange was a studious-looking and pleasant-mannered man whose mild appearance was deceiving, as many a defense attorney could attest. He was recognized by his legal peers as a sharp, tough fighter in the courtroom, strong as a prosecutor. He frequently was called upon by his boss, District Attorney Joe Grubbs, to handle trial duties.

Lt. Royce Gothard and investigator Johnny Cruz arrived at the courthouse and told Strange they needed to get an arrest warrant for a suspect in the murders of Christina Benjamin and Brian King.

The entire county was shaken up and talking about the horrible killings, and Strange was surprised but very glad that the investigation had reached this point. When he and the district attorney's investigator, Phillip Martin, had gone to the location where the bodies had been found last Thursday afternoon, the prospects for an arrest any time soon had seemed dim.

Strange told the investigators to have a seat in his office and informed his colleagues they would have to conduct the class without him. The warrant would take time to prepare.

The three men sat around Strange's desk and Cruz outlined the information they'd gathered that pointed to Jason Eric Massey, twenty, formerly of Ennis and now living in Canton, Texas, as the suspected killer of the two teenagers.

Along with the arrest warrant, the CID men wanted to get an evidentiary search warrant. They believed they would find stuff in Massey's residence and automobile that would strengthen the case they already had.

Cruz handed over the statements from Mark Gentry and Chris Nowlin about the remarks made by Massey and his voiced intention of wanting to rape and "kill women" and mutilate their bodies. The remarks seemed to be partly consistent with the autopsy results on the body of Christina Benjamin.

Massey had met both teenagers at their Garrett home only ten days before their slayings. He had planned to pick them up at a late hour that same night after driving by and honking twice, a signal for them to go to the nearby all-night One-Stop food store, where he would stop for them. It was the same signal and plan presumably used on the fatal night, except they apparently had entered his car at their house. Massey's car generally matched the vehicle that Brian King's father had seen pulling away from his residence the night the teens had vanished.

Moreover, the detective explained, a carpet fiber found on the boy's shoe probably had come from the carpet in Massey's Japanese-made car. Buddies of Massey familiar with his car told Cruz the carpet was tan or light brown.

Cruz told the assistant D.A. about the Ennis incident a few days before the murders when Massey was stopped by officers who found a live cat with a rope around its neck in his car and several possible weapons in the trunk that could have been used later in the decapitation and mutilation of the girl.

Cruz had located two sisters who knew Massey and said he had been in town on July 26. Massey had visited the girls at their house about 6:30 P.M. He later went to McDonald's, where one of the girls worked, and talked to her during her evening break. He left about 11:15 P.M.

That put the suspect only a few miles from the home of Christina and Brian a short time before they'd apparently left in a light-colored car.

The girl at the fast-food restaurant recalled Massey had been drinking beer and acting strangely.

There was also the anonymous call to the Ennis police dispatcher saying that Jason Massey was the one who should be investigated, that he'd actually talked about wanting to kill and mutilate Christina Benjamin.

"It is possible we might find the weapons that killed these kids in this guy's house or car," said Cruz. "And it wouldn't surprise me if he has the girl's body parts and clothing stashed away somewhere. We know from witnesses that he kept the heads of the animals he killed for trophies."

Strange conceded the investigators had enough circumstances to justify a warrant for Massey's arrest. Unfortunately, searching Massey's residence and car was going to be more complicated. It required an evidentiary search warrant, which was far more involved than the usual search warrant for contraband. Strange said he had prepared only one such warrant in all the time he had been with the office, and would need to follow the style of a similar warrant written by a predecessor.

Studying the warrant from the past, he noticed that any writings of a defendant—including diaries or letters—were evidence that could be hunted under the warrant. This was vitally important to the current investigation: if Massey had killed the youngsters, he fit the profile of killers who were inclined to write with egoism and pride about their misdeeds, keeping journals or letters.

Cruz glanced at his watch. He and Gothard were worried that

Massey might run before a warrant could be served. Massey's home in Canton was about an hour's drive east of Waxahachie.

The Canton police had given Cruz the address and a description of the house, a one-story red brick home with a white roof and an attached open carport—enough information to put in the search warrant. They also said Massey's tan 1982 Subaru bearing license tag Texas 270 XVG was parked in the driveway.

As time dragged on and Strange worked on the search warrant, Gothard phoned Van Zandt County Sheriff Pat Jordan and requested his department keep the address under surveillance until the Ellis County officers could get there. Once there, they still needed to get a local judge to sign the warrant. Justice was grinding too slowly, Cruz thought.

Strange, between thumbing through law books, was working as fast as possible on the warrant, making sure everything was covered. They wanted the warrant to be all-inclusive, to cover any possible evidence that might be found, and it was beginning to read like a discount store order catalogue. It asked for the authority "to search the house, outbuildings, mobile home, trailers, etc. . . . front, sides, back yards . . . for any items that might constitute a weapon used in the commission of the offense, including axes, hatchets, knives, bayonets, saws, letter openers, screwdrivers, any other sharp-pointed objects or tools; any and all firearms, pistols, rifles, shotguns; any items that might constitute evidence of offenses involving assault, sexual assaults, mutilation, abuse, cruelty to animals, obscenity, pornography, sexual performance; any or all books and publications, journals on child abuse, sexual abuse, murder, capital murder, or kidnapping."

Also, "any books, journals, pamphlets, magazines, photographs, pornographic papers, film, negatives, registered correspondence, catalogues having to do with pornography, and sexual acts, satanic culture, satanic acts, satanic slayings, membership in satanic organizations or serial murders or multiple killings, correspondence, diaries or any other writings, tape recordings or letters related to any juvenile or adult which would show identity of same engaged in any kind of sexual conduct between juveniles and adults. . . ." The list went on and on.

At last the warrant was being typed by a secretary when Strange, still flipping through law books and case histories, exclaimed: "Oh, damn. This can wreck the whole warrant."

In article 1802 of the Texas Code of Criminal Procedure, adopted in 1975 by the state legislature, he read that "the warrant does not apply to the personal writings of the defendant." That clause had been inserted as part of a compromise between state prosecutors and defense attorneys, necessary to get the bill passed; any "personal writings" were out.

Looking for loopholes, Strange hoped the intent might be that "personal writings" would be allowable if they weren't specifically mentioned in the warrant, but he found one case that shot down that idea.

Finally the warrant was finished with what Strange hoped was legal phrasing on safe ground. The arrest warrant was signed and issued by District Judge Gene Knize at 5 P.M.

Strange, Gothard, and Cruz, D.A. investigator Phillip Martin, and CID investigators Brian Thompson, Butch Smith, and Clint Tims piled into their cars and headed to Canton.

After being alerted by the Ellis County sheriff's officers, Van Zandt County Sheriff Pat Jordan personally headed the surveillance of Massey's red brick house on Big Rock Road. One of the county jailers lived next door to the house and Jordan and his chief deputy parked in the jailer's yard.

As the afternoon wore on, the officers observed several people leave the house and drive off. From the description they had been given of Jason Massey, the watching officers were sure that none of those leaving was the murder suspect.

While they waited, a young boy rode from the yard of the house on a bicycle and pedaled by the officers sitting in the sheriff's car. He looked at them closely, continued down

the street, then turned around and came back, again staring hard
as he went by.

Thirty minutes later a lanky youth, with long blond hair and
wearing jeans and a T-shirt, came from the house, got on a bicycle, probably the same one the smaller boy had been riding,
and rode past the stakeout.

"That's Massey," Jordan said. The lawmen watched as the
bike rider continued down the street, then turned at a corner and
was out of sight.

"Let's get him," the sheriff said. As their car rounded the
corner, they saw the youth get off the bike and walk rapidly
toward a hedgerow. It looked for sure like he was taking off.

The lawmen got out and called for him to stop. The youth
halted.

"Are you Jason Massey?" the sheriff asked.

The youth answered that he was.

"Ellis County wants to talk to you," Jordan said.

Massey said, "What about?" He didn't say anything else after
that.

The officers shook him down, snapped on handcuffs, gave
him the Miranda warning on his rights, and walked him to their
car.

At the county jail, in the booking room, as his mug shot was
being snapped for the records, Massey was told that he was
being held on a warrant charging him with capital murder. Hearing these words, he smiled widely as the jail camera clicked.
The photo showed a beaming Jason Massey. The jailer would
remember it as the strangest jail photo he'd ever seen of a new
prisoner.

Jordan could not believe that the suspect had grinned when
told of the serious charge against him. He had never seen that
happen before. Jordan advised the Ellis County officers who
were en route that the suspect was in custody and apparently
happy.

Seven

In an era where single mothers are hard put to raise their children without a supporting spouse to help, the birth and rearing of Jason Massey was not all that uncommon.

Jason's mother, Nancy, then about twenty-one, partied and drank before Jason was born. One of her female friends at that time, Jane Peters, then eighteen, recalled that "We ran around probably three or four times a week. We would run around at night together. I would go pick her up when I got off work about five or six. I had the car. I had the funds, and I more or less provided the car and money. We would just go riding up and down what we called Gilmer Street there in Sulphur Springs. Then we'd park on a big parking lot and meet and talk with friends and guys during that time."

Becoming pregnant didn't make a difference in Nancy's lifestyle. "We still did it while she was pregnant—some drinking, smoking, just things like that . . . usually stay out 'til two, three, or sometimes four in the morning."

Massey was born on January 7, 1973. It was an uneventful birth. He was a pretty baby, normal in every way, apparently. Nancy would place her newborn son in the back seat of the car when she and Jane went out. The baby slept most of the time, but if he woke up, one of the women would get him back to sleep.

"After Jason was born, we'd take him with us," Jane said. "He'd usually be asleep because we wouldn't go out until seven or eight P.M. Sometimes he would wake up, and one of us would pick him up and get him back to sleep. She had the child, you know. He was there, so she had to take care of him. It was like an obligation, you know, not affection."

Jane remembered that Nancy's pattern of life then was to sleep during the day and "party" at night. "At noon I could never arouse anybody. She always kept the TV or radio on, so it was noisy in there. But I couldn't get anybody to the door or to the window. The best I knew, she was asleep and the kids were either in their room or the living room. They had to be in there, and far as I know, there was no one watching them."

Jason never knew for sure who his father was. "I don't think that Nancy really knows, or knew, who Jason's father was. There was certain times, you know, if we went out, she had a lot of guys who came over. That's why I say I don't think she knew who his father was—there were so many different guys who came over and stayed the night."

Two years later, Jason had a sister, Johanna Nicole. Nancy and the kids were always short on money, Jane said.

"I tried to help out as much as I could. I bought the kids coats and shoes and toys, but I never did approach Nancy about how things were. You know, I was young at that time, and if I look back now, I see definitely there was a problem then. But at that time I didn't realize there was.

"Nancy would get a job every once in a while in a nursing home or a restaurant somewhere. And she would keep it just a few weeks, then she would call in or she wouldn't go, and then she was out of a job again. They lived basically on food stamps and Medicaid. I know his grandmother also helped a lot, you know, financially, where she could."

Jason and his sister lived in dismal surroundings. "When I'd go into the house, there would be dishes in the sink, clothes laying around, beds not made, things like that."

When Jason was five years old, he was sexually molested by a man who was babysitting him. The man performed oral sex on the small boy and tried to get him to reciprocate. Jason hit him and ran.

While they were small, the children were spanked frequently, with a big wooden paddle wrapped in masking tape, or with a belt. Their grandmother finally threw the paddle in a lake. Meals were irregular and the kids cooked for themselves, scrounged what food they could, or went hungry. They got themselves off to school.

One day when they lived in Sulphur Springs, Jason had an idea. There was an old shed near his house that he used as a clubhouse. It was a bright, sunny day and he was by himself.

He decided to climb on top of his clubhouse, pull his pants and shorts down, and suntan his penis. As he lay stretched out, his naked front exposed to the warming sun, he was thinking strange thoughts. He looked at himself and felt a twinge, the first stirrings of sex. He played with himself. It was a strange day, somehow.

He also played with a dead dog.

In the summer of 1982, when Jason was nine years old, he was playing with two younger boys along a creek bed not far from the mobile home park where they lived.

Jason suddenly overpowered the youngest boy, stripped him naked, and tied him to a tree. Using a tree limb, he whipped the boy hard, then harder, as he screamed in pain. It was a funny, exciting feeling.

The boy's brother ran home and told his startled mother that "Jason's hurting Jim, Momma. He took off all his clothes and said he was going to sacrifice him to the devil!"

The mother ran to the creek bed. The crying boy was still tied to the tree, but Jason had fled. She saw that her son had red welts over his body, the skin broken in places. After freeing her son, she took him home and called the Ennis police.

A responding officer said that "not much can be done because your boy's not hurt all that bad, and considering their ages and all, you know how kids are."

The officer and mother went to Jason's house to talk to his mother, but found no one at home.

Being unable to contact Jason's mother was a familiar situation to teachers who had Jason in their elementary school classes. The teachers felt sorry for the "scruffy-looking" boy who seemed to be so much on his own. They had trouble getting any response from his mother when they sent notes home reporting Jason's learning problems.

The teachers wanted to place him in special education classes. Reading, writing, and spelling were his biggest weaknesses in the fourth grade, and the teachers wanted to get him special tutoring.

When a teacher asked him if he had help at home with his assignments, Jason said no, there was no one at home, no help, none at all. Sometimes he didn't even know where his mother was.

They would have been horrified to know what Jason had on his mind at that time in his life: he'd killed his first cat.

The yowling, scratching, bloody animal was not easy to finish off, but its suffering and the warm blood established an appetite in the boy. He had never known such sensations, such satisfaction, the thrill that took his breath away, the wonderful feeling in the pit of his stomach.

He wondered how it would be to kill people, to watch them in fear and agony, to torture them like he'd done with the cat.

On his mind much of the time now was the desire to kill people. He wondered how it would be to kill a calf or a cow, cut its stomach open, and have sex with it.

Masturbation in the midst of his sexual fantasies was no longer enough. He needed to know the satisfaction of torture and death and actual sex with a girl, maybe with her cold body after she was dead. He looked in magazines that he would find sometimes, or get from older boys, that showed pictures of naked, cut-up women.

In his early years in school, teachers often noticed Jason, standing alone, waiting for a ride after missing the school bus, long after other students had gone home—a solitary figure in the dusk, with a hopeless expression on his face.

As he increasingly fell behind his classmates, he was often truant. When he *was* in school, he was sullen and stayed to himself in the halls or during recess.

Hatred and strange longings were raging inside a boy who found himself failing in school, without school friends, enduring harsh living conditions at home, and the target of ridicule by other youngsters and, more subtly, some adults.

Whereas his father, or the man who his mother said was his father, ignored him and turned from any relationship, he was nice to Jason's younger sister and gave her things as if she was his daughter. Their mother had told Johanna that another man was her father.

Jason received loving treatment from his grandmother, Sue Wickliffe. "Granny" was a good churchwoman, taking him to church with her whenever she could. She talked to him about the Lord and how Jason needed Him, how everybody needed Him and His love that never failed. Granny bought them food and clothes when there was no money at home.

Throughout his life, Jason would have an enduring love for his "granny," and for his little brother, who was born in 1987. Jason's diary contained entries about how he "worshiped" his little brother, and an observation about small children in general, "I believe the only innocence in our world is in small children."

Eight

Anita Mendoza, a pretty thirteen-year-old schoolgirl, answered the telephone in her home in Ennis, Texas, one afternoon in 1989. She had just come from school, and the phone was ringing as she dumped her books on the sofa.

After a second of silence, a boy's voice said, "I guess I got the wrong number." Actually, Jason Massey knew who he was calling, and why. He wanted to kill Anita Mendoza, violate her in every sexual way he had fantasized about, mutilate her corpse, and then make love to it. He also had a yearning to eat her sexual organs and drink her blood.

His quiet voice and words conveyed nothing of this. Before Anita could hang up, he quickly asked, "Aren't you Anita Mendoza? I know you. I know your voice. Hi, Anita. I go to school with you. I'm Jason Massey. I've seen you lots at school."

Anita, a vibrant seventh-grader at Ennis Junior High School, hardly got in a word. She managed to say she didn't think she knew him. She was sure he wasn't in any of her classes or extracurricular school activities.

"I've got a friend I think you know," Jason persisted, naming another student whom Anita knew only casually. He had to keep her talking. *God, her girlish voice was making him hard.*

She was in a hurry but tried to be polite. "I don't guess I know him very well, either. Listen, I've got to go. I—"

"Wait just a minute, please don't hang up."

"Listen, I'm sorry, but I've got to go. Goodbye." She hung up. The boy had been nice enough, had spoken softly, had seemed to know her. But she'd never heard of Jason Massey and wouldn't know him if they met face to face in the hallway. He'd been courteous, but kind of strange sounding.

The clean-looking town of Ennis, population 14,000, is in Ellis County, Texas, an agricultural region of rolling hills and level fields, with the rich black soil of the Trinity River bottom-lands. The countryside is spotted with thick woods. Ennis is a quiet little town of nice people, quaint homes, Sunday-packed churches, and good public schools. A community totally unprepared for Jason Massey.

Jason called Anita again the next day. He started with the same mundane chatter. She interrupted. "Really, I don't know you, and I wish you would quit calling. I'm getting ready to go with my folks."

"Wait just a minute, please. Do you have a boyfriend? I would like to be your boyfriend. A pretty girl like you should have a boyfriend."

"Thanks, but I have a boyfriend, and please don't bother me anymore. I'm not interested in you, period." She hung up before he could say anything else. He was getting on her nerves.

Over the next few weeks, the phone calls increased. Over and over, Jason asked Anita to go to a movie or go get a Coke. She always refused. *Any guy with good sense would have taken the hint long ago,* she thought. The guy wasn't only a pestering nerd, he was creepy.

After a let-up of several days, the calls started again. Making only suggestive remarks at first, Jason switched to obscenities. "You've got beautiful, long dark hair and the prettiest little ass. I want to sleep with you. I love you so, Anita. I have these hot dreams about you, baby. They're wonderful." She slammed down the phone.

Anita told her parents and schoolmates about the calls. Two of the bolder students told Massey to quit bothering Anita. The police were notified, but no legal action was taken against

Massey. A patrol officer told the Mendozas that "somebody will talk to the boy and warn him about making calls."

The Mendoza family finally moved to another address and got a new telephone number. Anita was relieved when the calls stopped. Maybe her life would be normal again, free of the fear that she was beginning to feel.

Anita's complacency was jolted by the arrival of a letter, forwarded by the postal service to her new address.

The writing was illegible in places; misspelled words and bad grammar also made it hard to read. But the signature was clear. Jason Massey wrote:

"What's your phone number? If you don't give it to me, then I'll get it myself by the end of this month and that's a promise, and as you will soon see, I'm a man of his word.

"Do you remember I told you that I had several dreams about you? I should have told you what they were. So here goes.

"We were sitting on the floor at this guy's house. You were saying something to me, then I grabbed your arms and laid you down. Then you said, 'I've been taking Karate,' and then I said, 'Have you ever heard of a f——g gun?' Then I put my tongue into your mouth. Then you started crying, so I left.

"The other dream is better though. I was in a garage looking out the window. I saw your mother leave. When she did I saw your father sitting in a chair in the yard. He told you to take some trash to the garage. When you came in I put my hand to your mouth and my knife to your throat, kissed you on the side of your face and said good-bye and started cutting your throat. But my knife would not cut your throat very well, so I pushed it through the back of your skull. Well, I think you can figure out what did or didn't happen. By the way, my knife is very sharp.

"I want to see you at the movies the 2nd of this month. I will pay for your way and whoever else you bring. But don't bring your whole family . . . Two of your friends have called me and said I needed to leave you alone. But how could I ever leave you behind? How could I leave the only person I really love behind?

"There is only one way for us. To be dead. Like I said, you're all I ever think about. It's 6 A.M. Wednesday morning and you're probably just getting up for school and I'm getting ready for bed. I do love you, Anita. Write me back, please."

Massey got Anita's new number and the nightmare of phone calls resumed, sometimes a dozen or more a day. Anita always slammed down the receiver as soon as she heard his voice. Jason didn't call at night, when he knew her parents would be there.

Once he exploded in anger before she could hang up, raving, "I'll get you, one way or other. I don't take no for an answer. If I can't have you, no one will have you."

Anita received a letter with a name and return address that she didn't recognize. With the letter, there was a picture of a mutilated woman with her decapitated head placed on her chest. The picture looked like it had been cut from a book or magazine.

"This is how you will look when I get you alone," read one scrawled sentence.

"Anita, I will go ahead and get to the point of this letter. I want you to know one thing. I love you. I always have, but now it's more than love. It's an obsession. You are my life. I live for you, hoping that someday soon we will be together forever. I've only thought about you and have been lucky enough to dream about you several times. I'm sorry for the phone calls I've made in the past, but that is the past and people have changed.

"Hope you forgive me. I would be very honored to be forgiven by a beautiful god like yourself. I put another name on the envelope so you would open it and not your family. The address on the front is real, so write me back. You look beautiful at the movies."

The letter was signed Jason and had a triangular symbol underneath his signature.

The last line chilled her. She was frightened at the thought that this weirdo was following her around and she hadn't even been aware of his presence.

She still had no idea what he looked like. He could be right next to her and she wouldn't know it.

None of her friends knew anything about Massey. He was a non-mixer. One friend pointed him out to her, walking by himself and unaware of them. He was plain and non-threatening in frame and facial features, skinny, and not very tall. He had long blond hair and pimples. People had told her he had a funny stare out of his blue eyes. *Scuzzy looking,* Anita thought.

The attempts by Anita's friends to discourage Massey's harassing conduct only brought another offensive letter.

"Anita, I got word that your boyfriend wants to kick my ass. I could not believe it when I heard it. He must be joking. Tell him I said thanks for the laugh. Why would he want to f—— with me, to stand up and protect his lady? What a noble cause. I don't think that's the reason. I think he wants to prove to you that he's a man because he's really not. He's just a stupid little fu——g puppy ass kid with a big mouth.

"You still have not written me, and for some reason I don't think you will so I will try other things to get your attention. I will not stop writing. That is one thing you should remember about me. I never give up and I always get what I want, one way or the other.

"And as you know, I want you and will have you one way or the other. I'm sure you know what I mean by the other.

"When you were at the movies on Thursday did you know I was sitting behind you. Your cousin Marilyn was to your left, and I remember you were wearing red fingernail polish."

The next words turned Anita's stomach.

"I remember when the two of you walked in I could smell your blood. It smelled sweet. I would love to spill your blood and sip it like a fine wine.

"I think about you all the time. I don't know, deep inside my head is a split decision that will end with you dead. You see the agony in my eyes protruding. I think it is time to die—die, love."

The wildly scrawled handwriting, misspelled words, and almost incoherent sentences caused Anita to wonder if he was doing drugs.

One Saturday afternoon when Anita and some girlfriends were at a theater, she left her seat to go to the rest room. She was startled to see Jason Massey leaning against the wall at the side of the rest room door, his hands in his pockets. He grinned but didn't speak. She hurried past him without speaking.

When she emerged after staying longer than she'd intended, he was gone and she sighed with relief. But why did he keep up this relentless and senseless pursuit? What was the matter with him?

She was nervous most of the time, especially alone at home or anywhere else she was by herself, even in the empty halls at school when classes had ended for the day.

The first thing she did at night was to pull the window drapes and make certain all the doors were locked if she was alone. She tried not to be by herself. If the house was empty, or even if a family member was there, an ordinary phone call would make her jump, sending her heartbeat racing.

Whenever she felt the injustice of the growing fear caused by this idiot and his stupid calls and letters, she hugged her pet dog, Frosty, to her. Frosty was company, but Anita didn't know just how much protection he would be.

Her father pulled another letter from their mailbox that appeared to be in the stalker's handwriting. Newspaper clippings of photos of Anita, her father, and a girl cousin snapped at a recent Ennis school event tumbled out.

Smeared across the front of the photos was something that looked like blood. Strange symbols and numbers that might be a code were on the back of the clippings. Whatever the stain was, it was smeared over their faces and name captions.

Part of the letter read, "Here's a song I wrote for you and a picture of yourself when I catch you alone." A song followed.

> Lying, dying, screaming in pain
> Begging, pleading, your blood flows like rain
> And mine explodes
> Pain shifts through your brain
> Stakes drive through your chest
> Soul of misfortune
> Honey, faded breath
> Vile smell and taste of death
> Dead bodies, dying and wounded
> Litter the city streets
> Shattered glass and bits of clothing and human deceit
> Dying in terror, blood's cheap
> It's everywhere
> Mandatory suicide
> Massacre on the front line.

* * *

On August 4, 1990, Anita Mendoza arrived at her house after having been away for several hours. It was a dark afternoon. A summer rainstorm had poured down and thunder still rumbled in the distance.

As she started to walk inside, she saw something on the driveway. She screamed and began sobbing. Frosty was lying near her mother's car. The poor dog's body was grotesque. There was blood on the driveway where it appeared the dog's head had been smashed against the concrete.

Anita would notice the details later. All she saw now as she cried was Frosty dead, dead, with only bloody pulp where his head had been. It was the most horrible thing she'd ever seen.

Even as her sobbing continued, the teenager was struck by terror as she saw written on the back window of her mother's car, apparently with blood from the mutilated dog, "Anita's dead." There was no doubt in her mind who had killed her dog and scrawled the crude message with the dog's blood. Jason Massey might as well have left his name at the bloody scene.

The Ennis Police Department was notified. Although family members said they were certain that Jason Massey, who had terrorized Anita over many months, was responsible, no legal action against Massey was forthcoming. There was no hard evidence linking him to the deed. The police said they had nothing to prove it, so no charge was filed.

"As bad as this is, we can't act on assumptions or what people think they know to be a fact," one officer said.

The Mendoza family felt deep frustration, for it was obvious that the violent phone calls and letters from Jason Massey had escalated into actual killing, intended as a stark warning to the young girl he had terrorized and said he wanted to be his "girlfriend."

Jason Massey had started keeping a diary in 1989. In a spiral notebook he regularly recorded his activities, thoughts, fantasies, his plans to kill girls.

On August 5, 1990, Jason wrote in his diary:

"Yesterday I went to Ennis . . . [A friend] took me to Anita's. I sat out in front of what I thought was her house & went to her window and knocked a couple of times and no one answered . . . [So I looked inside] & it isn't a room at all. So I went next door and got a bag of trash and found out where she really lives.

"I also went up to her back porch & grabbed a dog by the throat & strangled it, then beat its head against the concrete.

"Then I took it and wrote 'Anita's dead' in blood on the back of a car in her yard. I don't know if she seen it or anyone else because it rained about 5 or 6 P.M. So the rain probably washed it off. If anyone does know about it, I should find out pretty soon.

"I forgot to write about my .380. I got it about the 3rd or 4th of this month, August."

Nine

He roamed the dense woods around Ennis in the brightness of the summer day. The birds and other daylight creatures grew silent when he came near. The searing heat and humidity bathed the trees, brush, vines, and his own body in soaking wetness like rain. He never was aware of the sweat that drenched him on the long walks.

At intervals the day's brightness gave way suddenly to a kind of twilight in the thickest parts of the woods where the sun didn't penetrate the canopy of trees. He walked for long periods, bending aside hovering tree limbs, pushing through entanglements of vines that were grasping and smothering the other growth.

There were mosquitoes, thick swarms in the swampy places, but he hardly noticed them, brushing at them with his hands, in deep thought as he looked and sought the private retreats he needed: a place to bury a body when he was ready, several bodies when his campaign began, a place hidden enough for a private graveyard for his "girls," a point of rendezvous with the dead, when and if that time came.

It had to be far enough into the woods to be undetectable by searching police, yet close enough for him to conveniently visit when he wanted to be with his collection of "trophies," those beautiful bones that would cry to him from the dank earth.

To him there was no "if" about his mapped-out campaign of slaughter, only a "when"—when he could begin at last.

He often explored the woods, searching for the "cemetery" site during the day. But it was the night—when the woods were shrouded in blackness except for the rare openings in the over-shadowing tree limbs that admitted patches of bright moon-light—when Jason Eric Massey felt closest to his destiny of serving the Master.

The Master gave him "knowing," made him watchful, made him careful and cunning. It was in the woods on moonlit nights that Jason felt the tug of spiritual strangeness. It was here in the woods where he once heard the voice of the demon as he knelt at his crude stone altar on which a candle flickered and made the shadows all around dance like wildly leaping demons. The voice of the demon calling his name had risen above the intensity of the nighttime insects and frogs.

He felt at home in the darkness where patches of moonlight painted shadows at their sharpest. It was here, away from people, all the fuckers who hated and despised him and taunted him and talked about him and beat him up sometimes, that he felt a sense of peace and purpose.

It was the proper setting, the true kingdom, for one who meant to be the world's greatest serial killer of beautiful young girls and women. He had even set age limitations—from ten to forty years—but he might make exceptions if something truly fine and good came along.

It was in these dense woods that dozens of cats and dogs died savage deaths at Jason's hands, following orgies of torture and disembowelment and decapitation and skinning. Their last shrieks and howls and thrashing sent the adrenaline surging through his system, especially at the moments when their hot blood gushed forth in throbbing spurts to drench the gloves he wore.

He had become philosophical about these animal sacrifices; they were just killings for his pleasure. He had noticed, while killing some thirty-eight cats and dogs and five cows, that they were just like people.

Some fight like hell. Most just fight a good little bit. But a few hardly fight at all. They just accept death and go on to the other side. Some don't accept it until life is completely gone.

Jason Massey liked most of all to raise the knife in the moon's glare and watch the blood, dark in the lunar light, drip from the blade. It gave him an erection.

To abduct, rape, torture, kill, mutilate, and violate in every dreamed-of sexual manner the living and the dead young girls, this was his destiny, his calling in the Master.

His thinking about pain and hurting started when he killed his first cat at nine. In his early teens, Jason began thinking of murdering human beings, young and innocent girls most of all.

But his developing plan to murder countless young females—to outdo serial killers such as Charles Manson, Henry Lee Lucas, Ted Bundy, the Green River Killer, and other sex murder champions whose lives he followed in books and movies—was going far too slowly for him. In comparison, his list of potential girl victims was growing too rapidly. If he didn't get started, he would never be able to do them all. He loved them all so much, with an intense passion, but the only way he could possess them forever was to murder them and mutilate their sweet, beautiful bodies filled with warm, sweet blood.

Anita Mendoza was first on the list. This pretty, innocent girl with the long dark hair and cheerleader body had told him before she'd banged down the phone, "You're just a piece of shit that only picks on girls!"

Well, she was right about him picking on girls. And that delicious little girl, she would be the first. He would have her body and soul, as she feared.

Ten

Edith Robinson was twenty-two, dark-haired, pretty, and winding up her second year as a schoolteacher. During the last half of the 1988 school term, she was teaching two classes at Ennis High School: correlated language arts, and fundamentals of math.

The vibrant young teacher could have been mistaken for one of her high school students. Her very youthfulness fostered an easy relationship with the teenagers in her classes. Students were comfortable talking to her about things not connected to school-work—their interests, ideas, and sometimes problems.

She encouraged this friendly openness, engaging in a game she called "Topic of the Day" to get to know her students better, especially the quiet ones. Students and teacher asked each other questions and gave answers. These talks took place after class-room assignments were done.

One freshman boy in particular, Jason Eric Massey, seemed to enjoy testing Edith with offbeat questions and talk. Edith believed that if she taught for the next fifty years, she would never have a stranger student than Jason. The fifteen-year-old with the long blond hair and light blue eyes was an enigma. He was in both of her classes, first period and sixth period.

Jason wasn't a disruptive student. He was quiet, personable, and polite. He had artistic talent, though it was manifested in sketches of swastikas, inverted crosses, skulls, daggers, and crossbones drawn on the homework papers that he turned in. If anything, he was shy, always saying "Yes, ma'am" and "No, ma'am." He didn't mix in the usual give-and-take of school life.

But he took to the one-on-one talks with Edith. Early on, it was apparent that he liked to shock her with stories about satanic cults, satanic handbooks, devil worship, and sacrificial rites involving animals. He said he was involved in cult activities, but Edith wasn't sure he was being entirely truthful.

He said he had become a cult member because "If they want to sacrifice somebody, they favor blond hair and blue eyes. That's why I have to be a member, so they won't want to kill me."

However, what seemed to be on his mind most of all was killing people. Some of his questions were unforgettable.

"Do you think you could kill someone?" Or, "If you knew you were going to be killed—not just die, understand, but be killed—would it bother you?"

He always heated to the subject, leaning forward as he asked, "Would it bother you to watch someone die?" and then volunteering his own reaction, "I don't think it would me. I think it would be neat, really cool, if you know what I mean."

Once he asked Edith how she would go about killing a person. Another time he said, "Wouldn't it be easy to kill somebody if you didn't know them? The police couldn't track you because you couldn't be connected to that person."

Edith knew that Jason's hero was Charles Manson. He carried around a newspaper story and photograph of Manson in his notebook. The teacher noticed that as soon as he sat down at his desk, he pulled out the Manson article and placed it on the upper right corner of the desk. She made Jason put away the article; otherwise, he wouldn't do his class work.

Jason liked to argue that Manson wasn't guilty, that he might have had a good reason for the murders, that "It's okay to do it if you have a good reason."

Edith had difficulty with Jason when she assigned her language arts class a research paper about their favorite hero. Jason chose Manson. Edith decided the Manson-mania had gone far enough and refused to accept a paper lauding the sadistic killer.

"Then I won't write about anybody," Jason flared. "You can't be the judge of who my heroes are." He refused to do the assignment.

The youth's growing classroom resentment and refusal to do assignments led to a meeting of Jason, his mother, a school counselor, and Edith Robinson. Jason had often mentioned that he didn't like his mother. During the meeting, when Jason reached for a pen on the counselor's desk to write something down, his mother suddenly slapped his hand and berated him. Edith Robinson thought it was an overreaction by the parent, and she felt a pang of sympathy for the mixed-up boy. It was the first of several counseling sessions.

Subsequently, the teacher had a conversation with Jason that raised her concern even more about his strange mental patterns. While the math class was working on a unit that included negative numbers and integers, Jason asked her about subtracting larger numbers from smaller numbers.

"Instead of subtracting 3 from 9, couldn't you do it this way?" Jason asked, smiling and handing her a piece of paper. On it he had written a 3, then a minus sign, a 9, an equal symbol, and a 6. "Instead of subtracting the three from the nine, couldn't you do it the other way around?"

"Yes, but you would wind up with a negative number," Edith answered.

"Well, let me show it to you this way." He still was grinning. He reworked the figures on the paper. "If you do it this way, you get sixty-nine, see?"

"Well, not really." She wondered what he was trying to prove.

"Well, I guess not really, but sixty-nine is very important. Sixty-nine is a good number."

"Why is it important?"

"Don't you know? It's a sexy number, has a sexual meaning.

You know . . . important—what it stands for. Besides, it's the year that Charles Manson went on his killing spree, and nine and three, the year '93, is going to be important as the Manson killings in '69, I can tell you that."

"You need to work on your math lesson, Jason," Edith said, ending the conversation.

On a morning in late May of 1988, students were arriving for the first-period class. Edith glanced up from the paper she was marking as Jason sat down at his front-row desk opposite her own. She noticed he was perspiring heavily, not unusual, considering the stifling heat in the classroom. The air-conditioning certainly was no help—it was blowing hot air instead of cool.

Dressed as usual in jeans, a button-down shirt, and an undershirt barely visible at the neck, Jason looked miserable because of the heat. Edith was irritated that the cooling system hadn't been repaired. Kids had trouble enough concentrating on lessons this late in the term without having to endure such discomfort.

"Jason, why don't you roll up your sleeves or untug your shirt?" she suggested. "It's awfully warm in here."

"I can't do that, Miss Robinson. It would scare too many people," he said. It was a strange reply, but then, what should she expect from Jason, she thought.

In sixth period, the last of the day, Jason lingered after his classmates had left. He told Edith he had been thinking that he should explain why he had been worried about "scaring people" in first-period class if he'd unbuttoned his shirt or opened it to cool off.

"I'll show you, if you won't tell anybody. I was at this ritual last night with some guys and a dog and a cat were sacrificed. One of these days, though, we're going to have to kill a person.

"I didn't just watch, I took part this time. I got my undershirt bloody, and I didn't have time to change before I came to school. That was the reason, Miss Robinson. I'll show you, but don't tell nobody."

He unbuttoned the outer shirt and pulled it back to expose the undershirt. It was covered with a brown stain which gave off a terrible odor: dried blood, old and smelly dried blood—not just blood spatters. The undershirt was saturated, as if it had been dyed the color brown. Shocked at the sight, the young teacher managed to keep her composure and tell Jason that he should not do such things.

She later made a report to her immediate supervisor and the school principal about the incident and the student's consuming interest in the occult, cult violence, and even murder. She was assured she had acted properly in allowing the boy to talk about what surely was a growing problem in his life.

Jason wasn't there when school started the following autumn. He had said he didn't get along well with his mother and might go live with his grandmother in Canton, and Edith surmised he had done that.

She hoped something would help him.

Eleven

At one point, when the world seemed down on him and all the attention at home seemed to go to his new little brother and his sister, Jason got an unexpected break.

It came almost like an angel from heaven in the form of an Ennis woman, who was a good friend of his grandmother, Sue Wickliffe. Finances were at a critical low when his granny, who had done all she could, took things in her own hands and phoned Roberta Adams.

"Roberta, can you help the children? Things are pretty bad right now." The family friend said she'd be glad to help. So with their mother's permission, Roberta Adams took into her own home the suffering children to live for a while. Their grandmother took Jason and Johanna to the Adams's house.

The first thing Roberta did was sit them down in the kitchen for a serious talk. "I'm sorry at this age that you have no direction, you have no goals, that your home life and school life are like this. John [her husband] and I want to help you, but let me tell you right now, we can only help you so much, and the other help will have to come from yourselves."

It was an optimistic and encouraging talk, and the kids were eager to live a different kind of life. But Johanna returned home a few days later.

The Adamses discussed with Jason what he wanted to do in life. He said he wanted to enter military service, so they contacted the army recruiter at Corsicana, the nearest recruiting station, and inquired what Jason needed to do to qualify for enlistment.

When told that Jason had not finished high school, the recruiter said he would need to obtain a G.E.D., a certificate equivalent to a high school diploma.

The Adamses purchased the necessary books for Jason to take the G.E.D. test and pass it, and Roberta's husband started working with Jason at the kitchen table. Jason studied hard and learned fast. When John asked him the G.E.D. questions, he was able to answer every one. They did the work while Roberta was cooking dinner every evening. When she glanced at them, she saw a new look on Jason's face.

He seemed to luxuriate in the newness of someone doing something to help him. Jason finally had the feeling that he had real family love and caring.

There was something else to do, too. He couldn't go into the Army with stringy, not-too-clean-looking hair down to his shoulders.

Roberta took an apprehensive Jason to a beautician and instructed the hair stylist to "give him a short haircut." Jason didn't protest.

When it was finished, the woman operator stepped back to look at the work. Jason was a different boy.

"That looks so nice," she said. "He could pass for your son."

Hearing those words, Jason looked toward Roberta with a smile on his face.

Jason was supposed to take his G.E.D. test on his next birthday, but once again his mother decided to move, this time to Dallas, and to take her children with her. The Adamses were disappointed. They felt that Jason was on a new track, for the first time looking forward to doing something that would make him a new man with hope for the future. It might have been the best period of his life. It had lasted only two weeks.

Not long after they left, Roberta Adams went to Dallas to visit Nancy and her children.

Roberta called first to see if she could take Jason and his sister to dinner, wanting to talk with them away from home, to get a true picture of how life was going. Their mother said taking them to dinner would be fine.

Roberta Adams was shocked when she entered the apartment to pick them up. Bugs and trash covered the kitchen counter and stove, and dirty dishes filled the sink. In the living room was a worse mess. She saw with disgust that excrement was on the floor, and the baby boy was walking through it.

She couldn't believe Nancy wouldn't at least have made an effort to clean up the apartment, knowing a visitor was coming. *What a pitiful way to raise children,* she thought. She left as quickly as she could with Jason and Johanna. When dinner was over, she hated to take them back.

Whether it was the influence of his Christian granny, and his going to church with her, or the sudden impact of the violent suicide of someone he knew, Jason's entry in the first volume of his diary on October 13, 1989, was very different from his future railings about lust and murder:

"Time to start a diary again, because I can't keep all inside, especially after what I found out today. I found out this guy who was only 21 shot himself. I really didn't know him that well, but it really hurts inside.

"I think I have just realized what God wants me to do. Defend the weak, help the misfortuned, comfort the old and the small children, and promote God's word."

In frequent entries in his diary, Massey wrote about wanting to get away from his mother as fast as he could, and he was insultingly critical of her conduct toward him during his early life. Yet in retrospect, he later wrote that she was not to blame for his being what he was today.

Following several paragraphs of sordid fantasy about what he would do to a girl after killing her, he observed:

"I do know good and evil, right and wrong. My mother

taught me these things. She's not at fault where my up-bringing is concerned. She's done everything and more a loving mother should do. My personality is just me. I was killing [animals] before I listened to Slayer, before I knew what death and sex was."

Sue Wickliffe, Jason's grandmother, said that the life of Nancy and the two children in those earlier years was not as bad as some people thought.

"They had a good life . . . they were poor, they didn't have money, but they had a good life. I've seen a lot of kids who had a lot worse life, you know. Jason worships his little brother. He's eight years old now, and a straight-A student in school.

"Jason used to be the escort for his sister to all the little proms, beauty contests, Cub Scouts, those kind of things. His mom was a Cub Scout den mother. Jason was such a beautiful child, a good child, and a sweet child. His mother has pictures of him that are out of this world."

Twelve

Jason Massey and his mother had moved to Dallas after he dropped out of school in Ennis. It was probably prompted, in part, by his mother's constant need to find a new job. Her changing jobs was something he was used to. Moving was nothing new to him, either. It seemed like he'd been doing it most of his life. He and his younger sister lost count of how many times the family moved, often being evicted for failure to pay the rent. Once the children and their mother lived out of an automobile for a while. He wondered if that had anything to do with his wish to head for the Pacific Northwest, Seattle, and the big-woods country, then Canada.

But he knew his nomadic background had little influence on this compelling desire to travel to far places. It was that thing growing inside of him, eating at his innards, demanding to be filled, before it burst forth in complete devastation wherever he might be.

He was going to have to kill a young girl. He was hungry to do it. Do it, or admit to himself that he was one of those bullshit talkers who never did anything about what they told themselves they were going to do, had to do.

In October 1989, he began in earnest to keep a diary. He wrote in it almost every night, his fantasies building to a high pitch and eventually becoming lost in the wild scribbling that swept across the pages of the spiral notebook. He wondered what Miss Robinson would think about what he wrote now.

The illegible entries always occurred during bouts of heavy

drinking, tripping on acid, or floating on marijuana. He couldn't read some parts of it the next morning.

His diary reflected his private wars with the world and, more specifically, his mother. He lived with her out of necessity—he didn't have or keep a job long during some periods of his restless life. He felt she bugged him, always sticking her nose into what he was doing, always bitching, as much a monkey on his back as the drugs he began doing more frequently.

She must have seen some of the pages of his diary. He wrote:

> "It looks like everything is going as planned, with the exception of my mother. Yeh, she's been ripping parts of my history out again. That's how she reacts in any situation. She childish. It really is fucked. Now my thoughts aren't private."

Jason was still making trips regularly to Ennis; his life was rooted there.

He'd started serving the Master there, killing cats and dogs in sacrificial rituals, or sometimes, just for the plain hell and pleasure of it. He would do it in quiet spots in the woods, lighting a candle at his "altar," the small flame flickering as he did the bloody work. Usually he wore gloves, and when it was over, the cat's life was over, its screeching was over, and its gutted body lay there. He would cut off the head. His trophies were increasing, as were his desires.

He knew that beautiful women, as much as he enjoyed looking at them in their shorts with their beautiful asses, hated the very sight of him. He wrote:

> "When I'm in public and see a beautiful woman, I look at her and smile. Then by the expression on her face I know she's saying that little pimple-face punk actually has the nerve to look at me. Then I frown and disgust fills that once beautiful face! Most girls in school, too."

He had not forgotten pretty Anita. He was going to do that little bitch any time now. She was no. 1 on his list. After a visit to Ennis, Jason wrote in his diary:

"I just got back from Ennis, and, yes, I done it again. I found out where my baby lives; she tried to move.

"She changed her number, then I got it and called her, so she changed it. Now I *know* where she lives. I even know where her bedroom is! She had better realize two things. She can't ever hide from me, and two, I will have her soul as she fears."

At night when his mother was snoring in her room, Jason reported faithfully to his diary. He had named it "Slayer's Book of Death," in honor of his favorite death metal band, Slayer of Los Angeles. He jotted down his growing frustrations with his life in general:

"I'm 17 years old; a dropout dope head with almost glich to look forward to. If a man don't do what he says he'll do, then he's nothing. When I took Tommy [a child relative] to the park the other day, the children's parents looked at me like I was going to snatch up their kids and fuck 'em or something!

"Every since grade 4, children and old alike have despised me, laughed at me, whispered behind my back, made stories of 'sick' Jason Massey.

"I heard people say they heard I fuck my own sister! They have babies! . . . probably more lies that haven't surfaced yet. They have betrayed me, spit in my face and upon my name. Those so-called 'friends' are the seeds of these lies."

On a cool day in November 1990 Jason had a new secret love. Her name was Tessie and she lived next door in another apartment at the complex. She was only ten years old, pretty, with long black hair and a childish, innocent little face. Yet sometimes there was something in her eyes, her smile, that made him sure that some little girls grow up fast.

A guy he ran around with mentioned that he thought Tessie really liked Jason. Jason began thinking maybe he was right; this little girl was really getting close to him, coming on. He couldn't believe it; she was only ten!

He was fighting against it, though. He and his buddies went to Flagpole Hill to shoot the shit and smoke weed and drink beer. After one trip to the park, he wrote in his diary:

"I swear, every time I go to Flagpole Hill some goddam fag tries to pick me up. But I have a hard time trying to get pussy. Decent pussy is all I want. Not 10 years old, or some damn fag."

Paul was one of his Dallas friends, an all-right guy who liked the same bands and songs, liked to talk about killing and doing bitches with Jason, and was heavy into drugs. *Too much,* Jason thought, *that's all he's living for, the coke and stuff.* They were planning to take off for the Pacific Northwest, but nothing was getting done.

Paul had a mind; he knew things and was able to read people. Jason talked to him every chance he got about getting out of town, running off, and camping in the outdoors of the Northwest or Canada—survival living—and doing drugs and girls. Paul wanted to do these things, but he was slow getting around to it; his brain was fried all the time.

But Paul agreed, when Jason told him, that Tessie probably was coming on to Jason. Jason felt he now had about 35 percent of her trust—he wasn't sure just how he hit on that figure. He'd accidentally burned her on the lip with his cigarette, and knew he'd lost ground, though it wasn't his damn fault.

Once Tessie had playfully pulled his pants down. *I'm getting there,* he thought. *She'll be okay in two or three days, forget about that little burn that made a cute mole on her lip.* He hoped she would let him fuck her. He thought she might. *So she's ten years old, so what the hell?*

Few people thought well of Jason. Even one of his favorite relatives, an uncle, said he thought Jason was doomed and would be dead or in the pen in five years—"and that's long-range." But Jason told his diary:

"I say, fuck you, fuck you all. I'll never go to the pen. I know the odds are against me, but Anita, you are the only reason I care to live. And Tessie. My time is short & I have all these girls to get. Hell, Lucas killed over 260 people, and he started in 1960. Shit, I should be able to do at least that many. Maybe not. It's all up to the Master. [. . .] I may end up killing 'til I'm dead . . . I don't care as long as I get my chosen girls. I'll get away with it all. Murder is my love . . . I'll *never* ever rest until I've got them all. There's something in me that won't let them go until they're dead, mutilated and mine. If I let them live then they've escaped. If I kill all of them, that's the only way I'll keep them FOR-EVER!!!"

He heard the demon again one night. It was the first time since that time in the woods near Ennis. He woke up at 3 A.M. and heard the voice calling, *Jason . . . Jason . . . Jason.* Three times.

He whispered, "What?" And the voice didn't say anything else. But he was sure it was the same demon who had called to him in Ennis, there in the woods.

Thirteen

Working in the convenience store would have been like serving a jail term for Jason if it hadn't been for Lynnette, a cashier. He was a package clerk in a Tom Thumb store. It was one of several jobs he would hold for short periods while living in Dallas.

Lynnette was pretty, a year younger than he, and one of the few girls he had met who did not seem turned off after he'd known them for a while. They both lived in separate units in the same apartment complex and had become friends. Jason wanted to make their relationship more than that, but when he asked her for a date, she told him it would be better if they just stayed friends, since they worked at the same place.

Her answer came as a blow to his already suffering self-image, but he tried not to show it. *Another rebuff, just like they all do,* he thought.

"Okay, fine, whatever," he said.

The next morning Lynnette discovered a dead cat on the walkway of her apartment, right at her doorstep.

When she saw Jason later that day, she asked if he had left the cat as some kind of macabre joke. He said it hadn't been him.

He visited often when they were off-duty. He didn't get out of line after she turned down his date and said she wanted to be just friends.

But now she regularly found on her outside step a yellow rose with a green thumbtack stuck into it. Jason admitted to leaving the roses. He explained the rose and thumbtack was a symbol of satanic love.

One morning at 6:30, she sleepily answered the door and it was Jason. He said he wanted to tell her that he had put a letter in her black jacket.

She asked him in, then went to get the letter that she had not noticed earlier. Jason sat on the sofa while she read. The letter was weird and full of dirty ramblings. He'd written he wanted to kill her and have sex with her body because that was the only way he was sexually aroused.

"Are you scared?" Jason asked. He looked funny; his blue eyes always seemed to look through you. She could smell that he had been drinking. Maybe he'd been up all night, but she didn't know or care.

"No, just tired," she replied. But she *was* scared and was trying not to show it.

Jason pulled out a knife and moved toward her. "You shouldn't have turned me down. Girls as pretty as you don't deserve to be alive. I'm going to scramble your brains, bitch." His face was contorted with anger.

Lynnette was strong and had spunk. She struggled with him, bit him on the neck, and somehow as they wrestled around the room, she got the knife away from him. As she snapped it shut, the blade cut her fingertips. She ran to the door and flung the knife outside.

"Get out of here, you creep, and don't ever come back!" Lynnette shouted.

She slammed the door after him and bolted it. Then she gave way to tears. She debated calling the police, but decided not to.

Jason never tried to see her again, and he didn't show up for work.

Dallas was a merry-go-round of hell-raising for Jason. The big city suited him. Dallas had the prettiest girls and women of anywhere in the whole damn world. Some of them, like

Lynnette, lived in the apartment complex where he and his mother lived. He was meeting his share now, and he was going to *get* his share.

There was no problem finding dope, whatever he wanted, especially with Paul and his contacts.

Jason had made another friend, Aaron, who he'd recruited to his satanic beliefs by playing some of Slayer's songs to get him interested. He even got him into animal killing, something a lot of guys didn't want any part of. Paul also liked to do it, but he was tripped out too much of the time.

Aaron was going to join Jason and Paul on their trip to the Northwest and Canada, where they hoped to raise a marijuana crop, live in the wilds, and use all the survival ways of living that Jason liked to read about.

Paul was glad he'd met Jason at a friend's house. He was one screwy dude, and they were interested in the same music, the same movies, in doing drugs, and in wanting to rape and kill girls. Jason talked about killing girls all the time, enjoyed telling what he would do to them.

Paul would never forget one thing that Jason had said, how he would like to cut off a girl's head and drill a hole in her head and fuck her brains out, literally.

They had favorite movies, like *River's Edge,* the one where a body is found and some teenagers go back and look at it. But their favorite was *Angel Heart,* about a man doing voodoo killings in Louisiana and New York and meeting the devil.

One time Jason cut the heads off two kittens. He was always killing cats, either stabbing them straight through the gut or chopping their heads off. He and Paul took the heads over to Aaron's house, and they played golf by knocking the kitten heads all over the yard like golfballs.

Another time, Jason got a kitten and put it next to the front wheel on Paul's car. Paul ran over it, mashed it flat, with all its guts running out.

Aaron had a new whore—well, she was his wife now—and she was squeamish and wanted them to stop, but maybe she'd get over that, if she wanted to hang around Aaron and his friends.

Paul told Aaron he knew one thing for certain: if Jason had done all the things he'd talked about, he was wild, man, wild. Jason told him how one time at Ennis he'd poured gasoline on a dog and lit it and watched the burning dog run howling into a field where it thrashed around and died. Set the field on fire, too.

Jason liked fires. He started a little fire when they went to Flagpole Hill one night. He said he'd set a bunch of grass fires in Ennis.

Jason wanted to show his friends where he'd killed cats and dogs and calves at an "altar of sacrifice" in the woods behind McDonald's when he lived in Ennis. He had spent many hours in the woods, hunting, camping, or just seeking isolation from people.

Paul remembered one bloody night. He, Aaron, Aaron's wife, and Jason drove to Ennis and parked. Jason had spotted a calf. He was carrying a knife and a machete. He started running after the calf, and when it stopped, Jason started beating its head with the machete. The calf fell to the ground and Jason was on it like an animal, slashing with the machete and then ripping its stomach open with the knife. The animal's insides fell out. He stuffed a beer bottle into its gut, then sliced the calf's throat open.

Paul joined in. He thrust a buck knife directly into the calf's heart. He left the knife there and they watched in fascination as the embedded knife moved to the beat of the heart until it stopped. He remembered that Jason was sweaty, breathing hard, and had a funny look on his face.

Another time Jason and Paul chased after a full-grown cow in the field and Jason shot it several times in the neck and head with a .9-mm semi-automatic pistol. They stood and watched until it "pleaded out."

* * *

Massey's diary entry on May 1, 1990, read:

"I was just counting how many animals I've killed, at least 18 cats, more likely 20 or so, 18 for sure that I can remember; 9 dogs and 6 cows. What a fuckin' trip."

Fourteen

In January 1991 Jason was doing drugs frequently, getting high on marijuana, coke, speed, and LSD. And Tessie was an obsession with him. He'd decided he would kill her because he felt she'd rejected him. It didn't make sense to him: he loved her so much, but he had to kill her.

Writing in his diary, he said:

> "I am going to kill Tessie. I hope I am caught. If not I won't be able to stop, and I know there will be so many more. I love them all, too, but Tessie will be my first. I want to see her face when I cut her throat and drink her blood. Tessie, I love you and I want to kill you & drink your blood.
>
> "I will always remember two things Tessie said. The first thing is she asks me if I will kill her soul. Two, she just told me I was evil. Yes, maybe I am, but little girl I'll kill your soul, too, and yes, I'm evil. You're not the only one I love and I'll kill."

The next night he went to Tessie's apartment house to kill her, but he couldn't break the window and he was afraid neighbors heard the noise. He ran away into the night in frustration.

He started a new volume of his diary on January 22. He noted the day as a milestone:

> "I am about to start my career as a serial killer. Yes, I'm about to start my campaign of mass murder.

"I will be the best at what I'm to do. Out of all the killers before me surely I'll be in the ranks of the most high. [. . .] Even if I kill only Tessie, my campaign has only began."

He went to her place again on January 25 to kill her, but this time, she was walking too fast for him to get in position and do it. He thought he could have gotten her, but he decided he wasn't ready.

It was one of many dry runs he would make. After a while, the tension inside eased, and he made no further efforts, even halfhearted ones. He was becoming what he feared: a bullshitter to himself.

He liked to write about it, to rave on and on about it, but doing it was something else. He agonized over being chicken.

On February 6 he tripped for his thirteenth time on acid. Before that he went over to see Tessie. He wrote later:

"When I went over there . . . she peeped out the door and went inside like I just asked her to fuck, just playing the game. *WHY?* I know she likes me, maybe not enough to sex me but mom and probably her mom and others told her I was on drugs and shit. She probably thinks I'm some wild crazy beast who will rape her and kill her . . . I have gut feeling she likes me, but she's scared because she's got a stereotype on druggies."

Jason was in one of his frequent rages toward his mother:

"I'm getting tired of my mom. She's starting to piss me off. . . . I can't stand to even think of her . . . Let's cut the bullshit. She hates me & I hate her."

He was thinking he would have to put her six feet under. Jason remembered that his grandmother once told him,

"Whatever you do, you better make your mark." That was what he had in mind. He planned to engrave his name in history; he would be the country's greatest serial killer ever. He wanted to "grab society by the throat and shock 'em with terror until [. . .] they realize what's up. So they'll remember who I am & why I came their way."

He was sure the Master had his eye on him. He'd give him a "knowing" and smooth the path for him to do his bidding. After all, he was not asking too much. All he wanted was "to murder countless young women."

At times he felt like going to the high school in Ennis and to kill some of his intended victims all at once, massacre them on the spot.

Even if he died, if the pigs shot him down, he'd like to do it just for the shock and memory that would result. But he hoped it didn't come to that. He'd rather do it the way he'd been planning for the past five years.

By March 13, 1991, he was becoming overwhelmed with his fantasies. He was high the night he wrote in his diary:

"The number of girls I've decided to get [is] getting higher. It's just when I see one I know I have to get her, and I just fall in love with her and thoughts of killing, torturing, and mutilating them . . . I'm not very interested in 10-year-olds but Tessie is special. After her I will go only for 17 and well—it, age—really don't matter because when I see the *one* I'll know it's the one."

He was worried that if he didn't act soon, God would return to earth and it would be too late. God would kill him and Jesus would take his girls to heaven in the Rapture.

They would be separated by heaven and hell.

* * *

Jason learned suddenly that violent death is not like it is depicted on TV. One day about 5:30 P.M., in front of a bar near his home, he witnessed a man killed by gunshots.

He had seen the man only a few times before, but to see him shot down in the street affected him deeply.

"Death is really dead serious," he wrote. He didn't know how God could allow it. Witnessing the murder frightened him to the point that "if I don't begin to serve God he'll take my life. [. . .] He wants me killed because I don't worship him."

He was his old self the next day, wanting to rape and kill Tessie. But he was wondering if maybe he had a problem; maybe should see a shrink. He was thinking he did have some kind of problem, thought he might even be demon-possessed.

That night he wrote in his diary:

"I must be demon-possessed because I come up with these good ideas how I can rape, kill her and shit like that. They just 'pop' inside my head. I just know something that I couldn't 'know' without the demons."

By the next week Tessie was shoved to the back of Jason's mind. As he put it in his diary, "It's been a hell of a week!"

He had met a beautiful redheaded woman named Rita. What a sexy, sexy bitch! Older than him by several years, he guessed, but what the hell!

The night they met, they got high. He couldn't believe how her talk turned so quickly to sex. She asked him if he liked her tits. Damn, did he like her tits. Then she told him how her ex-husband liked to come home and eat her pussy. And just from the way she talked, he bet that she could suck a lawn sprinkler up a water hose.

That night was one of the wildest nights he'd ever spent with a woman. She was all that his fantasies were about. He had never been loved by any woman like that before.

But even better than that, this same week he realized a big

goal in his life: he got a gun. He couldn't believe it was true—it was too easy. It must be broken. He still hadn't shot it. A .9-mm model.

All of this and Barbara, too. Barbara was Rita's daughter. She was only twelve years old but mature for her age. Jason was mowing Rita's lawn when he met this gorgeous little girl. Rita told him that Barbara had started having her period when she was eleven. He knew if he was to get this young one, this really delicious-looking one, he would have to manipulate her carefully. He thought he could do this, and he wouldn't kill this one.

Impossible as it might seem, he still had Tessie on his mind. It had to be her childlike innocence. He didn't understand why he wanted her so, but he loved her body, her face, her hair, her pert cheerleader looks. He still remembered when she'd pulled his pants down, and when she'd said he was evil, and when she'd asked if he was going to kill her soul.

After Rita and after meeting Barbara, he couldn't believe that he still was thinking about Tessie.

Jason had heard that somewhere in the world, perhaps Korea, a religious cult was sure that the world was going to end on May 15, 1991. One week before, he wrote in his Slayer Book of Death:

> "THE CHASE HAS BEGAN! . . . If I live past the 15th, then I and only I alone will make the biggest change in my life. If I'm still here after the 15th then I'll take it that the Lord isn't going to kill me . . . is going to let me live and thusly I will truly begin the chase and live out my 'fantasies.'
>
> "Tomorrow I'm going to see if Tessie still lives in the apts. where we lived. If so she's dead by next day."

The days went by and he lived after May 15 and Tessie lived on. On May 21, he wrote himself an alibi: "I've put off killing you because I want to fuck you violently, kill you and drink your blood from your neck." He needed to get Tessie so he could concentrate on Anita.

"I've said the chase has begun. It hasn't. Not yet, not until I've taken off [. . .] this bracelet as a vow. Tessie gave me this bracelet."

Fifteen

In June 1991, Jason Massey's personal world fell in on him. It might as well have been the end of the world.

The police picked him up for unlawful possession of a weapon, a gun, in a tavern, a third-degree felony. His mother was looking in his closet for some money to post his bond when she accidentally found his diaries. When she read through them, she was shocked and disturbed by the contents. Those warped and twisted fantasies, as recorded by Jason, about raping, torturing, and killing young girls, and killing and mutilating animals, caused her great concern that her son was suffering from possible mental illness.

After he was freed on bond, she took him to Parkland Memorial Hospital on June 10. As a voluntary patient, he was interviewed in the psychiatry emergency room by Dr. Kenneth Dekleva, a staff psychiatrist on duty that day.

The youth's mother turned over the diaries she had read. Dekleva interviewed both Jason and his mother about his background, then leafed through the diaries.

The lurid entries covered the period from January 1991 to June 1991, in which Jason outlined his plans for becoming a serial killer and listed the names of several intended female victims, as well as Police Chief Dale Holt of Ennis.

Jason hated Holt because of the way in which the police chief had talked to him once when he was brought in for questioning. The pig had called him an asshole. He didn't realize Chief Holt had been playing the "bad cop" role in the good cop-bad cop routine for quizzing a suspect.

The psychiatrist later reached the conclusion that Jason was both homicidal and suicidal in his thoughts and writings and was dangerous not only to himself, but to others as well.

To the young doctor, the most alarming thing about the diary entries was the progression from fantasy to specific, deliberate planning, including the purchasing of weapons. And Jason had been arrested only a few days before his mother'd brought him to the hospital for possessing a gun on the tavern premises.

Dr. Dekleva believed Jason Massey might be suffering from mental illness.

Several hours later, Massey was transferred to a mental diagnostic center in Dallas, now known as the Dallas County Psychiatric Intensive Care Unit. There he would have additional examinations and it would be decided at a hearing whether he met the criteria for commitment.

But other doctors who examined Jason failed to concur with Dr. Dekleva, and Massey was released.

Massey temporarily discontinued his diary, fearing his mother would discover the new volume. However, he started again and on November 5, 1991, Massey was philosophical about his dysfunctional life as he wrote:

"Mom had one chance to help me. 'The system' had one chance, too. So what can I say? It's not my fault. After reading all the shit in those two books they had a reason to get a court order to get me some help.

"But now, I have a chance to beat them. I have the mind and I know what I have to do; but for me it's just a matter of doing it.

"Almost always in the past I have gotten in a hurry to get on with it, getting on the road and heading up north to the mountains. Now I'm on probation for 3 years and why not take these three years of probation and turn them into something positive?"

Massey had received the probationary term on the illegal possession of a weapon charge. Now he had to report periodically to a probation officer and undergo a urinalysis for signs of drug use. If drug usage was detected, he could go to the pen.

Rita had invited him to move in with her and he decided to take her up on the offer.

Ever aware of the strict provisions of his probation, Jason was more nervous about using drugs or other activities that might end his freedom, but it did not harness him when the urges became too strong. He might have been more careful to a degree, but he was not the kind to be pinned down by the law.

After all, he had the Master on his side, the "knowing" that came from him, the feeling that he was anointed by Satan to do his bidding. He obtained another gun, needing it for the 'jacking, as he called the planned robbery, of Popeye's, a fast-food chicken place where he'd worked for a while before being fired.

It was only one of several jobs Jason had held over a period of months; he'd worked in a convenience store and had also mowed lawns. He needed another job now to satisfy the terms of the probation. But first, he needed money to satisfy his growing drug habit.

Jason and Paul started planning the Popeye's holdup two weeks in advance, casing the restaurant and making sure each knew his part in the heist.

On a summer night they struck.

Jason, with his semi-automatic, waited in front, in the shadow of an abandoned pizza joint next door. He would give a whistle and signal when the restaurant employees came out the door. Then Paul would run around and join him to help keep an eye on the employees and take the money from the safe after it was opened.

When the workers came out, Jason and Paul moved on them quickly.

Jason gestured with the pistol he held, ordering them:

"Turn around and don't look at me or you're dead!" He ordered the manager, "Don't look at me. Head straight back to the door!" Herding the employees, Jason followed them into the restaurant.

"Manager, you open the safe. Hand me every penny you have."

Paul handled the money. When the safe was empty, Jason ordered the employees, "Stay facedown on the ground for at least five minutes and nothing will happen to you."

He ripped the phone from the wall and threw it on the floor. Then he and Paul ran from the building. They dashed across the parking lot and down an alley and ran for several blocks into a darkened residential neighborhood.

"Let's take some cash and hide the rest," Jason said. "We don't want it on us if the pigs happen to stop us." They concealed the sack of money in some shrubs, noting its location so they could retrieve it later.

They continued their flight on side roads and alleys until they spotted a public pay phone. Jason called a cab, which delivered them both to their homes. The cabbie was paid from the loot.

They returned for the stashed money a few days later, when they felt they were in the clear. They split the take, each getting about $750. The money was spent on drugs, beer, and food, and gas for driving around. Jason was exuberant over the success of the robbery, but he didn't write about it in his diary. It was about the only time he showed any discretion about what he recorded.

Jason was drunk out of his mind. He was smoking weed on top of the booze. Rita was drinking, but she still knew what was happening. She was helpless to stop Jason when he was this far gone. They were in Barbara's bedroom and Rita was glad the girl wasn't home.

In recent days, Jason had raved on and on about gruesome stuff—killing female cows, having sex with them, slaughtering cats and dogs and cutting off their heads for trophies. He had even showed her some heads in various stages of decay stored in a shed. Rita knew then that he should go.

She accidentally came across the journal he was keeping in a spiral notebook. When she glanced through the pages, she couldn't believe what he'd written. She decided he was crazy, crazy as a bedbug, when he was high. Sober, he kept all that rambling madness inside, but now . . .

As Rita looked on with fear and horror, the youth who so many nights had been her lover dragged a dog into the bedroom and tied it to a post of Barbara's bed.

"Jason, what are you doing?" she yelled.

"Shut up and watch."

She slapped his face hard.

He grabbed her and pressed the butcher knife in his gloved hand to her throat. "I oughta slice your belly open, bitch!" His face was contorted and his blue eyes were blazing. He let her go and turned back to the dog.

He grinned as he cut the dog's throat with one sweeping slash of the butcher knife. Rita screamed and covered her face with her hands. He laughed and ignored her crying and pleading. She ran from the room to get rags and a pan of water to clean up the horrible mess before her daughter returned. In her alcoholic daze, she thought the gory room had to be cleaned. Saving herself didn't occur to her.

He dragged the dog out. As she scrubbed, she didn't want to think what he would do next.

Before she finished mopping up, Jason came in with a second dog, tied it to the same bedpost, and almost decapitated it. Terror overcoming the sickness that engulfed her, Rita fled from the nightmarish scene. She heard Jason go out and she ran to lock the door. He walked away, dragging the dog's corpse into the night. She knew he'd stay away for several hours. She had never seen anything to match this horror. After a drunken or dope explosion, he always left to return later composed and acting as if nothing had happened.

Jason had told her he did such things when called by his Master. She had thought it was the rantings of a doper stoned out of reality, until the day he showed her his "trophies."

During the long night, as her head cleared to be replaced by a reverberating headache and disabling nausea, she knew she had to do something about getting him out of her house forever.

Their sexual relationship and Jason's love when he was sober had clouded Rita's thinking even when she was sober—until now. The crazy pervert was finished living with her.

Jason Massey, at various times, was disgusted with himself for talking too much or carelessly leaving his diary where someone could read it. He was doing stupid things for someone who planned to become the world's greatest serial killer. He dwelled on the bad habit of talking too much in his diary:

"I told Rita about all the dogs & cats & cows and she believed me. I've not told her my biggest secret & I won't [apparently a reference to his girl killing ambitions]. The only one I've ever told is Paul, and he's not my destiny—as much as I wish it were it's not. I want to think I'll have another [killing partner] but I'll probably end up just being solo. [. . . Paul] won't be going with me to the Pacific N.W. or Canada. He's into drugs *too much* anymore, I believe. I know he's frying his brain with all the crack and shit he's doing. I think all he does is try to get or do drugs."

Jason also decided he trusted people too much.

"I'm so sick of people. I trust them with all my thoughts and people are to be distrusted. I want to trust 'em but I can't.

"Rita hit me in the mouth for no reason last night and I won't ever forget it and I want revenge. Stupid bitch, she said thanks for not killing me. I'd like to put a butcher knife in your chest. I'd probably chicken out in the end. Boy, Jay, what a great serial killer you'd make. . . .

"I want to be a killer. As odd as it may seem I want to

be a killer who's very strong & handsome. [. . .] I feel so stupid for leaving this out for Rita to find. Now she knows everything. She read my book.

"NEVER SPEAK YOUR *TRUE NATURE!* The *least* friends you have the better. You used to not speak your nature to anyone. But now everyone and the police have copies of names and my twisted and sadistic 'lust' for Anita on them."

Jason never expected it to happen, but one day Paul told him he was ready for the big trip to the Pacific Northwest and Canada. Paul laid out his plan to Jason and Aaron, who was going with them.

He would steal his mother's car, some gasoline, and some get-along money and pick them up at Flagpole Hill. Jason and Aaron got their things together and stashed them in the woods near the rendezvous site.

"If he backs out this time, it's going to be too bad for him," Jason told Aaron as they waited.

But Paul pulled up in his mom's car. They heaved their stuff into the trunk, and they were doing it at last. With Paul driving, they headed out of town on highway 287 toward Amarillo, and from there points west and north.

But the great expectations came to an abrupt end in Oregon, where they were nabbed by police who had received a stolen-car report on the car owned by Paul's mother.

The runaways were returned to Texas, but no charges were pressed by Paul's mother. Once again one of Jason's big plans had run off the track.

Rita gave in to Jason's pleadings to return. In spite of his emotional vows to straighten up, Massey soon was doing things that made Rita regret it.

He did stay relatively sober for a while.

But then he did something strange one evening. She couldn't understand at all why he crawled under the kitchen sink and watched her through the open bathroom door in a bathroom mirror while she took a bath. He told Rita afterward that the voyeurism was exciting to him.

He told her another time that she couldn't satisfy him sexually anymore because it never could be as good as it would be with a dead woman. He raved on about how he would like to have sex with Rita while she lay on top of the dead cow he had cut open in a field in Ennis.

Still another time, when Rita confronted him about doing extensive damage in her bedroom with a baseball bat and cutting the end of her box springs with a knife, he began babbling and crying and wound up pressing a knife sharply into her stomach. He ordered her to climb out the bedroom window and not return until she found some "rock."

She never called the cops. She didn't think they would understand why she was having anything to do with a guy like that in the first place.

Sixteen

At the beginning of 1992 all Jason's thoughts were on Barbara, not Rita, her mother. On January 2 he noted in his diary that his nineteenth birthday was only five days away. During the next few days, he wrote of his longing for Barbara:

"She laughs at my love. Loving never works. Even one I love never loves me. It was not meant for me . . . I will do what I must . . . I don't want to kill Barbara, but she don't love me. She rejected me. She laughed & sneered at me. [. . .] She never even gave me 1 chance. Now I have finally made my choice. She must die. [. . .] If only you would have listened telling you how much I love you. You had to be bitchie. You have defied me.

"So far, just thinking of killing a lot of young girls makes me happy, but it's at a point where it's going to be reality. . . . I guess it's going to be hardest to do the first ones . . . Barbara, I still love her. I guess that's why I want to do her."

Jason had nothing but anger now for Rita. She had given him herpes, he was sure. The disease he'd gotten from Rita, it would be with him the rest of his life. If not for Rita, he'd have Barbara instead of herpes. He'd make Rita pay with her life the very first chance he had.

In July 1992, Jason's fantasies of young dead girls, of violating their youthful bodies before and after death, ripping and tearing inside and out, were building like an unbearable boil about to burst. He had to have a car to do it all. He wrote in his diary:

"I want to get drunk, drive, pick up a fine female victim, rape her, kill her, then make love to her once again. It seems my desires for the death of untold numbers is growing. I want to kill just to have sex, and now that I have herpies that desire of sex with the corpses of beautiful young girls grows. . . .

"So I will just kill her before sex. Plus I just have this picture in my mind of this dead girl lying on back, eyes and mouth open, naked, the moonlight shining down through the trees and how so romantic it would be to climb on top of her lifeless, naked, pale, cold, clammy corpse and make love to her throughout the night. . . .

"I will have Barbara. . . . I can see her crying already. I know what I'm going to do to her. I've even figured about where I'll bury her. And hopefully all the hurt she's put me through, I am going to hurt her. I want her to cry, beg and tell me she loves me. . . .

"I guess I'll stun her and drug her and carry her out in the yard. Take her to my ALTAR OF SACRIFICE, rape her, kill her. . . ."

Jason and his mom had moved back to Ennis in the spring of 1992. Maybe it was the separating distance (although it was only about forty miles from Dallas) that made his deviant longings for Barbara, his personally envisioned Lolita, rage beyond control.

He still visited Dallas frequently. And on one of these visits in late August, Jason's weeks of fantasy erupted violently into reality.

They were alone in the house while Rita was out on an errand. Jason and the now thirteen-year-old Barbara were talking in the living room and watching TV. Barbara was miserable. She could see that Jason was really drunk, and she was feeling uneasy. She became more worried when he started saying that she didn't care for him or their friendship.

That wasn't new—he was always feeling sorry for himself, especially when he was boozing—but he was acting strange tonight.

Finally she said, "Jason, I'm sorry, but I need to go to bed. I have to get up early in the morning, need to get to school early." She said goodnight and walked to her room.

Five minutes later she was in bed. Jason walked in and said, "Barbara, I'm sorry if I upset you. I came in to make up. Give me a goodnight hug, will you?"

She sat up, hugging him as he bent over, and as they embraced, he put a knife to her throat.

"I should have killed you a long time ago," he said, pressing the knife point against her skin hard enough for her to cry out.

Her scream sent a surge of triumph and sexual excitement through him, an adrenaline rush not unlike the one he felt when he cut off a cat's head. "Don't you move, or I'll kill you."

She fought inside to stay calm, even in her rising panic. She was sure that if she tried to run or scream again, he would kill her. She had begun fearing him when he lived in their house, ever since she'd heard the awful stories about him killing animals. When he'd told her those things, she'd cried, but he'd kept telling her more and more horrible things, talking dirty, enjoying her wide-eyed repulsion and fear.

Now he wasn't telling her terrible things; he was doing things that frightened her. He pulled at her clothing, breathing hard, his foul, sour breath sickening her. He yanked down her pants, then slashed away her panties.

He had taken off his jeans and was fumbling with himself as he struggled with the crying girl. He ran his tongue over her exposed shoulder, up to her face, licking at her salty tears.

Just then, Rita came home.

Jason grabbed up his pants and hurried from the room.

Barbara told her mother about Jason coming into her room and talking to her and frightening her. An enraged Rita ordered him to leave. She said if he didn't leave, she was going to call the police.

"Never come around here again, you no-good bastard," she shouted.

Massey left, aching with the frustration of how close he had come to the ultimate joy of his sick dreams, knowing he must take the life of the girl he loved so much.

Jason recorded the attack in his diary:

"Well, the act itself occurred around 12:30 A.M. It's about 6 A.M. Saturday morning. Well, Jay this is a day to remember. This is what I did.

"I smoked some stones for a while, then I drank about a 12-pack. Anyway, I went into Barbara's room to get to myself. Before long I began to imagine and more realistically plan a 'rape.' She came into her room and I was caught. Then a while later I drank a beer or two, then I went into her room. Before I knew what I did, I just put the knife to her throat. She kinda thought, well I guess she thought I was B.S. . . .

"Before long I had her so scared she began to cry. And I put my knife to her throat and told her 'If you scream I'll kill you. [. . .] it got her believing I was going to kill her.

"I remember [. . .] hearing her gasp, telling her not to move, climbing onto her, terrorizing her for so long, then making her take off her pants, and then I cut off her panties, pulled off mine and then Rita comes home as I was seconds away from raping her. God, I came so close I don't know what would have happened if I did of raped her. God, I love her so much. It hurts me to think I probably won't ever win her love. . . .

"I'm afraid Barbara's going to talk. She told Rita about

it, all but the attempted rape, I think. It's going to be a sad time when I have to [. . .] kill her. But if I can't have her, no one will."

Somehow, he and Rita made up enough for another visit. But it was the last one. He recorded it in his diary on September 10, 1992:

"I left Rita, again; for good, too. Shit was really crazy there at the end. I hit her in the eye, and last night she pulled my hair. And before I knew it I had her on the ground by the throat strangling her. Came within literally seconds of raping Barbara, and during all of it I was drunk.

"I just get uncontrollable when I drink. . . .

"I have a feeling that in 1993 I will kill two people. Barbara is one, Tessie #2. . . . I just have a feeling once I get started my confidence will overwhelm me. Then I'll begin to kill regularly. Maybe uncontrollably!

"My lust to kill women and have sex with the dead consumes me and my thoughts daily. When I see a woman on TV being strangled, it excites me sexually. . . .

"I think of the time when I travel in my car to other towns to lure and kill many young girls."

Seventeen

Back in Ennis, it was easy for Jason to return to the life of his earlier years. He was happy to go again to the woods behind McDonald's, where deep into the trees he had his "Altar of Sacrifice."

On one of his first visits to the woods he symbolically buried Barbara, to see how he would feel when she was gone. He was more optimistic and felt as if his life was finally turning around.

Right now, his aim in life was "to stay clean," improve his reputation, exercise, eat right, and stay off drugs. He remained on probation from the Dallas County weapon charge, which was mostly responsible for his good intentions. "There will be things I can't control, but I can control my choice to stay clean."

But one thing didn't change: his lust for young girls was strong as ever. He dreamed one night that he entered a church and saw a girl, ten or eleven years old, with long hair. He forced her into a bathroom, strangled her to death, and had intercourse with her body.

Sex and death filled his thoughts. He wrote:

"I guess these things are all I think of.

"It kinda scares me and makes me sad to think of what I am capable of inflicting on humanity. It scared me to think when I get my driver's license and drive, a killing will be all I can think of."

Autumn was in the air. The trees and shrubs were still green and it was hot, but the sun was moving to the south, clearing the way for the crisper weather of the holidays, his favorite time of year, for some reason. He wanted badly to kill a girl and feel her cold flesh after the body was exposed to winter's cold. He wanted to do Barbara in the winter so he could touch her cold skin.

He believed that after his first murder, when he lost his virginity as a nonkiller, "I won't feel nothing for taking folks out. They'll be like another dog."

He knew that if he drank enough beer, "I feel no emotion and I could kill a girl with little or no second thought, but I want to be sober so I can feel all the emotion."

Jason visited the man said to be his father, and the man's wife. He really liked her. He told her about Barbara and his love for her, and she seemed to understand. He didn't mention anything about wanting to kill her, of course. He began wondering: if he killed another girl, would he forget Barbara?

Writing in his diary, Jason recalled that one month and one and one-half hours had gone by since he'd almost raped Barbara in Dallas.

"I remember the power I felt when I got on top of her. I remember it felt like I had done it a hundred times before. I remember how she cried and how I felt on her right tit as I went down on her neck, up her face and the taste of that tear. I remember how she took off her pants so fast, almost in anger. [. . .] But more than anything I'll remember the pain and the pleas for her life. [. . .] But I'll remember how she died the most."

He still was undecided where to bury her. He wanted the spot to be close enough so he could visit her, but far enough away that if the police suspected him of murder they couldn't find her. He guessed it wouldn't matter, as long as it was a deep hole.

* * *

Jason wanted to create a new image for himself. That was the way he would get all he wanted, get on with his life, and forget the past mistakes.

He had a job and received his first paycheck on October 15. He paid his bills. He attended Alcoholics Anonymous meetings. He liked the AA people. They'd put bad problems behind them. Attending the meetings also pleased his probation officer.

He saved his salary, going so far as even to drink water instead of soft drinks at work. All the things he wanted—a car, camping gear, guns—took money. He read books and articles on police and FBI operations, especially on serial murder. He watched all the cop shows on TV.

He looked forward to the day when he could say he'd killed a human and was a murderer. In God's eyes he guessed he already was a murderer because he'd killed a cat when he was nine years old. Only a cat, but nevertheless, a life of some value, he thought. But to him there was a big difference between humans and animals.

He counted up five sexual killings of cows he had done, which convinced him he had the capabilities of a "to be" serial killer. He cut out pictures of mutilated women from the crime magazines and looked at them at night in his room.

Masturbation gave him little relief. "I'll be the first serial killer in Ennis," he prophesied in the diary. "But there's so much killing I want to do now, it's hard to wait, especially when I look at these pictures."

He dreamed about a Dallas girl who had taken his knife from him. That was an embarrassment. He had not forgotten her, and he vowed that after he moved north, he'd return and kill her.

He wrote:

"I love 'em all, that's why I have to kill 'em. They'll never love me, and I can go see bones any time.

"Rape is not enough. I must have a body for the next

day or two, to hold, talk to and make love, bones to talk with, burial sites to remember, towns in fear. [. . .] The bones will cry to me from the earth. Their sorrow is my joy. Their tears my fountain of youth."

Jason's smouldering hatred for women flowed like acid in his written words.

"Women, bitches of the earth, all these whores from hell with their damning curses. I hate them. . . . I've found out there are few good girls anymore. Most girls over 18 have had multiple sex partners. Whores deserve to die."

The day before Thanksgiving, Jason wrote:

"Almost all my family will be there. It's going to be nice to see everyone. I would like to see Dad thanksgiving.
"But I'm sure 'they' all have their own little deal so I won't interfere."

Thanksgiving, as he predicted, was a flop for Jason. He wrote on Thanksgiving night:

"I asked my dad to come out tonight. He said no. It pisses me off. I love him, and he, too, seems to push me away. Fuck him! I'll give him one more chance, then to hell with him."

Jason planned to get his driver's license and some eyeglasses. He was still saving for a truck or car.

He dreamed he raped a fourteen-year-old girl at knifepoint. He had forgotten to write about the dream in which he shot another little girl in the head with an Uzi. He knew his dreams reflected his desires. In other dreams, he'd "killed a lady and her two boys," and "killed Lois and cut her throat viciously in a bathtub. I did it so hard I cut myself."

Various diary entries stressed the type of young girls who drew his attention:

> "It's their vibes they give off of a carefree, laughing, fun, outgoing, life's-a-party cheerleader type with long, dark hair, a lot of laughs and smiles, that attract me, innocents."

The third day into 1993, he was worried that the Holy Spirit was working on him. It offended him, because he believed he was "very demon-possessed." Jason believed he had not been killed yet because Satan's demons rested in him. Powerful ones, he was certain.

He felt as if he were losing his mind. He wanted to die, and he wanted to live to kill.

On January 14, he had what he considered "The Final Solution."

> "I have come up with the master plan. It is truly the final solution. I don't recall a plan so devious and ingenious, too, I've ever made. I'm sure it will work."

The plan was how to "do" Barbara: he would strangle her. Then, before burying the body, he would "f— her brains out literally, eat some of her brain, heart."

Also, cut out her vagina and, "after preparation, eat it and her ovaries, stab her in the thighs, breasts, butt."

He would "live out my fantasy, this one last time with her. . . . I'll show her . . . just how sick old Jay is."

Jason had a new girlfriend, but regardless, he needed to keep budgeting his money if he was ever going to do what he wanted.

He had a special fantasy about his new girl, Marti. "I really get off thinking of Marti putting on the blood-soaked gloves I used to skin 'Baldy,' Dog No. 31."

Marti was a "good" girl, church-going, resistant to sex, and closely watched by her mother. But Jason was optimistic: she would give in to sex in three months, he figured.

"If not, I'll continue to date her for social reasons. I need to keep a good, damn good, rep[utation] and at the same time, some way, people must know that when J. M. says something, don't question him."

One Sunday he went to church with Marti, then the two of them and some of her church friends went to the lake. He and Marti did some French kissing, which gave him an erection.

The way she talked, Marti was thinking about marriage, but he wasn't ready for that. He wondered if he would ever have a normal relationship with a woman, if he would ever lose his desire to roam and kill.

"I don't understand it. I guess it will always be there like my drinking problem."

But he knew, because of his herpes, he would never be able to have intercourse with any girl without using a condom.

Jason's life was going well and he was working thirty-eight hours a week. However, with all the frustration of Marti refusing him sex and talking about marriage, he slipped up and got drunk, even did some drugs.

He guessed AA wouldn't work unless he spoke at a meeting and got some of this off his chest. He felt AA was a good deal and could help a guy if he wanted help badly enough.

Jason wanted to join the Army and serve a few years before he ever got married. But getting married, having kids, and a dog named Spot, that wasn't for him. And there was his "career" of killing he had to think of. He admitted he wasn't like other kids, never would be.

But he felt his reputation was being "healed." Paying his granny back money he owed helped a lot; she didn't believe he would, Jason thought.

He planned to do more for her this spring—wax her car, mow her yard, go to church. That would make her happy. She had been attending church as long as he could remember, had started in church years before he was born. She was one relative for whom he felt a deep love. She was always there to help, to give him a lift up. She always witnessed for the Lord, too. He loved his Granny Sue.

His mom and his grandpa were proud of him, too. He was proud of himself. But he noted: "I'm in good with everyone except me and Jesus."

By late winter, on the brink of spring, the restlessness was there again, strong and unrelenting.

His having a girlfriend didn't help. Barbara still haunted his mind, his desires. He drove out to see the place where 34th and Chambers Creek met, an isolated spot with woods and brush, a good area to bury a body. There was a car wash in Avalon where he could clean up a car in some privacy.

But first he had to keep building an image. He was working on what he described as a "good Ted Bundy image," but it would take time. Bundy had fooled everybody with his clean-cut college-boy looks and demeanor, and it had enabled him to kill girls everywhere he went. Bundy was cool.

He decided he didn't need to drink to kill. He prayed his drinking was over. He didn't know when or where, but he knew before long that he would abduct, rape, torture, and kill Barbara. "Then stay with her corpse the night and make love to her, then sleep 'til noon or so, play with her body for more sex, before sundown sex once more, then I must dismember her for eating, then behead her, finally disembowel her before burying her."

* * *

In March 1993, a year had passed since he'd left Rita, or Rita'd left him, and he was "doing good." He had a job, a girlfriend, and a driver's license, and he would have a car soon, and glasses.

Jason believed he had learned much since he first started keeping a diary in 1989. He continued to study criminal investigation and serial murder. And he was about to get off probation.

"May it all come to pass. I want to kill over and over again, years of it, hundreds of victims. [. . .] Next summer will be worse on them than this one, and the summer of '95 will be the worst year for Ennis, TX. ever!"

In three weeks he would have a car. But he was concerned about the money he was spending hanging out with Mark Gentry, Chris Nowlin, and other guys.

They got together regularly, with whoever had a car, and drove around for hours, drinking beer, doing coke, and smoking primos (marijuana cigarettes laced with coke).

They did wild things when they were doped up and drunk, boasting what they would do to girls, and at times getting mad at each other. One night Jason and two other guys were riding around the Bristol area when they stopped to take a leak. Jason spotted a calf nearby, went to the car for a hammer, and hit the calf in the head. He dragged it to the car and pounded it again with the hammer. The youths put the unconscious calf in the back seat of the four-door Subaru.

When the calf moved, Jeff hit it with his fist. Everybody was into the fun. Later, they dropped Jeff at his house. Jeff never knew what happened to the calf. He thought Jason probably had his usual fun with it. Jason liked to screw dead animals. Damn, he was queer. Talked about killing women, too.

* * *

In April, the same trio went calf hunting again, this time near Telico, in Ellis County. Jason spied two calves near the wire fence just off the road. He stopped the car, got out, and slugged one calf in the head twice with a billy club.

Then he saw a car coming down the road and quickly got back into the Subaru.

He drove down the road until the other car's taillights had disappeared. Then Jason turned around and came back.

He pulled the calf into the road, and Jeff hit it across the neck with an ax. Then they loaded the calf into the back seat. They drove around drinking, ending up in a little town called Alma. They drove around there for about an hour, boozing and talking about what they would do with the calf.

"You know, I'd like to know how it feels to kill somebody, a human, a girl," Jason said, gulping down his brew. *He's always saying things like that,* Jeff thought.

They were used to Jason talking about killing women or wanting to, and doing dirty things with their bodies. If you hit *him* in the head with an ax, a pussy would fall out.

Jeff mentioned he wanted to go home, so he was dropped at his house. When he got out, he turned and hit the calf several times.

Jason was getting drunk and said he wanted to call it a night.

Driving his buddy Joey home, he fell asleep at the wheel and the car bounced off the curb and a tire went flat immediately. Jason never drove slowly. They fixed the flat, then Joey took Jason home and got a ride back with a friend.

Later, an Ennis detective talked to Joey about a dead calf found near McDonald's, where a guy was seen running away early in the morning.

Joey gave a statement about the previous night's activities and was released. He never learned if anything came of it.

On Friday, April 9, 1993, Jason went to church at his mom's and Granny's request. During the invitation, when the preacher asks people to come forward and get right with Jesus, Jason walked down the aisle and told one of the deacons a lot about himself, mentioning no names. He confessed to the attempted rape on Barbara and told of his involvement in Satanism rituals and worship.

Later, he wrote in his diary that he had been saved.

> "Anyway, I love the Lord. To hell with Satan and his army. The same with drugs. I will not alter my conscience with that shit. Any of it. I've been saved. I still want Barbara. I want to marry her. If it ever happens, it will be of God. I still want to kill. Maybe just Barbara."

Three days later, Jason wrote:

> "I have my car fixed and running. I haven't had much time to write with all the shit going on. Marti and I had a big talk yesterday about me never seeing her. Her mom's pissed."

In the early summer of 1993, Jason Massey found himself in trouble. Mark Gentry was angry because he thought Jason was messing with his girlfriend. Jason had broken the unwritten code—You don't mess with a buddy's girl, or even ex-girl, without asking the guy if it was all right.

Gentry was sure that Jason had busted the code. Jason had been visiting with Gentry's ex-girlfriend, who Gentry wasn't sure he was finished with. Jason hadn't asked him if it was okay.

One night Gentry, Nowlin, and two other guys went looking for Jason to beat the hell out of him in retaliation.

Gentry and Nowlin were known to the Ennis cops as small-time troublemakers. When the booze was flowing or dope was being done, they could be spiteful.

Nowlin explained the falling-out later in court this way, speaking of Gentry and his girlfriend:

"They was girlfriend and boyfriend, and they broke up. We all, you know, we all hang around each other, me and Mark and Jason Massey and a couple other dudes, and we broke up with a girl, then we'd go to each other and say can I mess with her and stuff, me and her mess around. Jason Massey didn't do that. He just went straight to her. You know, Mark was trying to get her to be his girlfriend again. And he [Jason] was going over to her house, you know, trying to mess with her and stuff like that."

On July 18, 1993, Mark Gentry went hunting for Jason. Nowlin and two other guys were with him, in one of the other guys' cars. They drove to a house where Massey was, but Jason saw them and took off in his car.

Nowlin later testified in court:

"We was in, we was cruisin', we went after him, you know, he took off in his car, so we jumped in our car and was going behind him, and, you know, when we lost him. And then we seen him again on this one road, and we going behind him, and then we kept on getting in front of him with our car."

He said the driver wheeled into the side of Massey's Subaru to try and stop him. They chased him a couple of miles out highway 34 near Ennis.

The ramming of Massey's car did extensive damage, including breaking windows on one side. Massey swerved to the side, then took off toward Ennis. The group in the other car followed Massey, but when he stopped and went into a house in Ennis, they drove on. The fight was over for the time being.

After that night, Jason Massey was on the run from his former buddies.

Two days before that falling out, Chris Nowlin and Jason had been together to smoke some weed and do some coke. They drove around, sucking down beers on top of the dope, looking for some of their pals to visit, but they didn't find any of them at home.

Chris had the idea to go see a thirteen-year-old girl that he knew, just as a friend, not a real going-out girlfriend. That sounded good to Jason, especially her age, and Chris said she was a pretty blonde.

Nowlin and Massey went to her house, and Nowlin introduced Massey to the girl.

Jason Massey's destiny was set.

Eighteen

Execution of the evidentiary search warrant after Massey's arrest in Canton on August 2, 1993, had its share of headaches. District Judge Tommy W. Wallace, who would have to sign the search warrant before it could be served in that county, had left his courthouse office to see his son in a baseball game at nearby Grand Saline.

A Van Zandt County deputy sheriff drove Clay Strange and Johnny Cruz to Grand Saline to find the judge. Luck shone on them. The deputy spotted the judge driving along a street.

Back at 527 Big Rock, the search warrant was executed. An elderly man was the only occupant at home when the officers showed up, but Massey's mother, Nancy James, appeared there within a few minutes. She was shocked and visibly upset at her son's arrest earlier and the search of the house and premises.

The hunt for evidence began in a back bedroom where Massey was staying. The room was topsy-turvy even before the searchers started—newspapers, magazines, books, and clothes scattered everywhere. As they sorted and dug through the mess, the investigators found "girlie" and soft-porn magazines stuffed under and between cushions of a couch and between the mattress and the bedsprings.

Articles about the teenagers' murders from two newspapers also were found under the mattress of Massey's bed. One of the more ominous finds was a pair of handcuffs that appeared to have blood on them.

Books and magazines that indicated the suspect had a strong

interest in serial killers, satanic cult activities, and the techniques of homicide investigation were found in the bedroom and in a small storage building at the back, where Massey had cardboard boxes filled with his belongings.

Massey's library included *The Stranger Beside Me,* the story of killer Ted Bundy; *Confessions of Henry Lee Lucas,* the book about the killer who'd claimed at one time to have slain up to 600 people, then had recanted on most of them; *Whoever Fights Monsters,* case histories of serial killers; *The Search for the Green River Killer; Satan Is Alive and Well on Planet Earth; Satan's Angels Exposed;* and *Who Killed Precious?*

Other books were *The Holy Bible, The Book of Mormon, The Living Bible, Child of Faith, Will You Be in the Rapture?, Married Love, How to Make a Man Fall in Love with You, Four Horsemen of the Apocalypse, Poems of Modern Youth,* an alcoholics anonymous book (and AA attendance records), *Games People Play, Self Hypnosis,* and *I'm OK, You're OK.*

Revealing Massey's interest in police procedures were booklets, pamphlets, and papers such as *Law Enforcement Handgun Digest, Military Small Arms,* a folder containing police radio frequencies and signals, and a pamphlet titled *How to Abduct People.*

Other items were knives; a knife-sharpening stone; two small cooking pots; an army totebag; a metal water canteen; a road atlas; a state guide to Alaska; a 1992 issue of *Practical Survival;* city maps of Dallas and Ennis; three Halloween masks; a partially burned candle; a silver flashlight; a folder containing profiles of women with names, addresses, and phone numbers; newspaper clippings about serial killers and slaying victims such as Charles Manson; obscene photographs of women; a pair of women's white shorts; and two pairs of girls' panties (underneath the bed).

While the search continued in the house, Strange and Dep. Smith peered inside the 1982 tan Subaru parked in the drive. To

Strange's surprise, the interior looked to be spotlessly clean. A window on the side had been broken out, but no glass shards were present.

There had been speculation that the slain girl's missing head and hands might have been kept in the car trunk by the killer. However, when the keys were obtained and the trunk was opened, officers saw only ordinary items that might be found in any trunk, all neat and orderly.

"All neat as a pin, can you imagine that?" Strange asked Smith. "Would you say the young man has been to a car wash recently?"

The car interior and the trunk had the look of having been vacuumed carefully. Cruz was equally surprised by the neatness of the Subaru's interior, since all Massey's running pals said his car always was messy, piled with all kinds of junk from beer cans to dead cats in bags.

Meanwhile, arrangements were made to have the Subaru towed by a local wrecking service to the Dallas County Sheriff's Department, where it would be impounded and gone over inch by inch by criminalists who had the expertise and the latest in equipment to run a thorough search for trace evidence. The car was parked in the sheriff department's sally port at the Lew Sterrett Criminal Justice Center.

Lt. Gothard posted an Ellis County deputy to stand guard over the vehicle from the time it was hauled there until the search and examination could be done. With evidence it was necessary to maintain the all-important chain of custody integrity, meaning the state has to prove that no evidence was tampered with in any way or changed from its original condition.

After the house search was finished and evidence bagged and loaded into the investigators' cars, Gothard, Cruz, and Strange drove to the Van Zandt County Sheriff's Office to talk with Jason Massey.

The first sight that Gothard had of Massey was the grinning jail photograph. *Something is wrong here,* Gothard thought. The kid was grinning right after being told he was charged with capital murder.

When Massey was brought down from the jail for arraignment before a local judge, Gothard and Cruz were not impressed by the suspect's appearance.

Gothard saw that he was a small-framed youth with dirty blond hair and dirty jeans and T-shirt. Not filthy, really—just unkempt. Gothard had pictured him as a larger person. But what caught the attention of both officers was the suspect's blue eyes: cold eyes that stared right through you.

Gothard spoke briefly with Massey, then the youth was taken into an interrogation room. Johnny Cruz sat down in a chair across from Massey with a table between them. Sheriff Jordan was present for a few minutes, then went out.

Cruz gave the Miranda warning again before beginning the questioning. Massey spoke quietly and did not seem upset. He denied knowing Christina Benjamin or Brian King. When Cruz countered by telling Massey about the statements Gentry and Nowlin had given, the suspect said the statements were not true, that the two were trying to get back at him.

He said Gentry was "trying to get even with me because he thought I was messing around with his girlfriend" after the girl had quit seeing Gentry. He also denied ever killing cats or dogs or keeping their heads as trophies.

"How about the time you were arrested by the officers in Ennis?" Cruz asked. "When you had a live cat in the front seat, with a rope around its neck?" Cruz also enumerated the knife, axes, hatchet, hammer, and a satanic bible found in the car trunk by the Ennis patrolmen.

"They're wrong about all that," said Massey. "I didn't have no stuff like that in my car."

Cruz tried a shocker question. *What did you do with her head and hands, Jason?*

"I don't know anything about no head or hands," he replied.

The investigator noticed that although Massey denied having known the teenagers, he never once denied killing them. He never admitted it, either. But he spontaneously switched to talking about what a "third party" or "they" might have done with the head and hands.

"I know where they would bury the head and hands," he said.

The statement startled the investigator. Massey asked, "Are you familiar with the low-water crossing on Ensign Road?" The detective nodded.

"From Ennis you take highway 34 and turn on Ensign Road, follow that road to the low-water crossing, turn left on a dirt road, and follow the dirt road for a little way. The head and hands will be buried at the base of a tree in the trees near the creek, in a shallow hole, I can show you how to go."

Cruz studied the cold-eyed suspect as he talked. He had long blond hair not well kept, a pale-looking face, and the strangest stare he had ever seen; he was real calm—no body motion at all, no change of expression. Most people the detective had questioned showed some body movement—crossed their knees, changed position, avoided eye contact or looked away and back. This guy was impossible to read. Steady, quiet, polite, soft-spoken, weird—lying like hell, too, but doing so with control and ease.

It was late when the caravan of cars headed back to Waxahachie, with a stopover planned at the low-water crossing where Massey said he would direct them to where the killer would probably have buried the body parts. The handcuffed Massey rode with Gothard and Cruz, the lieutenant driving. Massey seemed to want to talk to Gothard.

They didn't talk about the murders. Gothard had related well to the men under his command during his Marine service. The older investigator was an open-faced, plain-spoken rural type who people found easy to talk to.

When the lawmen pulled on to the dirt road near the low-water crossing and got out, Massey led the way. The moon was bright, but when the seven investigators and the murder suspect entered the woods there was sudden blackness. No moonlight penetrated the thick canopy of tree branches. The officers had only three flashlights.

Strange, whose hobby was hiking, knew he wasn't outfitted for a nighttime walk in the dark and reptile-infested woods, but he went anyway. Foremost on his mind were snakes—deadly rattlers or other snakes that could strike suddenly if you walked too close or stepped on them.

The insects and frogs were in full chorus as the men slowly pushed through the dense brush and trees to a spot where Massey thought the parts "might" be buried. But they found nothing.

Ill-equipped for such a search, the group nevertheless spent two hours in the woods, looking under one tree and then another at Massey's direction. They wondered if the murder suspect had taken them for one big moonlit ride, without moonlight.

It was about 2 A.M. before they reached the Ellis County Sheriff's Office. Massey acted as though he still wanted to talk with Gothard. They sat in the lieutenant's office for another hour—Massey in a chair in front of Gothard's desk, Gothard leaning back in his swivel chair, hands behind his head, talking casually, as if he had the rest of the night.

"I think he wanted to tell me about the murders but couldn't bring himself to do it," Gothard later recalled. "At times he acted right on the verge."

Then Massey said, "I'm tired, sir. I need to sleep some."

Gothard knew that once a prisoner tells you that, that's it. You don't deny a man when he says that. Gothard was courtroom experienced and careful. He had even reiterated the Miranda warning to Massey when they'd sat down in his office.

Gothard was glad to call it a night. He was exhausted from the search in Canton and the stress of the trip through the woods. The tightness in his chest was there, too, along with a tiredness he had never felt before. At almost 57, he wondered if he was getting old.

The next morning he was back early, as was Cruz, but Massey's inclination to talk ended when he conferred with an attorney that morning.

Nineteen

That same morning after Massey's arrest the night before, the trace evidence people in Dallas went to work on the suspect's 1982 Subaru. When they were through, there would not be a speck of dust inside or outside the car that was not accounted for.

A photographer in the physical evidence section took photographs of the vehicle, exterior and interior, from different angles. Close-ups were taken of specific areas where possible evidence was seen. The vehicle was dusted for fingerprints.

Charles Lynch, the trace evidence analyst from Southwest Institute of Forensic Science, then took over. Lynch was moderately famous in Texas as the criminalist in several sensational murder cases, including the cross-country spree of serial killer Henry Lee Lucas.

The first thing Lynch checked was the carpeting on the floor. It was tan, just as he had thought after viewing the carpet fiber on Brian King's shoe. From a naked-eye look, Lynch didn't have much doubt that the shoe fiber was going to match fibers from this carpet.

He gathered several samples from the carpet, then turned to the rest of the car's inside. From the right front seat and right front floorboard he collected two plastic cups, a pair of sunglasses, a pair of prescription glasses, and one New Testament Bible.

From the trunk the criminalist removed a jacket, two pairs of gloves, a mask, a pair of shoes, and a pair of men's shorts. Other items included a green toolbox with tools, an orange reflector, a Phillips screwdriver, a roofing hammer, an ax, a matchbox, three sheets of paper, and a paper bag with a green leaf inside that appeared to have a blood spot on it. Another hammer and a roll of duct tape were in the bag with the leaf, and both appeared to bear blood spots. The floorboards were examined for soil and vegetation samples.

Taken for examination also were a knife (from the glove compartment), a roll of electric tape, an adjustable wrench and socket, the driver's floormat, three samples from the driver's seat covering that looked like blood, taping from the vehicle seats and carpeting, and carpet, paint, and glass samples.

Next to go over the car was Michelle Skidmore, a forensic serologist with the Southwest Institute of Forensic Science.

The attractive brunette, 25 years old, was an accomplished horsewoman. When she'd enrolled at Texas A & M, she had originally planned a career as a veterinarian, taking biology courses toward that career goal.

She had become interested in serology, the scientific study of blood, and after graduation, had taken a job with the institute.

She, like Lynch, recognized the three spots in the front seat as blood. She learned later from tests that the hammer, the duct tape, and the leaf from the bag in the trunk had spots of blood on them. There were traces of blood on the steering wheel, the doorstep of the car, the passenger's floorboard, the dashboard, the console, and a seat belt holder. There was blood on the knife in the glove compartment, the electrical tape, the crescent wrench, the screwdriver, the orange reflector, the denim shirt, the soles of the shoes from the trunk, the green jacket, and the gloves—no large quantity on any single item, but enough to identify it as blood.

As to *whose* blood it was on various items, some scientific obstacles lay ahead in establishing that information with the use of the latest DNA techniques.

* * *

While the forensic team in Dallas was processing Jason Massey's Subaru, the CID investigators in Waxahachie took to the woods once again with cadaver dogs and their trainers.

Because of the extreme heat, a dog could work only fifteen minutes before it had to be relieved and another dog was sent in its place.

The search was first concentrated on the low-water crossing where Massey had led officers in the pitch-black of the previous night to a spot where he'd said a "third party" might have buried the girl's missing head and hands. Even with the dogs, who are trained to sniff out human flesh in all kinds of environmental conditions, the search was again unsuccessful.

That same day, investigators Cruz and Smith conducted horseback searches of an area in Summerwood Addition, just north of Ennis, where Massey once lived, on the theory that the murder suspect might have returned to his old haunts to bury the head and hands, considering them his most magnificent "trophies."

The wooded area where the bodies were found was combed again, along with another area in the woods where, at an earlier time, Massey had once been spotted by witnesses, roaming the woods in a suspicious manner.

But nothing was found.

Two days later, Gothard and Goss drove to Canton. Gothard heard a report that Massey had planted a tree in the woods behind the house where he was staying before his arrest. Gothard speculated that the suspect might have also "planted" the girl's missing parts beneath this tree. But the site yielded nothing.

Again the heat and humidity were fierce. While walking through the woods at Canton, Gothard suddenly felt the tightness in his chest that was becoming so noticeable at times, especially when he was engaged in strenuous exercise. The tight feeling persisted longer than before but finally subsided.

When Gothard arrived home that evening he was more fatigued than he remembered ever being. After a quick dinner, he was sitting in the den with his wife Sharmin and his fifteen-year-old son Aaron, talking and hardly aware of what was on the TV.

Suddenly Gothard's chest hurt badly. The severe pain did not let up. Thinking it might be indigestion, he went to the kitchen, poured some milk, and drank it. Then he lay on the couch. The pain seemed to be getting worse, and it felt as if the very air of the room was closing suffocatingly around him.

Gothard had never had any medical symptoms of heart disease in the past, other than the tight feeling in his chest during those stressful hours in the heat.

As he lay on the couch, the phone rang. It was Johnny Cruz on the line, and Gothard's son handed him the receiver.

"Johnny, I don't feel like talking to you right now. My chest hurts real bad. I don't feel good. I'll talk to you later."

Johnny had called to report he was on his way to question some more witnesses. He was puzzled by the lieutenant's words.

Thoroughly frightened by his dad's color and intense chest pain, the teenaged son called 911 and asked for an ambulance.

When it arrived, within minutes, paramedics administered oxygen to the pain-wracked CID commander and rushed him to the Waxahachie hospital. There it was quickly determined by doctors that Gothard had indeed suffered a severe heart attack.

Gothard was in very serious condition. He remained in the intensive care unit for two days, then was transported by ambulance to Baylor Hospital in Dallas, where further tests could be run. The around-the-clock murder investigation, especially the hours beneath the blazing sun, had taken their toll.

Cruz was stunned when he finished his interviews that evening and phoned back to talk to his boss, only to learn he had been struck down by a heart attack and was in serious condition.

Cruz suddenly found himself in command of the biggest murder investigation that he and the other unit members had ever worked.

Cruz is a modest man, and he couldn't help wondering if he was up to the job.

* * *

Gloom prevailed among the investigators in the CID office on the Monday after Gothard's heart attack. One of the gloomiest was Cruz, whom Gothard had named lead investigator.

It was Cruz who now had to plan follow-up interviews and the search for more evidence in the capital murder case that was making big headlines in state newspapers and on national TV.

The news media had poured into Waxahachie to cover the developing investigation of the teenagers' murders, in which the female victim had been decapitated, disemboweled, and mutilated. With rumors of satanic rituals and the horrible condition of the girl's body, reporters were hot after every detail they could get.

But reporters were the least of Cruz's worries. As Gothard had told the newspeople at the press conference on the day Massey was charged, "A lot of people think you make an arrest, and that's it.

"But that's really when you just get started. You have to keep beating the bushes—that's what it amounts to."

Also, Sheriff John Gage had made a statement after Massey's temporary attorney had told the press that he was certain his client was innocent. Said the Ellis County sheriff: "We've got a good case—a very good case. If it wasn't a good case, we wouldn't have filed a capital murder charge against him. All the evidence we've got right now points to this individual."

But he added that his detectives had not ruled out the possible involvement of others: "We're not going to preclude anything. We're going to be looking at everything."

The follow-up on the forensic findings by the criminalists in Dallas would be a major job, one vital to the prosecution of Massey when he was brought to trial, assuming he was indicted by the grand jury soon to be given the case.

There was also the task of trying to pinpoint Massey's whereabouts and movements before and during the time period in which the slayings were thought to have occurred—to prove he had the weapon, the method, the motive, and the opportunity to have committed the murders. No one thought there were eye-witnesses.

No one was more aware of the tremendous job facing investigators and prosecutors than attorney Joe Grubbs, D.A. for the 40th Judicial District. At the time the bodies were found, Grubbs believed it would be a tough case to crack and a tough case to try in court.

There plainly was no crime scene, as in many homicides, where at least some clues are left behind by the killer. As investigators had first speculated, the D.A. thought the killings had probably happened someplace else and the bodies dumped in the woods.

Even the motive was up for grabs. The naked girl suggested a sex motive, but the terrible things done to her body pointed to intense hatred on the part of the murderer.

When it was found by the pathologist that the girl's body was too badly ravaged by the elements to determine whether there had been a sexual assault, the sexual motive became even less provable. No tracks, no weapon, and the girl's head, hands, and clothing missing—there was practically nothing at the scene by which to track a killer.

Positive identification of the girl would be difficult, too, until the ankle X ray of a missing girl became known when Cruz and Gothard talked to her mother.

Grubbs was worried. He did not lack legal experience, although he had taken office as district attorney only the previous January 1.

Before his election, Grubbs had served two years as an assistant in this same office after graduation from the law school at Baylor, had been elected an Ellis County judge, had served nine years, and had then put in two more as a judge of the County

Court at Law. He decided to go into private practice, in which he spent some eight years before his election to the D.A.'s post.

Grubbs preferred enforcing the laws of the land over a practice of defensive law. As a strong Christian, he felt there was a certain amount of good feeling involved in serving society and helping people. He was a personable, serious official who chose his words before speaking.

In the Massey capital murder case, he knew they were facing the most difficult circumstantial evidence case he had ever seen. And from the early reports he had from forensic experts, it was going to require DNA techniques that were extremely complicated. Introducing that evidence would be about equal to dumping the hydrogen bomb formula on a jury of laypeople.

Grubbs named Clay Strange chief prosecutor in the case. He knew him as an excellent trial lawyer whose mild mannerisms and studious appearance did not warn opponents of the battler he was before a jury.

Strange had been with the office only a year longer than Grubbs but had quickly established himself as a prosecutor. A graduate of the University of Texas law school in 1973, he had been assistant and senior assistant city attorney in Austin, Texas, for six years; after that, he'd spent twelve years in private practice in Austin and in his hometown of Colorado City, Texas, and he had been a Mitchell County attorney in Colorado City from 1987 to 1992.

Grubbs called a meeting of his staff, and they began planning how to proceed in what appeared to be an impossible prosecution at this point.

Cruz went over the latest reports on the case. The report from serologist Michelle Skidmore disclosed that trace elements of blood had been verified on the pair of handcuffs from the house where Massey was living; on a knife found in his possession when he was arrested; and on items from his car, including the pair of shorts; the roll of duct tape; the hammer and the leaf in the paper bag; and on several other articles from the trunk.

Traces of blood were on the running board on the driver's side of the Subaru, possibly left by the foot of someone entering the car, and the steering wheel, console, and dash bore blood traces. The spots on the driver's seat cover were blood.

The blood in the car and on the handcuffs indicated that one or more bodies had been transported in the car, and one or more victims were bound by the handcuffs, laboratory examiners reported. It was believed the blood on all the items and inside the car was that of one or more victims.

The findings of Charles Lynch, the trace evidence analyst, confirmed that the fiber he found on the right shoe of Brian King matched fibers from the tan carpet of Massey's Subaru. They had been compared microscopically under polarized light.

Cruz nodded as he read the report. He was not surprised that the fiber on the shoe matched. When he first learned from the medical examiner's office in Dallas of a tan fiber on Brian King's shoe, Cruz had talked to witnesses who had ridden in Massey's car; they said they thought the car had either light brown or tan carpeting. The scientific comparisons confirmed what Cruz had suspected.

There was bad news, too.

Cruz got on the phone and talked with Skidmore, Lynch, and Jan Reznizek, a DNA expert with Southwest Institute of Forensic Science. He learned that the blood samples from some items in the car were minimal, to the point that it could not be determined if the blood was human or animal. But most of the blood could be analyzed.

Lynch also reported he found a foreign hair strand on Brian King's pants and other hair in the car. The expert technicians had obtained samples of blood from the victims, and now they needed blood and hair samples from the murder suspect to make comparisons.

As for the hair samples, at least twenty-four from various locations on the head and twenty or more body and pubic hairs from Massey were needed for the hair tests. Dallas experts said it would expedite testing if Massey could be brought there so that a qualified technician could obtain the samples.

Later that week, Cruz filed an affidavit of support for a request for a search warrant seeking the hair and blood samples from Massey. The judge granted the warrant, and Cruz and Phillip Martin, investigator for the D.A.'s office, drove Massey to the Dallas lab for collection of the needed samples.

Massey had little to say on the trip and appeared to be at ease, Cruz noticed. Thompson was also present when the blood was drawn.

Michelle Skidmore, the serologist, supervised the taking of the blood samples. Later, she recalled that she had a strange feeling as Massey stared at her with his penetrating blue eyes. With his whitish blond hair, which contrasted sharply with his tan, and the stare, Massey was the object of curiosity from passersby in the lab building.

"I had the creepy feeling as he looked at me that he was wondering how I would look with my head cut off," the attractive blood expert later told a prosecutor in the case.

Meanwhile, a new mystery witness came into the intensive probe. Before either Massey's arrest or the initial surfacing of his name from the witnesses quizzed by Cruz in Ennis, an unidentified man called and asked to speak to Grubbs. When Grubbs came on the line, the caller, who sounded youthful, said, "If you are looking for someone in the murder of those two teenagers, you should talk to a guy named Jason Massey."

The caller refused to give his name but said he might call back and quickly hung up.

The caller did phone again, but he still would not identify himself. Working through an attorney, the young man again contacted the D.A. This time he gave his name and said he would give a statement to investigators.

It was Paul Anthony Demomio. He lived in Dallas and said

he had been a roommate and close friend of Massey's when the murder suspect had lived in that city.

They'd had the same general interests at that time, Paul said, but now he had turned his life around, was off drugs and going to college, and had gained spiritual faith. He said he'd accomplished this striking change of character through the faithful support and encouragement of members of his family.

Paul had been nervous and feared that he'd eventually be drawn into the murder probe. With his new lifestyle, he decided to come forward voluntarily and tell what he knew. This would prove to be a great deal, when D.A. investigator Phillip Martin later took his statement.

The news from the Baylor Hospital in Dallas where Gothard had been transferred from the Waxahachie hospital was not encouraging, though there was still a hopeful prognosis. A heart catheterization revealed that Gothard would require quadruple bypass surgery. "Immediately," the doctors said.

Even in his serious condition, Gothard was wondering how the Massey murder investigation was going. He had faith in Johnny Cruz and the other detectives, but he wished he could be there.

Twenty

The CID investigators fanned out in different directions to talk to possible witnesses who could fill in gaps in the activities of Jason Massey.

Cruz returned to Ennis to learn more about Massey and people he knew there, people besides Mark Gentry and Chris Nowlin who might have information that could help track Massey's movements during the time the teenagers disappeared from their Garrett home and were found two days later in the dense woods near Telico.

From the others who knew and ran with Massey, Cruz had obtained the names of two young women, sisters who had known and associated with the murder suspect. He introduced himself to one of the sisters, Christina Erwin, about twenty, a pretty girl who worked at a fast-food restaurant in Ennis.

Christina Erwin told the detective that she had known Massey only four or six months. She'd met him at Lake Bardwell through Massey's sister, and her own sister, Shawntee Erwin, who were friends.

On the night of July 22, 1993, Jason had stayed at their place. Her parents were working and staying overnight at the Lake Bardwell Marina, and her sister, Shawntee, was also away. Massey slept that night in Shawntee's room, because, as Christina explained, "I was scared to stay home by myself."

She said the relationship between her and Massey was strictly a "best-friend type of thing," and that Massey was a perfect gentleman the night he stayed over.

The next day, Christina Erwin continued, she and Jason decided to go into the country to target-practice with a pistol Jason had.

First, she and Jason had gone to the Wal-Mart store in Ennis to buy some ammunition. She drove her car.

"Jason bought a box of shells, which I believe were .22-caliber shells," the girl recalled. "Jason also bought two knives. One knife was rather large, with black grips and a folded-type blade. The other knife was a large dagger with a nonfolding blade. It was in a holster."

She remembered that Massey paid about seventy dollars for both of the knives. After making the purchases, they left Wal-Mart in Christina's car.

"Jason was going to show me a place where we could shoot the pistol," the girl continued. "He said the place was in the Telico area [a short distance east of Ennis], and there were some sand dunes there that would give good protection against any bullets going astray."

She said Jason instructed her to turn left on a road intersecting highway 34. Somehow, they wound up on Union Hill Road, and Jason told her he was lost. She turned around and they got on highway 660, going toward Ennis. They did no target practice, but Jason shot the pistol six times out the window while the car was moving, she said.

Jason apologized about getting lost and told her that if they had more time, he was sure they could find the place he was looking for. He said when he'd been to the location previously, he'd been with Mark Gentry and another boy and that they'd been drinking and using dope. Jason said he wanted to give up such bad habits and needed help.

They went back to Christina's house and that evening went to church. After that Jason left, saying he was going home.

Later, Cruz said, in recalling the interview: "This is my way of thinking about that incident. It's only a gut feeling. Christina Erwin, with the same name and who is a pretty blond girl like Christina Benjamin, was lucky they did not find the place. I believe his intentions, of course, was to kill the Erwin girl that day. For some reason or another, he got cold feet. I don't know why."

Cruz said the description given to Christina of the spot they were going to fit perfectly that of the wooded area near Telico where the slaying victims were later found. The "sand dunes" he mentioned probably were the large piles of dirt from the excavated gravel pits in the area. Massey, as he lay in a bed in another room in the same house with Christina Erwin the night before, had possibly concocted the plan to kill Christina after taking her to the isolated wooded area on the pretext of shooting his pistol. Did he lie in bed that night, fantasizing what he would do to the pretty blonde who was only a few years older than Christina Benjamin?

Cruz would always think that the young woman was extremely lucky to have escaped what he was almost certain was Massey's plan to kill her.

Christina Erwin had more to tell about her friend Jason. He had returned to their home again on July 26, 1993, around 6:30 P.M. Cruz noted it was the same date that Christina Benjamin and Brian King had vanished.

"We visited for a while, and I left for work at McDonald's about 7 P.M., and Jason stayed at my residence to talk with my sister, Shawntee. Then Jason came to McDonald's during my break time at about 10:30 P.M."

She said Jason had driven as far as Telico and then remembered "that he had to talk to me."

"He said he had bought some gas at the Telico store. Jason told me that he was in love with my sister and that he cared for both of us. We sat at a table outside and joked around and laughed. Jason told me he would do anything for me and Shawntee. He was acting a little weird. He said he had drank a couple of beers."

She recalled Jason had left at about 11:15 or 11:30 P.M., presumably, headed for his home in Canton, Texas, which is about a one-hour drive from Ennis.

Cruz realized that Jason Massey, who at the time was living with his mother in Canton, was in both the Ennis and the Garrett-Telico areas only a short time before the two teenagers got into a light-colored car in front of their home around midnight.

Christina gave Cruz a blue box that Massey had left in her car. Looking at the box, the detective saw a Wal-Mart label stating it had contained handcuffs and a price tag for $16.66. She said that after hearing of Massey's arrest, her stepfather had taken to the Ennis Police Department an empty box with one of the knives that Jason had bought.

Cruz thanked Christina for her cooperation. Next, he talked to her sister, Shawntee Erwin, sixteen years old, another pretty girl.

She had known Jason for a longer time, having met him about one and one-half years before, through his sister. The last time she had seen Massey was the day he'd come to their house on July 26.

"My sister, Christina, and my parents left the house about 7 P.M. Jason remained with me and my girlfriend to talk. He talked about wanting to change his life. He said he wanted to quit drinking and using dope and wanted to become a Christian, but there was something keeping him from doing it.

"Jason and I were playing around, and I was hitting him on the stomach. Jason told me, 'Be careful, you might hurt yourself.' I then raised Jason's pullover shirt and I saw a chrome or silver-colored pistol on Jason's waistline.

"Jason tried to hide the gun from me by putting his hand over it. Then he pulled the gun out and said it was a .22. I asked him why he was carrying a gun. He said that the gun was for protection, that he thought Mark Gentry was going to hurt him. I also know that Jason carried a large pocketknife in the glove compartment of his Subaru car.

"Before he left, Jason told me, 'Remember me every time you hear the song 'If Tomorrow Never Comes.' I thought he was acting rather strange. I gave Jason a a kiss on the cheek before he left my house at about 7:45 P.M."

Now Cruz had a witness who could testify that Massey was carrying a pistol, a .22, the same caliber with which the Garrett teenagers apparently had been shot, and acting strangely on the evening before the slayings. He'd also had a knife in the glove compartment.

Things were looking up for the detective.

After taking statements from the Erwin sisters, Cruz located the Wal-Mart clerk who had sold the handcuffs to Massey. Christina had not been sure whether the date was July 22 or July 23 when she and Massey had gone to the store, but Donald Murrhead, the clerk in the sports department, pulled the sales tapes and pinpointed July 22 as the date the handcuffs had been sold.

The buyer had also bought a box of .22-caliber CCI hollow-point bullets, Murrhead said the register tape showed. He especially remembered selling the handcuffs.

Later that day, the clerk looked at a lineup of several men at the Ellis County Detention Center and picked out Jason Massey as the customer who'd bought the bullets and the handcuffs.

"How did you remember this individual?" Cruz asked.

"Well, we don't sell that many handcuffs. When we do sell some, it kind of sticks to you. There was something about the individual that bought them. It was just the way he looked. He had a stare that kind of stuck to my mind. He had long blond hair and I remembered his eyes. I remembered how his sort of greenish eyes were very sharp."

Massey looked different in the lineup—he had a short haircut—but the clerk still recognized him. Murrhead said he had never sold a pair of handcuffs before.

John Mason was in the barbershop, waiting his turn, when he picked up a newspaper a customer had left behind. It was a Tyler,

Texas, daily, and on the front page was a photograph of a guy
arrested for the murders of two teenagers near Telico.

"Well, I'll be damned," Mason said, looking at the picture,
holding the page out to the barber and a customer. "That guy
was in my car wash the other night, cleaning out his car."

While Mason was getting his hair cut, the police chief came
in. Mason raised his hand under the cloth around his neck, indicating the newspaper on the chair.

"I seen this guy, the guy in that picture there, in my car wash
the other night, and he was dumping out bags and clothes and
stuff like that." *If you could call a bandanna clothes,* he thought.

"Do you want to make a statement?" the chief asked.

"Well, I don't know. I guess. You know, I seen him do it, and
I know what was there." Mason had mixed feelings about a
statement. You don't run to the cops every time you notice something a little offbeat, if you have a business in a small town. He
didn't want people to think he was watching every move his
customers made and popping off to the cops about stuff.

But this time he squared it in his mind: those kid murders
were bad—real bad.

The chief had one of his officers phone the Ellis County Sheriff's Department with the report.

Investigator John Goss took the call.

"There's a car wash operator here in town that says that guy
Massey, the one you got for killing the two kids, cleaned out his
car at his place a few nights ago," the Canton officer said. "He
says he can identify him and the car and knows about some stuff
he junked."

Goss promised somebody would be there to check it out. It
was about midnight when Goss, Brian Thompson, and Phillip
Martin, the D.A.'s investigator, arrived in Canton.

Mason told them he arrived at his car wash as usual around
11 P.M. to clean the trash bins and check the washers. The trash
bins were his biggest chore. It irritated him that people stopped
at the car wash to dump their trash and debris without ever using

the coin-operated car washes and vacuums. Like it was the city dump, or something.

Drunks cleaning up old puke, people throwing out beer bottles, sacks of stale, half-eaten food, baby diapers, you name it.

When he caught somebody in the act, he sometimes reminded them this was a business he ran and there were plenty of other places to dump their junk besides his bins, if that's all they were going to do. But he didn't usually raise too much hell because sometimes the deadbeats did use the pay vacuums.

He'd seen some strange sights, some strange people this time of night. One of those TV talk shows ought to set their cameras up here for a while. They'd get an eyeful. You got to where you knew people by what they threw in the trash.

Mason was washing one of the bays when a beat-up, old-model car drove in from the back way, between the bays and the wash area. The driver, a kid in maybe his late teens or twenty or so, with dirty, longish, blondish hair, jeans, and a dirty T-shirt, got out and began removing bags and tossing them in the trash containers.

Mason stopped what he was doing and stared hard at the kid. The driver got back in his car, light-colored, maybe from the eighties. The car wash owner could see him staring back in the car mirror. He sat there about thirty seconds, then swung his old buggy around, got out, and put money in the vacuum. Mason wondered why in hell somebody would bother to clean up an old wreck like that.

The kid went all over the car, under the seats, everywhere he could get to with the vacuum. He looked up frequently, acted sort of strange.

In a few minutes he drove off. Mason walked over to the trash bins and looked to see what the kid had dumped. Bunch of broken glass. He remembered the old car had had a smashed window. There was also a red bandanna. Nothing all that unusual.

The car wash operator said the trash bins had been emptied the day before, but he told the investigators how to get to the location where a private hauler took all the trash. They found a large mound of trash about a quarter mile long and ten feet deep.

"Looks like it's going to be a long night," Thompson said with a sigh. "I knew I should have been a garbage man instead of a cop."

The investigators began digging in the massive pile of trash and garbage.

They had some idea of what they were seeking based on Mason's recollection of what had been on top of the trash bin contents when he'd looked, after the blond driver had finished cleaning his car that night, including a red bandanna and the shattered automobile window glass.

They dug in the private trash dump until about 2:30 A.M. and found nothing that might have come from Massey's car.

Martin, Goss, Thompson, and Cruz returned to Canton early the next day. Checking the bin at the car wash, the officers discovered that some of the contents at the bottom had been packed in tightly and hadn't been removed when the rest had been picked up by the hauler.

It was from the bin that officers recovered the red bandanna. And they learned that the large industrial vacuum cleaner used by Massey had not been emptied out, either. It was there they found the broken window glass, a blue bandanna, and a Kentucky Fried Chicken payroll receipt bearing Massey's name and showing he had worked thirty-one hours ending June 22, 1993.

The investigators showed the car wash operator a color photograph of a tan-colored 1982 Subaru, taken at the Dallas County Sheriff's Department when the vehicle was impounded there. Without hesitation Mason identified it as the car that had visited his place that Saturday night.

The mystery of Massey's meticulously clean car, something noticed by Assistant D.A. Clay Strange and deputies when they'd first glanced inside the Subaru on August 2, was cleared up. Massey, known to always have a messy car, had cleaned it thoroughly one day after the teenagers' bodies had been found in the woods near Smith Creek. The red and blue bandannas would get a going-over from the forensics people.

They knew from Massey's running buddies that he wore both colored bandannas at various times, tied "pirate style" around his head.

Investigator Butch Smith took a statement from Anita Mendoza, a pretty girl who had been stalked and harassed by Jason Massey off and on from 1989 and over the next five years. The Ennis Police Department investigated the series of phone calls and obscene letters and threats aimed at Anita by Massey, and one incident in which Massey was suspected of killing Anita's pet dog.

The questioning of witnesses had a domino effect. One witness would know of another person who'd been involved with Massey in various relationships. Massey's former girlfriends in Dallas, or the girls he would have liked to have had as girlfriends, came to light as the probe widened. Rita gave a statement to investigator Brian Thompson about her eight-month affair with Massey that ended with nightmarish occurrences of two dogs butchered in a bedroom and Massey's violence toward her and her daughter. Barbara, her daughter, recalled the attempted rape by Massey, and Lynnette, a convenience store cashier who worked with Massey, gave details of the knife attack on her.

Massey's weird pattern of conduct with girls, women, and animals was coming into strong focus. Investigator Smith talked to the Ennis woman whose small son had been tied to a tree and lashed with a limb by Massey, who had then been only nine years old.

The CID detectives were compiling an increasingly clear profile of an antisocial personality hell-bent on the destruction of girls, cats, dogs—and himself.

* * *

While detectives were heading in every direction to do follow-up work on the double homicide, an investigator trainee, Dino Martin, had been designated to keep on top of the many other daily criminal offenses that cross the CID commander's desk. Martin assigned some of the cases, when possible, but he personally handled a big share of these routine and some not-so-routine reports. His supervisors said later that "Martin moved right in and took the load off the other guys who were busy on the murders of the two kids."

The CID bunch perked up when the latest report on the lieutenant came in. Gothard had had the quadruple bypass surgery and weathered it well, though it was touch-and-go for a day or two. Then it appeared he was on his way to recovery, facing four or five weeks of recuperation.

Twenty-one

The prosecution's case against Jason Massey depended on its proving that the blood spots in Massey's car and on several items from the car trunk were the blood of Christina Benjamin or Brian King, or both.

The rest of the circumstantial evidence the detectives were collecting would not be enough, even as violent and weird as it showed Massey to be.

If Massey was to be convicted of the heinous murders, Clay Strange knew that the dead would have to "speak."

That was possible only through confirmation by forensic evidence that indisputably placed the two slaying victims in the accused killer's car—that would identify the incriminating blood and hair strands in his car as having come from the bodies of the slain girl and boy.

Grubbs and Strange drove to Dallas and met with Dr. Sheila Spotswood after she'd completed the autopsy report. They looked at the autopsy photographs and discussed how best to correlate the forensic evidence. Spotswood suggested that the prosecutors might want to use DNA techniques to attempt to relate the victims' blood classifications to the blood in the suspect's car and elsewhere.

During the early testing procedures in Dallas, the serologist Michelle Skidmore and Joan Reznizek, head of the serology department, had advised Ellis County officials of a major problem: the DNA in the blood of the young victims had been degraded by body decomposition and the environmental conditions to the extent that regular DNA testing could not be done.

There wasn't sufficient blood from the car and related items to do the DNA test known as RFLP (restriction fragment length polymorphism), the preferred test that can produce a genetic fingerprint for positive identification.

Reznizek recommended another test that could identify genetic markers in the available blood. Known as the PCR (polymerease chain reaction), this test had come on the scientific scene in late 1991 and could be done with a lesser supply and lesser DNA quality of blood. She supplied the name of a scientist who was tops in the field, Mike DeGuglielmo, with a company called Genetic Designs in Greensboro, North Carolina.

Facing the problem of degraded victim blood and insufficient "questioned blood," as the blood in the Massey car was called, Strange said, "We decided we would be riding the PCR horse all the way. And the more discriminating test results we could get, the better."

The severe breakdown of the chemical DNA in the victims' blood was blamed on the deep body decomposition and the severe heat and high humidity to which the bodies had been exposed for two days after death.

DeGuglielmo, in addition to doing the basic PCR test called HLA DQ Alpha, had been doing a more recently discovered procedure known as D1S80. By combining the results of the two tests, the degree of accuracy in determining the genetic markers would be much greater.

However, when the victims' blood samples were forwarded to DeGuglielmo, he reported that he was unable to get the blood of either teenager to amplify. He suggested that heart tissue from the bodies be submitted.

The delicate PCR tests would take a long while. It was an anxious time for Strange and the CID detectives; the circumstantial case being built against Jason Massey hung in the balance.

With the heart tissue, DeGuglielmo was able to perform the

HLA DQ Alpha test. In PCR testing the goal is not to obtain a match of blood specimens, as in the RFLP test, but rather, to determine a ratio in which a certain individual cannot be excluded as the donor of the blood.

The HLA DQ Alpha test disclosed that on the accepted ratio basis, the blood of 20 of 21 people could be eliminated as that found in the suspect's car, but the blood of Christina Benjamin could not be eliminated.

The D1S80 test would narrow the possibilities even further. Once again DeGuglielmo had a problem with the blood samples to be analyzed. The heart tissue worked for the first test but would not amplify for the D1S80 test.

But there still was another technique the scientist could use. Every person has two genotypes—one comes from the father and one from the mother. By obtaining blood samples from both parents of each victim, the serologist could work backward to arrive at the victim's DNA classification.

Strange and his staff got on the phone and made arrangements with Christina Benjamin's father in Watertown, New York, and her mother in Ennis. When these samples were forwarded to DuGuglielmo, he was able to determine that the range of 20 out of 21 could be narrowed even further: the second test showed that out of 1,688 donors, 1,687 could be excluded, but Christina could not.

Combining the results of the two PCR tests meant that about 95.4 percent of the population of the North American continent could be ruled out as having the same blood genotype as was found in the blood inside Massey's car and on the hammer, duct tape, and leaf in the trunk, and in the blood clot formed on the hair recovered from the ground beneath where the girl's head would have been.

When the results were finally in, Assistant D.A. Strange was elated. It would be powerful evidence. The next thing would be to present the blood findings to a trial jury in a manner allowing jury members to understand the complicated DNA techniques that had led to the blood test results.

As the scientific side of the murder probe was pursued in Dallas by forensic experts, analysis of trace evidence from Massey's car and the crime scene gave prosecutors a further boost in the case.

Charles Lynch, trace evidence technician, completed his report on the hair evidence from the car. He reported that a long blond hair found on the front floorboard of Massey's Subaru, the blond hair strands entangled in the barbed-wire fence, and the clotted lock of hair from the ground all had the general fine microscopic characteristics of hair samples taken from Christina's hairbrush.

Lynch said the examination also revealed that the lock of hair had been severed with a sharp knife apparently at the time of the decapitation. Since it was found directly underneath where the head would have been when attached, this indicated the head had been cut off at the spot where the body was lying.

His report also revealed that the blond hair found on Brian King's jeans had the same microscopic characteristics as a sample head hair from Jason Massey.

Lynch's initial finding that the fiber on Brian King's shoe matched sample fibers from the carpet in Massey's car was confirmed by the FBI lab in Washington.

A noted forensic entomologist played a unique role in establishing the approximate time that Christina and Brian had been killed, an important element in proving a homicide case.

The bodies were not discovered until about 2:15 P.M. on July 29, or about two and one-half days after the teenagers had left their house in Garrett sometime around midnight of July 26. Time of death had to be pinpointed more accurately to tie into the accumulating circumstantial evidence.

Forensic entomologist Dr. Neal H. Haskell of Purdue University in Indiana had been recommended to the prosecutors by the blood and trace evidence experts in Dallas.

After calling Haskell and giving him the necessary facts

needed to compute a time of death, the pathologist in Dallas had forwarded specimens of larvae—the wormlike grubs (maggots) of the housefly deposited in a decomposing body—and full-grown flies found on the bodies. The specimens were killed in boiling water to preserve the stage of growth at the time of collection.

In his laboratory Haskell cultivated live larvae under heat and humidity conditions identical to those in the area where the bodies lay until the larvae reached the growth stage of the grown flies. This gave Haskell a time segment that would approximate how long the corpses had been there after death.

Observing the time from larva to grown fly, the entomologist concluded that the teenagers had been slain in a period from midnight July 26 until about 10 A.M. on July 27, or roughly a ten-hour period.

The convening of a county grand jury to consider the sensational murder case gave prosecutors an opportunity to question members of Massey's family about his activities on July 26, 1993, and before and after that day. Among those appearing before the grand jury were the suspect's mother and others who had been at the Canton residence on the day of the arrest.

Clay Strange had one angle that he wanted to pursue closely in the grand jury atmosphere of sworn witnesses. Massey's former buddies, Mark Gentry and Chris Nowlin, and the others they ran with, came under intense grilling in the grand jury room at the Ellis County Courthouse.

As Sheriff Gage had said at the press conference about two weeks earlier, investigators would examine all possible angles of the case, including the possibility that others besides Massey might be involved.

In the grand jury room, the witnesses fielded a barrage of questions from Strange. Grand jury proceedings are by law secret, and though there may be occasional leaks from the proceedings, what takes place in the sessions for the most part never sees public light—unless it is used in a trial to impeach a witness who testifies contrary to what he told a grand jury earlier.

Strange later revealed that attempts during the probe to administer polygraph tests to the former associates of Massey—after they voluntarily agreed to take the so-called "lie detector" tests—were unsuccessful. Gentry and Nowlin had taken drugs within the last few weeks, it was revealed, and the Texas Department of Public Safety polygraph examiner believed the results would not be reliable because of recent drug use.

After the grand jury interrogation and a check by investigators on the whereabouts of Massey's friends during the time period in which the slayings were thought to have happened, it was decided that Jason Massey had acted alone in the murders.

Alibis of the other possible suspects reportedly were verified.

The grand jury apparently was convinced that the brutal murders were the act of a lone killer: the jury panel returned an indictment against Jason Eric Massey alone, charging him with capital murder, kidnapping, and aggravated sexual assault in the deaths of Christina Benjamin and Brian King.

Later, after further investigation, the counts alleging kidnapping and aggravated sexual assault were dropped due to insufficient evidence. It could not be proved that the boy and girl did not accompany Massey voluntarily from their home, and the decomposition of the girl's body prevented confirmation that she had been sexually assaulted.

Massey was reindicted on a charge of capital murder.

One thing that had not turned up in the search of the house at Canton on the night Jason Massey was arrested or in the later search of his car was a firearm that might have been used to shoot the two teenagers.

After Cruz learned that Jason had been carrying a .22-caliber pistol in his waistband when he'd visited the Erwin sisters in Ennis on the evening of July 26, CID officers set out to locate the weapon.

A twenty-six-year-old man who referred to himself as a "cousin by common-law marriage" of Jason Massey was apparently the owner of the gun. But the gun still had not been found.

Robby Turner said he had purchased a .22-caliber chrome-plated revolver with a black pistol grip for seventy-five dollars from a pawnshop in Ennis. He was moving from Ennis and he had gone to Canton on July 18 to spend the night at his grandmother's house.

He had intended to stay with his grandmother for a few days but said "it was too crowded, so the next day I went back to Ennis. I was kind of like living in my car for a little while."

Jason Massey, his mother, and her common-law husband were among those staying at the house in Canton, Turner said.

After arriving at the Canton residence that evening, Turner said, he put a box of his belongings—books, some loose clothing, and accessories for his guitar—in the breezeway. He planned to leave the box there until he got settled somewhere.

He had also taken out the .22-caliber revolver to unload it before placing the gun in the box of personal belongings.

A friend who had ridden to Canton with Turner was present, as was Turner's small half-brother, who was living at the house. Jason Massey was also there, but Turner said he did not get to talk to him until the next day.

Turner found a job and a place to live in Ennis. It was several days later that he phoned his grandmother in Canton to tell her he was working and had a new address. He learned then that Massey had been arrested and the house in Canton had been thoroughly searched.

He asked about the gun he'd left in the box on the breezeway and was told it must not have been in the box, because the searching officers had not found any revolver on the premises.

He wondered what had happened to his gun.

The young boy who had been at the Canton house that night said he had seen Turner leave the gun in the box. The next day the boy saw the gun in the possession of Jason Massey. The chrome-plated revolver was tucked in Jason's waistband at the side, with his shirt over it.

The boy said Massey had briefly showed him the gun. "He said he didn't want no one else to know about it. He told me to keep it hushed. He told me that my half-brother gave it to him, let him borrow it. Jason stuffed the gun in the glove compartment of his car."

The boy said he later asked Jason what he did with the gun, "and he told me he got rid of it in Dallas. He said he gave it to a black person in Dallas, and that's all he told me."

The boy said he was the youngster who had ridden a bicycle in the neighborhood on the day [August 2] that "the police came." He recalled that Jason had been watching from the house that day. "I thought he was watching for cars coming down the street, or something."

The boy recalled he rode his bike back to the house and into the parking lot. Jason was outside, sitting on a car.

"That's when he asked me, he said he wanted to borrow my bike." He had last seen Jason ride the bike down the street and around the corner at the church.

Then the police came and brought the bike back and searched the house.

The investigators tried to track down the revolver in Dallas. But they never found the gun, which they believed was the same gun seen by the Erwin sisters during Jason's visit on July 26 and probably the weapon used to shoot the teenagers later that day.

Twenty-two

The case against Jason Massey was coming together nicely, but there was still a big mystery that bothered District Attorney Grubbs and Assistant Prosecutor Strange. The investigation had brought to light the possible method—the .22-caliber revolver, and the large hunting knife and an ax found among other items in Massey's car.

They had witnesses who knew about opportunity to commit murder—Jason had been seen in the Garrett-Telico-Ennis area only a few hours before the teenagers had disappeared from their house.

They had witnesses who knew he had met Christina Benjamin and Brian King just over a week before their deaths, and witnesses who had overheard Massey talk about wanting to rape, kill, and mutilate the girl.

But the motive for the murders remained an enigma.

Prosecutors knew the slaying of Christina Benjamin had overtones of a sex murder, certainly in light of the remarks Massey had made to Nowlin and others, and that her body had been nude when found. They were aware that rapists often become violent and kill their victims, either to avoid being identified or accidentally during the attack.

But decapitation, cutting off the girl's hands, ripping open her abdomen, stabbing and slashing all over her body, even inside, where stab wounds penetrated the liver with no outside wounds, and cutting off the nipples—these did not go along with the typical sex murder.

The extreme violence done to the body spoke more of vengeance and intense hatred. *But how could any man derive sexual satisfaction from such barbaric actions as the dismemberment and mutilation?* Grubbs wondered.

In January 1994, with the case moving toward trial, Grubbs and Strange discussed the case with agents of the FBI's Behavioral Science Investigation Support Unit, part of the Violent Criminal Apprehension Program of the National Center for the Analysis of Violent Crime at Quantico, Virginia, site of the FBI Academy.

The attorneys flew to Quantico, and for one full day, agents of the behavioral unit met with Grubbs and Strange and offered their theories on the teenagers' murders, based on the agency's experience with similar killers.

FBI agents reviewed details of the two murders and looked at photographs of the crime scene and bodies offered by the prosecutors. Attorneys outlined the evidence that had been put together so far.

Texans learned from the special agents that Jason Massey exactly fit the profile of a sexual killer, a lust murderer, an organized antisocial.

Everything the prosecuting team and investigators had dug up about Massey's life, his personality, his expressed desires, and his actions, dropped into place in the "lust killer" profile like a key made for a lock.

The agents explained that a lust killer is not a typical rapist-killer. The FBI had done exhaustive studies on this kind of killer.

One study done by FBI agents involved in-depth interviews with convicted serial killers. The interview answers allowed federal agents to look into the dark recesses of a sexual-serial killer's mind, to lay bare the thoughts and fantasies that preceded the actual murderous acts.

The study, along with previous projects aimed at revealing the mental makeup of a sexual killer, uncovered patterns that were strikingly similar in the killers' backgrounds and the murders they committed.

Of particular interest to Texas prosecutors was a relatively new finding that thought and fantasy play a major part in motivation for a sexual murder committed by a lust killer. Among the many common denominators found in sexual murderers was the number of years they had engaged in thoughts and fantasies involving violent acts—their fantasies often began in early childhood. This fantasy life preceded the first murder by a killer.

Another common characteristic among sexual killers was that they committed their first violent acts on animals. Serial killers were loners; they had negative personality traits, and in their self-imposed isolation from others, fantasy reigned supreme.

When violent murder was done, it was the result of always-present fantasies building to a pressure point that could be appeased only with the reality of the act.

Other common factors existed: a sexual lust killer was often a heavy user of alcohol, was extremely mobile and usually had a car in good condition, frequently changed jobs and towns, followed the investigation of his crimes closely in the news media, and had a fair or better intelligence. Newspapers with stories about their crimes often were found in a killer's residence by searching officers.

Lust killers often took souvenirs from the victims or the crime scenes. They also liked to set fires and were bedwetters into late adolescence. A perpetrator of a sexual homicide commonly had a fixed hatred toward society, a feeling of rejection.

A lust killer was classified as either an organized or a disorganized antisocial—the organized killer being the more careful to leave few clues behind and to act with preplanning instead of sudden impulsiveness.

Although FBI agents believed Massey fell into the organized antisocial category, some of the traits of the disorganized psychopath were also present in him, such as "average intelligence, socially immature, poor work history, sexually incompetent, harsh discipline in childhood."

* * *

Grubbs and Strange had the motive now, without a doubt. The ghastly murder of Christina Benjamin was definitely a lust murder. Massey had undoubtedly achieved immense sexual satisfaction in his decapitation and savage mutilation of the girl. Brian King, in all probability, had died merely because he was in the way.

Jason Massey had wanted to be alone in the dark woods with a nude and dead girl to live out all the desires of the deviant fantasies that had overpowered him since the age of at least fourteen and very likely since as early as nine or ten. His lurid fantasies had been building for years, finally erupting into gruesome, violent tragedy.

The prosecutors knew about his fantasies and perverted desires from the copy of a diary obtained from a Dallas psychiatrist. The murder investigation revealed that Massey's mother had taken him to the Parkland Memorial Hospital psychiatry emergency room in 1991 after she'd found the diaries in his closet and read them.

They were filled with scribblings about killing cats, dogs, and livestock; and about wanting and planning to kill young girls, decapitate them, cut off their hands and their nipples, disembowel them, cannibalize their sexual parts, and have sex with their bodies after death.

Fortunately for the prosecutors, the psychiatrist had copied the two volumes he had as part of Massey's medical records.

The realization that Massey was a lust killer whose sexual fulfillment was in acts that would sicken and disgust the average male seeking sexual satisfaction with a woman gave prosecutors their direction for trial of the case.

Grubbs said: "What was done to the body was horrible and evil to normal people—and, in fact, *is* horrible and evil—but once we understood that this individual had hewed his own values to the point that this is a satisfying sexual experience, we were able to get the case channeled in the right direction and get the proof going.

"At this point, we could look back and say, 'Well, we have a strong case.' "

Twenty-three

Back in his office in the Ellis County Courthouse in Waxahachie, Strange huddled with other members of the district attorney's staff to prepare for trial. The real nitty-gritty started now—studying and preparing for courtroom presentation of the complicated forensic evidence (including crime scene and autopsy photographs), sorting out witnesses and their statements and issuing subpoenas for them, putting the entire case-in-chief together so that it would flow smoothly and effectively before the jury.

Strange would lead the prosecution team and handle the extremely important DNA evidence. Lacy Buckingham, an assistant district attorney, assisted in putting together the trial "notebook," helping to organize the sequence of witnesses and evidence introduction, the intricate details that go into telling the story to the jury in the best order.

As an example, the state had witnesses who needed to be sandwiched between other very different witnesses. Important as their testimony would be, Strange said, the prosecution had witnesses "you wouldn't invite over to your house for dinner." He spoke of people with criminal records and drug habits. During the questioning of potential jurors, when the panel was called, one of the questions he would ask was, "Will you listen to somebody who doesn't look or act as you do or have the background that you have?"

Such a witness is a natural target of the defense, especially when the witness has testimony that could hurt the defendant.

The point in the witness parade when the "black-sheep" witnesses take the stand is an important part of prosecution strategy. Trial lawyers have a theory that jurors tend to remember the first and last things they hear in a trial. So prosecutors seek to work witnesses with obvious character flaws into the middle of the lineup, where jurors won't form an early opinion of the prosecution's case based on character or on what some witnesses look and sound like.

Cindy Hellstern, another assistant, was given the assignment of researching and handling the defense's DNA expert witness, which meant digging deep to learn where this witness stood on the varied techniques of the relatively new forensic science.

The defense had already tried to block admission of the DNA evidence garnered by the state. Failing this, the obvious move would be for them to question it with differing testimony from another expert.

Assistant Kamala Cromer was given the job of reading the books found in Massey's room for pertinent passages useful to the prosecution. Cromer was a fan of true-crime books and had already read some of Massey's books.

Strange was trying not to overlook anything in the trial preparation.

Massey's defense team was also busy. Waxahachie attorneys Mike Hartley and Mike Griffith were appointed by State District Judge Gene Knize to represent Massey because neither he nor his family had the funds to hire a lawyer.

Hartley, quiet-spoken and distinguished-looking, with a beard and mustache, had been in private practice in El Paso before moving to Waxahachie, where he was recognized as one of its most respected attorneys.

Griffith was a younger lawyer, not all that long out of law school. It would be his first capital murder case, and the judge felt he would give it an all-out effort.

Judge Knize knew he was naming competent attorneys in Hartley and Griffith.

The defense attorneys had earlier requested and been granted

Christina Benjamin at 11 years old.

Christina Benjamin in 1985 at six years old.

Christina Benjamin, 12, at aunt's graduation in New York.

Marker over Christina Benjamin's grave in family plot in New York. A color photo of her is on it.

Brian King at 14 years old.

Mug shot of a smiling Jason Massey taken immediately after being arrested and told he was charged with capital murder.

Mug shot of Massey taken after his arrest for murder.

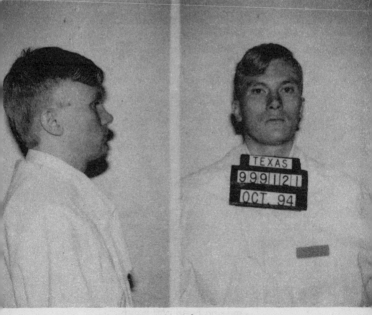

TEXAS
999 1121
OCT. 94

Prison mug shot of Massey.

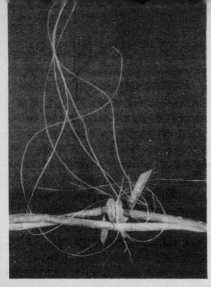

Strands of Christina's blonde hair were found entangled in a barbed wire fence the killer carried her over.

Cadaver dog, trainer, and officers search for Christina's missing head and hands.

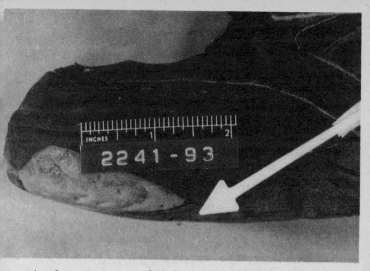

Fiber from Massey's car found on right tennis shoe of victim Brian King was a vital piece of evidence in the trial.

Rusty metal cooler which held Massey's diaries and animal skull "trophies."

March 13, 1991 Wenesday

The number of girls I've decided to get getting higher. Its just when I see one I know I have to get her, an I just fall in love with her an ~~thoughts~~ of killing, torturing, an mutalatin them. Especily between a sexy womans legs next to ~~he~~ her beutiful cunt. I wauld olove to cut there tits on there throats to drink these beutiful girl of there blood. I must say I'm not very interested in 10 years olds but Tory's is specil. After her I will only go for 17 and well it ~~(age)~~ rellig dont matter becase when I see the one I'll know its the one. Any way I think I'm going to make history with Pauli an Mark Gentry. 3-18-91

Continued ↓

The victims' blood stains and other clues were found in Massey's tan-colored 1982 Subaru.

Family home along farm road from which Christina and Brian disappeared.

Lead investigator
Johnny Cruz.

Evidence investigator
Brian Thompson.

Lt. Godarth

(Left to right) Assistant D.A.s Lacy Buckingham, Clay Strange, and Cindy Hellstern.

D.A. Joe Grubbs.

funds to employ their own DNA expert, as well as a firm of Dallas private investigators to interview the numerous witnesses scattered over the county and conduct a defense probe of the murders.

The defense was denied its request for a change of venue to another county, sought on grounds that the extensive publicity in the Waxahachie and Dallas area would prejudice jurors.

The defense also made a motion to exclude the DNA evidence on grounds that the results were questionable because of possible contamination and improper procedures in collecting blood samples. The judge took the request under advisement and planned to rule before the trial began.

Hartley and Griffith occupied a small suite of offices in a multistory building across the street from the old courthouse. Most of the town's lawyers had offices in buildings facing the courthouse square, which looked like a set from an early period movie. Waxahachie has surrounding rolling hills and woods. The town's residential streets, lined with beautiful old turn-of-the-century homes of Victorian, Greek Revival, Carpenter Gothic, and Queen Anne architecture, retain the look of the old South.

The square has two or three old-fashioned restaurants where the courthouse crowd drinks coffee and eats lunch, and there's a drugstore with an old-style fountain.

The homey, folksy little town was not at all in synch with the horror story soon to unfold in the ancient courthouse. One day around noon, as he watched from his window a crowd gathering in the rain with unfurled umbrellas to take part in a National Prayer Day observance in front of the courthouse, Hartley said to a visitor, gesturing at the scene below, "That is what Waxahachie is."

Selection of the jury started on September 6, 1994. A two hundred-member panel had been summoned, but legal exemptions and excuses, plus the usual number of deceased or persons who no longer lived there, cut the panel significantly.

Individual examination of the jury prospects by attorneys sent other voir dire members on their way after they claimed previously formed opinions of guilt or innocence or bias against the death penalty.

It took three weeks to pick the jury. The state announced immediately it would seek the death penalty for Jason Massey, who sat at the counsel table between his lawyers. He was dressed in a light suit, shirt, and tie and wore shined shoes. His shoulder-length blond hair was long gone, replaced by a neat, short haircut.

The youthful defendant wrote frequently on a notepad. He did not look around the courtroom.

Each day the defense lawyers entered with a purple folder used by Massey and handed a notebook from the folder to him. At the end of the day's session, his lawyer retrieved the notebook and folder.

Later on, when a jury was seated, one woman juror was startled when the neat young man at the table was identified as the defendant. When she had noticed him during jury selection, she had thought he was a law clerk or a junior assistant.

With the jury of seven men and five women and two alternate jurors complete, testimony was set to begin on Wednesday, September 28, 1994.

Twenty-four

Jason Massey was involved with a teenaged girl again.

From his jail cell, waiting to go to trial for capital murder, he was up to his old tricks—writing letters to young girls.

News of the startling development was learned by the district attorney's office on September 22, 1994, from two women visitors.

Phillip Martin, twenty-seven, chief investigator for the D.A.'s office, had been very busy the past few weeks. His workload had snowballed as the Massey murder trial had drawn nearer and with the jury selection already in the third week. He was getting together all necessary records, locating stored evidence, making sure subpoenaed witnesses were available, etc., for this major trial, in addition to working on the usual run of felony criminal offenses that came to the D.A.'s office.

The two women interrupted the flow of work. The younger woman gave her name as Veronica Meadows. With her was her mother, Lillian Flanders. Both were worried.

Worry was not new to Veronica Meadows's life. Her teenaged daughter had attacked and stabbed her three different times. The object of her worry had not changed, only the nature of her concern.

Her daughter, sixteen-year-old Laura Meadows, was confined in the state mental hospital at Vernon, Texas. Laura's mother and grandmother visited her regularly. A frightening thing had come out of the visits.

"I think my daughter is exchanging letters with Jason Massey," Mrs. Meadows told Martin. She went on to explain that Laura, during a visit, talked about having a "boyfriend." She mentioned no name, saying only that he was "awful nice and understanding." They had been exchanging letters, the girl said.

But she remained secretive about details. Once, while talking about happenings in Ennis, where the family lived, Veronica told her daughter that the trial of Jason Massey was about to start. She was surprised when Laura answered, "Yes, I know."

It was the grandmother who'd eventually gotten more information. Laura told her that the boyfriend's name was "Jason." Her mother confronted the girl, and she admitted that she and Jason had been writing to each other since late June 1994.

Laura had seen TV news segments about the case and was intrigued with Massey, who told her in his letters that he was "being framed for murder."

The relationship by mail had reached the point where Laura and Jason were planning to run away and get married in California, when both of them were free again, her mother learned. Massey was optimistic about being acquitted.

Veronica Meadows did not like the love-by-mail situation at all.

She was incensed that her daughter was corresponding with a man accused of capital murder, who was writing to her from his jail cell and had been for all this time. She wondered how such a thing could happen, how an accused multiple murderer could be the pen pal of a teenaged girl under treatment for mental problems. She wondered why authorities didn't regulate the letter-writing of such dangerous felons. How could they allow them to send letters to young female mental patients?

Laura had been sent to the Vernon hospital for counseling and treatment after the stabbing incidents. The hearing had been in juvenile court in Ennis. The girl's problems had included alcohol and drug abuse, primarily alcohol.

Martin promised he would look into the matter immediately. When he contacted the sheriff's department, he learned that the first letter from Laura had arrived in an envelope addressed only to the Ellis County Jail. It had been necessary to open the envelope and read the letter to find out to whom it was being sent.

Eventually, the letter had reached Massey through the jail underground. He had replied and the correspondence had blossomed. The district attorney's office knew nothing about it until tipped off by the anxious mother. The letters to and from Massey had been monitored, as is all mail of jail inmates. But for some unknown reason, the news of the letters had not reached the D.A.'s office.

Veronica said Laura had a large collection of Massey's letters in her room.

Finding that Massey was penning letters to a teenaged girl was a bombshell development for the prosecutors. They had to have those letters. Right now, they could only guess at the contents, but they had a feeling that if Massey's writings were anything like letters he had sent to schoolgirl Anita Mendoza, who was to be a witness in the trial, the letters to Laura would be spectacular evidence that could convict Jason Massey.

The Massey letters could be critical evidence to convince the jury that Massey was a continuing threat to society, one of the requirements for assessment of the death penalty.

Working with Bobbi Reilly, the assistant district attorney in charge of civil and juvenile cases for the prosecutor's office, Martin started preparing an affidavit for a search warrant for the room and any other areas of the state hospital frequented by Laura Meadows.

While the affidavit and warrant were typed, Martin contacted D. J. Victerson, who was the county juvenile probation officer in charge of Laura Meadows's case.

Martin knew he would need help in executing a search warrant for the quarters of a patient in the state hospital.

In the past, Martin had run into difficulty with counselors

and staff executives of some institutions who are concerned with the welfare of their patients. He could understand such concern by the medical people, but right now, Martin didn't want Laura inadvertently tipped off that prosecutors were interested in obtaining the letters.

In his capacity as Laura's supervising probation officer, Victerson agreed to assist Martin in gaining admittance without undue trouble.

On Monday, September 27, 1994, the day before testimony was to begin in Massey's murder trial, Martin and Victerson drove together to the state hospital. Victerson would take Laura to another location for an interview while Martin ran a search of her room. The juvenile probation officer would also deal with the hospital's security personnel.

First, however, Martin had to locate a local judge to sign the search warrant. The judge was in a trial and Martin had to wait as precious minutes ticked on. By the time Martin could get the warrant signed, Victerson's interview with Laura was over. Fortunately, it was lunchtime, so Laura was on her way to the dining hall.

The letters were not hard for Martin to find. Most of them were in Laura's footlocker that served as a closet. There was a picture of Jason on the wall in her room. There were also newspaper stories about Massey's pending trial.

When she returned, Martin informed her of the search and that he was taking possession of the letters under the warrant's authorization. The girl was furious that the letters had been confiscated. For a second, the investigator thought she was going to attack him with her long nails. Her eyes blazing, she said she thought her rights had been violated. Martin assured her the search was legal.

It certainly had been productive. When they examined the letters in the D.A.'s office, they saw how well-armed they now were for the punishment phase of the trial.

In one letter, Massey had come close to admitting the murders to his new girlfriend. There were no obscenities—he obviously realized the letters went through jail monitoring.

In one letter, he wrote:

Dearest Laura,

Hello babe. I thought I'd write you. *I've seen dead people's spirits, too. I seen one go to heaven and angels were taking her.* Well, Laura, I want you to be sure and not show my letters to anyone. Not even the friends you have there and elsewhere.

You always said once you get to know me you will begin to reveal all your secrets and fantasies. I think if you did it will help me to open up to you, so let me know them sexual ones. I'm tempted to tell you one, but I got to be careful, but there's a lot I want to tell you.

I could tell you something you would not believe. I mean, things you could not imagine in all your wildest dreams. I mean true things I've already done.

Love,
Jason Eric Massey

Underneath his signature was a symbol of some kind, followed by:

P.S. *July 27, 1994. It's one year since it all began.*

The prosecution would contend that Massey was referring to the date of the murders that he had hoped would launch his career as a serial killer of "countless young women," as he'd described it elsewhere. They could tell that he might be working up to writing some dirty stuff to the girl.

Another letter, in which Massey himself admitted that he was "dangerous" when drinking and "did crazy things," read:

Dear Laura.

No, I don't drink anymore. It's just too powerful for me.

I cannot handle it, plus, *I tend to get crazy when I'm drunk. I'm just dangerous that way.* I didn't drink much. A 12-pack was enough. I didn't drink often, but when I did I drank until I was drunk or passed out. I just don't drink because it seems to cause me so many problems. I'm not, or was not, addicted to it. And I just can't drink. Drinking possessed my own spirit. You did ask if I'd seen spirits.

Well, once here in jail I seen an angel of God, and I seen a demon looking in my cell before, just smiling at me. I just rolled over and went to sleep.

I seen about six angels take a girl to heaven, her spirit anyway. I was on a road, and I seen it at night in the woods. I'll tell it all to you in time.
Yours,
Jason Eric Massey
[With a symbol under his name.]

One line from another letter would be stressed by prosecutors:

The last time I had drank was July 26, 1993.

It was the date Christina Benjamin and Brian King left their home and died so brutally on a lonely, dark road through the woods.

Twenty-five

The crowd started arriving early. The parking spaces around the courthouse were soon full. Drivers were hunting for parking space blocks away.

The news media from Dallas, print and electronic, were out in force. Cameras were prohibited. Hoping to get seats, townspeople made their way up the old staircase to the courtroom on the second floor. The elderly and the more patient waited for the small, slow-moving elevator that had been installed near the stairs in the late 1950s.

The palatial courthouse had known violence in previous years. A bullet hole is present in the door of a first-floor office that at one time had been the sheriff's office. In the 1920s, a gunfight broke out in the courthouse. A deputy was wounded and another man killed.

On this warm and sunny day, out-of-town visitors flocking to the square stopped and stared at the startling faces sculptured on each side of the smooth red granite and sandstone courthouse. They were ugly, scowling faces, all except one, which had the fine, beautiful features of a young woman.

Some of the faces looked down with demonic expressions, and one face in particular appeared to be the face of the devil. When they asked old-timers about the bizarre sculpture that adorned the four sides of the courthouse, they heard a strange story.

The contractor who'd built the courthouse in 1895 had

brought three artisans from Italy to decorate the exterior with artistic carvings.

They'd carved the faces into huge sandstone blocks that were hoisted into place above the arches over the four entrances and continuing around the building.

One of the artists had stayed at a boardinghouse on the square run by a woman who had a beautiful daughter. Her name was Mable Frame, and the sculptor had fallen in love with her. He'd carved her face on a block above the east entrance.

But Mable was not in love with the sculptor; she'd married another man and the rejected suitor had sought revenge. He'd begun carving faces with lips contorted into snarling frowns. They were weird faces, some with eyes askew, glaring down at the town's citizenry.

The legend holds that the grotesque faces were sculptured to look like actual men of the town by the vengeful sculptor.

The faces, especially the devil-like face, added an ironic touch to the murder trial going on inside. The young man before the bar had believed—at one time in his life—that the devil was his master, urging him through demons to rape, torture, mutilate, kill, and cannibalize his young female victims.

He had heard demons call to him in the woods as he'd gone about his sacrificial rituals of butchering cats and dogs and cows at a crude altar.

He should have felt right at home with some of the grotesque engravings on the courthouse walls.

Clay Strange rose to give the state's opening argument. The crowded courtroom was silent. Over the next thirty minutes, the prosecutor started building the state's case against Jason Eric Massey.

He took the jury step-by-step through the events that had culminated in the murders of Christina Benjamin and Brian King in the lonely, dark woods near Telico, Texas.

Strange related how Jason Massey had been introduced by a

friend to Christina just ten days before she and her stepbrother had disappeared from their Garrett home forever.

After meeting the girl, Jason Massey had told his friend of his admiration and desire for the pretty blonde.

"What he said was this, that he thought she was cute, and I'm not going to use the exact words that he used, he said he wanted to have sex with her. He said that he wanted to kill her, that he wanted to sexually mutilate her and cannibalize that sexually mutilated body part."

The assistant district attorney went on to relate the evidence against Massey. He had stolen a .22-caliber revolver, bought ammunition for it, and purchased a pair of handcuffs only five days before the murders. Late on July 26, 1993, Massey had driven by the house and picked up the two teenagers. He had taken them to the isolated area on Cutoff Road, where he'd shot Benjamin King to death, shot Christina Benjamin, and then committed horrible acts upon her body beyond the imagination.

Speaking concisely, Strange outlined the investigation by the Ellis County Sheriff's Department: the tedious analyzing of blood, hair, and fiber samples; the unusual work of an entomologist in establishing the time period in which the youths were killed; the stories told by witnesses; the evidence gathered at Massey's house and in his car; and the highly technical work of forensic serologists and trace evidence experts in linking the murder victims to the car of the accused.

He mentioned the finding of witnesses who'd placed Massey in the area of the murders during the critical time period, and recovery of several items from Massey's car at a car wash in Canton where he had taken the Subaru for cleaning after the slayings.

"So you see, Jason Massey, the defendant, had a method to commit these murders, and the opportunity to commit these murders, but you would have to wonder why anyone would do such a thing," Strange said. "What person would even think of doing such a thing?

"At the end of the state's evidence, we are going to show you that only one person, only one person that you'll ever likely meet, would have, could have, and did commit the murders. Because you see in this trial, in the form of that man, you're going to encounter an evil that you've never seen before and hopefully you'll never see again—the darkness of evil murder and mutilation has brought us into this courtroom, but the light of justice is going to lead us into the day."

Strange sat down. Mike Hartley rose and stepped before the jury box to give the defense's opening statement. He lost no time in attacking the state's stated plan to prove the guilt of his client.

"Ladies and gentlemen, I have no doubt the state is going to bring you proof of many of the facts that Mr. Strange has spoken about. . . . The question you've got to ask yourself is what do these facts prove, individually and in combination."

He said the state would prove that two teenagers were slain and their identities established.

"They are going to prove to you that it was a gruesome situation. I don't think any murder is anything less than that. But that in itself is no evidence of guilt or innocence on anyone's part. What the state is doing is proving this case through their forensic scientists who they claim link my client to these individuals because they don't have any eyewitnesses who were there."

After the state relied on forensic experts, who reached limited conclusions, and had a finger pointed at his client through statements made by certain witnesses, they stopped investigating, Hartley told the jury.

"This case was too tailor-made to convict my client, not in the sense it was tailor-made to prove reasonable doubt or guilt beyond a reasonable doubt, but rather, they stopped when they had enough to say, 'We can point the finger at him. We have a suspicion of him.'

"These people who come before you can tell you what they think about the items they found, the items at the crime scene, or the items found in my client's car or home, but they can't say to you this is a certain person's hair, this is a certain person's blood."

Hartley again attacked the state's DNA case, telling the jury: "I think you will see that not only will the DNA not link these victims to the evidence found in my client's car, but because of what could have been done and should have been done, these tests prove directly the opposite.

"They, to an extent, exonerate my client."

Hartley then turned to the witness who the state said would tell the jury about remarks made by Massey that left no doubt that he wanted to have sex with Christina Benjamin and kill her.

"I think you are going to realize why the prosecutors have almost been apologizing for the last two and one-half weeks [of jury selection] for having to bring these people in front of you. The character of this young man and others who are involved in this case—their character and their background made them suspects at one point prior to when my client was involved. And you will find out that if anybody has got a motive, certain other young men you will hear about had a better motive to point the finger at Jason Massey than he had to take the lives of Brian King or Christina Benjamin. . . .

"I think you will realize why the state is being so specific during voir dire to say to you, 'Will you listen to somebody who doesn't look or act or have the background that you have?' I hope you will discriminate and check every witness that comes on the stand, listen to what they say and will admit when cross-examined before you, and make up your mind what they heard, what they claimed my client said, what they said he said."

The defense attorney also took a whack at the state's argued claim of "evil and darkness."

"Expect the state to bring people to tell you that they have a bone to pick with my client. They are not going to like him, and they have a good reason not to like him. But again, we are look-ing for proof that ties my client to this crime. And just because he may not have the background that you have, and just because there may be people that don't like him, that doesn't necessarily mean that's evidence of guilt or innocence. . . . Given the fact it is purely a circumstance case, you are going to want more than just inferences and innuendoes and even the best scientific evidence you will hear can offer.

"This is a case where you have to examine every piece of evidence and every witness's testimony in the cold, sober light of day. You're not going to have the kind of character information that will lead you to conclude there is guilt beyond a reasonable doubt."

The battle lines had been drawn.

Twenty-six

"Call your first witness, Mr. Strange," Judge Knize said, leaning back in his chair. The judge sat at what may be the oldest district court bench in the state. It is the original bench installed when the courthouse was built a hundred years ago.

The witness, Clint Tims, a former Ellis County deputy who went to the scene when the body report was received, was now a member of the Ennis Police Department.

Tims described how the bodies of the girl and later the boy were found.

"Have you been in this area at night?" Strange asked.

"Yes, sir."

"What's it like there at night?" Strange was seeking to show the atmosphere of horror in the eerie woods where the two teens had been slain on that black and terrible night.

"Well, it's pretty dark, pretty spooky, not much traffic. Not many people travel that road."

"Even with a moon at night, is it pretty dark there?" the prosecutor pressed.

"Due to the trees, yes, sir."

A hush fell over the courtroom as the next witness walked to the stand. She was Donna Lee Brown, mother of Christina Benjamin.

Her face was etched with the sorrow that had haunted her life, the ever-present knowledge—as if the savage butchering of her daughter was not enough—that the missing head and hands of the girl had never been found so they could be buried with the body.

The mother slowly related the remembered details of that night and the next day after Christina and Brian had vanished.

Another indirect victim of the horrible deaths of the children took the stand. Patricia King, the mother of Brian King, related under questioning by Strange the background and lifestyle of her son, a well-liked youth who was popular with both teachers and students and who was active in many school and civic organizations. The photograph of Brian on display in the courtroom showed a smiling, cheerful boy.

With tears in her eyes, she said: "He was going to be a comedian, so he worked on his imitations quite a bit. I guess you might say he practiced on the family as far as his comedy went."

Dr. Sheila Spotswood, the Dallas pathologist who performed the autopsies, took the stand. Her quiet, professional testimony was shocking to the jury and the court spectators. Relatives of the slaying victims left the courtroom as the pathologist displayed autopsy photos and described in detail how Christina and Brian had been killed.

It was a clinical recital, a very necessary one, but testimony that quickly brought into the present the horrible death Christina had suffered.

The girl had literally been butchered.

One woman juror put her hands to her face when the doctor said the girl had been decapitated, her hands had been severed at the wrists, her abdomen had been slashed open and her intestines exposed, her nipples had been sliced off, and deep slashes and stab wounds had been inflicted over her chest, abdomen, inner thighs, and posterior. The killer had apparently reached into her abdomen and stabbed viciously into the liver. No outside wounds matched the inside liver wounds.

"Could you determine how the head was decapitated?" Strange asked.

"It could have been done with a large hunting knife. There was some sawing component to the decapitation."

Holding up an autopsy photograph, Dr. Spotswood testified, "This is a view of the upper inner thigh region, including the genital area. It shows the two cuts are pretty symmetrical on either side of the upper thighs. It also shows a cut or wound that's in the right side of her external genital region."

An audible sigh washed across the courtroom when the gruesome medical testimony ended.

Van Zandt County Sheriff Pat Jordan took the witness chair to describe how he'd arrested Jason Massey in Canton on the afternoon of August 2, 1993, and booked him into the county jail. While Jordan was on the stand, Strange introduced a color mug shot of Jason Massey taken at the jail right after his arrest. It showed him smiling broadly. The sheriff said Jason smiled at the instant the photo was snapped. He had just been informed he was charged with capital murder.

Entomologist Dr. Neal H. Haskell testified how, using larvae, maggot mass, and grown flies removed from the badly decomposed bodies, he'd determined the approximate time period in which the two victims were killed. "Sometime between midnight on July 26, 1993, and 10 A.M. on July 27, 1993."

Strange was now ready to clear the way for the introduction of the DNA evidence, the key to the state's case and the primary target of the defense.

First, the science of DNA had to be explained to the jury as simply as possible. The jury listened and watched intently as Dr. Michael DeGuglielmo, director of forensic analysis for Genetic Design at Greensboro, North Carolina, gave a short course in the complicated forensic science of DNA testing.

"DNA is really nothing more than a complex chemical. It's present like a lot of other chemicals in our bodies and in the body of every living organism, be it plant or animal."

He said that DNA is a component that passes on information

from one generation to the next. "It enables you to be exactly what you are—all the physical characteristics, all the biochemical properties that make you an individual, and that is information that is coded in the DNA and it's inherited from your parents. DNA is a genetic blueprint. It contains the information necessary to build an organism and to allow that organism to live and function."

He explained the DNA relationship to heredity. "In other words, you might inherit your eye color from one of your parents, or your hair color. . . . If it weren't for DNA, we wouldn't be able to inherit those traits from our parents. DNA is the molecule which passes genetic information from one generation to the next. A gene refers to a specific piece of DNA."

Dr. DeGuglielmo said DNA is composed of four basic building blocks, abbreviated A, T, G, and C. "In a person there are approximately three billion of those from end to end, much like beads on a chain. The sequence variation, whether it A, T, G, or C, and the sequences it occurs in is what differentiates one person from the next."

Dr. DeGuglielmo explained further: "So there are cases where DNA evidence is very limited or cases where it's very degraded [the blood], meaning it's been exposed to a number of environmental conditions where it's such high humidity or extreme temperatures that DNA may start to degrade, to break apart the chain, thereby making a procedure known as PCR the only type of testing that we can do."

Strange watched the jury. They were attentive, but he wondered how much the lucid scientific explanation was getting through to the laypeople. Yet it had to be made, with hopes for the best.

Dr. DeGuglielmo described the two basic methods of PCR testing and made way for the state's introduction of his test reports linking the blood in Massey's car and on the items in the car to Christina Benjamin. The PCR tests concluded that 1,687 out of 1,688 people could be excluded as the ones who'd left the blood in the car, but Christina Benjamin could not.

From watching the jury, Strange believed that if nothing else, the impact of the tremendous odds on the blood in the car being the girl victim's had gotten through to the jury members.

Mike Hartley had prepared himself well for the DNA expert's testimony. Although he had been a biology major in college, Hartley had studied every book and article he could find on the subject of DNA to prepare for the case.

It was fascinating and complicated, and the defense attorney knew that even if you couldn't get certain points across to the jury, you could stress the aura of confusion that surrounds such high-tech tests.

In his cross-examination of DeGuglielmo, he bore down on the types of tests run to gain the results given by the DNA expert. Hartley raised the possibility of sample contamination from improper procedures in collecting blood samples. The defense lawyer questioned the professionalism of the sheriff's department investigators at the scene where the bodies had been found.

Hartley picked out specific slides used by DeGuglielmo in his testimony. The light was bad in several, he said. He quoted DNA textbooks that said certain tests were not reliable.

He told the jury to look closely at the test photographs.

Hartley quoted from DNA books about testing procedures and quizzed DeGuglielmo about several paragraphs.

The expert witness replied, "You have to read it all, Mr. Hartley," implying the quoted passages had been taken out of context.

Through Dr. DeGuglielmo and serologist Michelle Skidmore, the state introduced its bloodstain exhibits: the bloodstained hammer, roll of duct tape, and leaf found in a bag in the car trunk, and a blood sample from the front seat. These blood samples, along with the blood on the lock of hair on the ground, all matched Christina's DNA as disclosed in DeGuglielmo's PCR tests.

Through Charles Lynch, the trace evidence expert, the state introduced the fiber found on Brian's tennis shoe. Lynch said it had the same microscopic characteristics as fibers from the carpet of Massey's car.

Lynch also testified that a blond hair on the front floorboard of Massey's Subaru, the blond hair entangled in the barbed-wire fence, and the hair lock on the ground matched in microscopic characteristics the hair from Christina's hairbrush.

A long blond hair found on Brian's jeans was a match in the same microscopic comparison with sample head hairs from Massey, Lynch said. Also, the bloodstained leaf in the trunk matched other similar leaves on the ground at the body site.

The state moved forward, bringing witness Kenneth Jones, the road worker who described his discovery of the girl's decapitated body, and John Mason, the Canton car wash owner, who'd notified investigators that Massey had washed his car at his car wash and dumped various articles there, including Massey's red bandanna, which had a blond hair on it that was identified as matching, in microscopic characteristics, the hair samples from Massey's head.

When Strange called James Enoch King, Brian's father, the heavy-set, black-haired man eased into the witness chair wearing the expression the jury had seen before on the other parents of the victims. From an earlier statement King had given, Strange knew there were some unexplained or confusing points in the man's story that the defense was ready to pounce on.

King testified that his son Brian and Donna Brown's daughter were both at home when the adults retired on the night of July

26. Christina was asleep in a bedroom with her younger sister, and Brian was sleeping outside in a hammock.

Strange questioned the witness about happenings that night that had become a nightmare in King's memory.

Strange: Did something unusual happen later that night?

King: Yeah, I heard a car pull up and beep its horn twice as it went by. Then, when it came back, it cut its lights off. That's when I got out of bed and went to the front door.

The witness said he had seen a vehicle in front of the house, seen the driver's side of the car, and to the best of his recollection, the time was about 1:30 A.M. He recalled that the headlights were off, but the parking lights were on.

Strange: Could you tell anything about the kind of car it was or what the car looked like? Do you remember anything about it?

King: I know it was a tan-looking color. It had a luggage rack and the windows were a little tinted in the back. I did see heads bobbing up and down in the back seat, all right. But I couldn't make out nothing.

Strange: Now, at one time when the police were there . . . did you tell them that it might have been a Ford?

King: Yes, sir. It was the wraparound turning signals that made me think that.

Strange: Okay. I'll show you a photograph and ask you if that vehicle also has wraparound turning signals.

Strange handed King a picture of Massey's 1982 Subaru.

King: Yes, sir, it does.

Strange: You said that you saw people inside the car. Did you see your son out there?

He had, but he hadn't seen Christina outside, only Brian, walking back and forth by the car, to the driver and then to the back of the car. He identified the photo of Massey's car as the one he had seen at the front of his home that night, or early in the morning.

* * *

During cross-examination by Hartley, King said the car passed by his house the first time, its honking waking him up. King recalled that the lighting outside his house was poor.

Hartley: You saw heads bobbing up and down?

King: Yes, in the back seat.

Hartley: So there was more than one person?

King: Yes, sir.

Hartley: That's two people in the back seat or three? How many did you see?

King: I know I seen one.

Hartley: One in back?

King: I seen one in the back seat. And there was the driver.

Hartley: I understand [in] the statement you gave, the person in the back seat had blond hair?

King: Uh-huh, bushy hair.

Hartley: And what did the driver look like?

King: You got me there.

Hartley: You didn't know what the driver looked like?

King: I couldn't see the driver. All this was just outlined in the back seat.

Hartley: You remember telling Johnny Cruz that person in the back seat had blond hair?

King: Yes, sir.

King said that his son was sleeping that night in a hammock in the front yard. "That's the only night he's ever been out there."

Hartley: How was Brian dressed?

King: Blue jeans, shirt, tennis shoes. I believe he had a shirt on. I don't know if he did or not. The car drove off. I went back out there and Brian wasn't there. I was worried and sat there for a little while, about an hour, hoping he'd come back. But he never did . . . I just went on back to bed and lay down. Soon as I got out of bed about six, I went straight to that hammock and I went right straight to her room [Christina's room]. They was not there. I got worried then. Then we sat and waited and figured they'd be back by morning. That's when we went and called the police. The following day, somewhere along in there. It's been a year.

Hartley: So that morning, when you discovered them missing, you did not go to the police department?

King: No, I figured they might come back later.

Hartley: Where did you think they had gone to?

King: Didn't know.

Hartley: Had either one of them ever been out of the house before like that?

King: Just for a short time . . . an hour, something like that. It wouldn't be late at night, too late at night. It'd be about an hour and they'd come back.

Hartley: So in other words, there were times when they'd leave without telling you?

King: There was one time like that, two times.

Hartley: They never ran away from home.

King: No, sir. No, sir.

It was a somewhat mixed-up recounting of that fateful night, but the father had told it as well as he could, as well as he could remember.

Strange took a deep breath and said, "The state calls Chris Nowlin."

The witness, now eighteen, walked to the witness chair and sat down. He was wearing orange jail coveralls. He appeared to be nervous, looked down and around, and sat slumped in the witness chair.

Answering Strange's questions, he said he was at present confined in the Ellis County Jail because the probation he had been given on a robbery charge a year ago had been revoked. He also admitted he had alcohol and drug abuse problems.

Strange was over the initial hump with the "put them in the middle" witness, on whom so much of the state's case depended to establish a motive for Jason Massey killing Christina Benjamin. He knew he was on dangerous ground, with an astute defense attorney just waiting to jump in.

Strange asked if there was a time in July when Nowlin was with Jason Massey and Christina Benjamin.

Nowlin answered yes and explained, in reply to another question, that Christina was "just a friend. She used to write to me when I was at home, you know."

Strange asked him if he had been in the Texas Youth Council (the state's juvenile detention agency) for a while, in a series of halfway houses, and if Christina had written him while he was there and if he'd written back.

Nowlin answered that that was the limit of his relationship with Christina—she was never his girlfriend, they never went out on dates, that sort of thing. He said that he and Jason Massey had gone to Christina's house while out riding around on July 16, 1993.

Nowlin: We was riding around in the car earlier in the day. Most of the people we knew were not at home. So we went over to her—I told him we could go over to her house. So we went over to her house. She came out to the car and started—we started talking to her. She started talking to us. Jason was driving the car.

Strange: What sort of thing did the three of you do after you got there, to her house?

Nowlin: Well, we—on our way there I told him she was about fourteen years old. When we got there, he asked me how old was she, and she said how old did she look, and he was saying eighteen, nineteen, or twenty years old, flirting with her and stuff, then she wanted to sneak out. And he said, yeh. About twelve o'clock tonight he was going to come by her house, and I was going to be in there [the car], and me and him were going to go by her house. He was going to honk the horn, and she was going to go to the old Fina station at I-45, near her house. . . . We was going to go by and pick her up and cruise around and go riding around, but we never did get to that, because we went over to one of my friends' house, Mark Gentry's house, and something, we never did get over because one of my friends, Mark Gentry, had to go to the hospital.

Strange: Okay, when you left Christina's house, did you and Jason Massey have any kind of conversation?

Nowlin: Yes, sir. After we left her house he said he would like to— [hesitates].

Strange: You're going to need to tell the jury exactly what he said.

Nowlin: He said he would like to fuck her, kill her, cut her pussy lips off, fry them, and eat them.

There was a gasp in the courtroom.

Nowlin: Then we, you know, I didn't pay much attention to it then, you know, it was weird.

Defense Attorney Hartley launched a blistering cross-examination intent on demolishing the witness's testimony, concentrating on Nowlin's character. In his questioning, Hartley brought out that Nowlin had run away from a Dallas halfway house five times.

Nowlin said that he and Mark Gentry ran around together, sometimes joined by Massey. He said they would drink and take drugs, including LSD, marijuana, and something called "primo," which was a mixture of cocaine and marijuana in a cigarette.

Nowlin testified that the group usually got beer and drugs and went "out in the country." The witness said that on the afternoon before they later went to Christina's, he and Massey were drinking and smoking primos. Describing that day after the meeting with Christina, Nowlin related:

"Everything was cool and set up and that night Mark got cut, you know. She was going to go over to that Fina station. She was going to go over there, and we was going to pick her up at twelve or one o'clock, or around there. And then we went and smoked some more primos at this one dude's house. We picked up this black dude and took him to the other side of town, and we rolled a weed and some coke. There was bunches and bunches of coke this time, man, and I got so messed up I started puking and stuff, and then I was gone. That's when we went to Mark's house and someone had cut him."

Responding to more of Hartley's questions, Nowlin said about Massey's comments concerning Christina, "No, I didn't pay any attention to it because he talked about killing girls all the time, so I didn't pay no attention to it. When I got around him, he started drinking, he started saying, 'I want to kill.' He was always talking about killing girls. Nobody paid much attention to him."

Hartley now asked Nowlin about an incident that the attorney wanted to bring up for a possible reason why Massey had been carrying a .22-caliber revolver that had been mentioned in witness statements.

In a series of questions, the defense attorney elicited details from Nowlin about a wild car chase in which Massey's car had been slammed in the side by the pursuing vehicle on July 18, 1993.

Nowlin said that he, Mark Gentry, and two other youths were after Massey because Gentry wanted to beat him up for "messing with Mark's ex-girlfriend."

The witness explained that the group had an unwritten law that no one would mess with another guy's girlfriend after a breakup unless the boyfriend gave his okay.

He said Massey "messed" with Mark's former girlfriend without asking, and that's why he wanted to chase him down and give him a beating that night they spotted Massey in his car on the highway near Ennis.

Strange felt Nowlin's testimony about Massey's stated intentions with Christina was still intact, but he was thankful he had put Nowlin in the middle of the witness lineup, though he doubted even that would help jurors forget the witness.

Next, the state called Christina Erwin to show the jury that Massey had a .22-caliber revolver in his possession several days before the murders. She had been with him on July 22 when he'd bought ammunition for the gun at the Ennis Wal-Mart.

She testified Massey had bought bullets because she wanted to shoot the revolver. "My dad is a hunter, and I have shot rifles, but I've never shot a pistol before. And I just wanted to see what it was like."

She said it was a silver pistol, a big pistol with a black grip. The girl said Jason made his purchases while she was in the fabric department. Later he showed her two knives and a pair of handcuffs he had also bought that day.

To shoot the gun Massey suggested they go to a spot near Telico, near some gravel pits. He told her he was familiar with the area: it was isolated and there'd be no danger of accidentally shooting somebody. But they got lost and returned to her house, Christina Erwin said.

She saw Massey again on July 26, when he went to her house, and later that same evening, when he stopped by McDonald's, where she worked. They visited while she was on her break, and he left around 10:15 P.M.

Strange: Had the defendant been drinking when he came by?

Erwin: He had a six-pack in the front seat and one of them was missing.

Strange: Was the defendant acting normally that night, or how would you characterize it?

Erwin: Everything was pretty normal until he got ready to leave. He said he cared for me and my sister, that he loved us both, and he said he just needed to declare his thoughts and how he really felt about my sister, and that he would do anything to protect us and never hurt us. That was just strange for that particular goodbye.

She said he left about 10:25 P.M. Previously she had told a detective it was 11 or 11:15 P.M., but checking the work time sheet as to when she'd taken her break, Christina decided she had been about an hour off on the time when Massey had left.

"Up until that night were you still Jason Massey's friend?" Strange asked.

"I would like to say I'm still Jason Massey's friend," she replied. The defendant at the counsel table smiled.

Under cross-examination by Hartley, Christina Erwin said she and Jason spent "a lot of time" together that summer, "swimming, go playing around, watching videos and movies, just whatever there was to do in Ennis." Usually her younger sister, Shawntee, was with them, and one or two other girls who were friends.

"It was almost every day he was out at our house," she said.

In answers to Hartley's questions, Christina said Massey told her he'd purchased the .22 because he was afraid of Mark Gentry and Gentry's friends, who had rammed their car into his Subaru several nights earlier. She said he bought the ammunition because he did not have any when Christina asked to go shoot the revolver. She said he did not try to hide the two knives or the handcuffs he'd bought. He had left the empty boxes in her car.

In re-direct, Strange asked if Massey said where he'd "bought" the gun. The girl said he did not say.

Strange: Did he say how long he had had the gun?

Erwin: He hadn't had it long.

Shawntee Erwin, who followed her sister to the stand, told of seeing the "shiny" revolver in Jason's waistband that same July 26. She said Massey acted strange when he left the house, telling her to remember him every time she heard the song, "If Tomorrow Never Comes."

Douglass Murrhead, a clerk in the Wal-Mart sports department, testified that he picked Jason Massey from a lineup as the customer who'd bought a box of .22 ammunition, two knives, and a pair of handcuffs on July 22, 1993. The clerk said it was the only pair of handcuffs he had ever sold.

With the next two witnesses, the state showed its version of where Massey's .22-caliber revolver had really come from, the gun Massey said he'd purchased.

Robby Turner testified that he'd purchased a chrome-plated .22-caliber revolver with black grips from an Ennis pawnshop for seventy dollars. Turner said he'd later left his gun in storage with some other belongings at a relative's house in Canton, the same house where Massey was living. The gun had disappeared.

Shawn McIntosh, a young boy who was the state's next witness, knew what had happened to the gun.

"Did you see Robby leave the gun in a box on the premises?" Strange asked. The boy replied yes, and added he'd seen the same revolver the next day, July 19, 1993, in the possession of Jason Massey. The youth testified that Massey had briefly showed him the .22, tucked under his shirt.

Strange: Did he say anything when he showed you the gun?

McIntosh: Yes. He didn't want no one else to know about it. He told me to keep it hushed.

Strange: Did he tell you where he got the gun?

McIntosh: He told me that my half-brother [Turner] gave it to him, let him borrow it. . . . Jason stuffed it in his car in the glove box.

The boy said he later asked Massey what had happened to the gun, "and he told me he got rid of it in Dallas. He said he gave it to a black person in Dallas, and that's all he told me."

That same day, Massey was arrested by the sheriff's department after he had asked to borrow Shawn's bicycle and ridden away on it. Later, the officers had come to the house and searched it, after Jason had been arrested.

Twenty-seven

In many murder trials the jury has to be excused from the courtroom while the attorneys on both sides argue a motion before the judge. Such motions usually concern the introduction of evidence that needs clearance by the judge on its admissibility before the jury hears it.

Clay Strange advised Judge Knize the state's motion concerned "extraneous bad acts," which meant bad acts over and above the act of murder with which Massey was charged. The "bad acts" the state had in mind were not violations of the law per se, but they would show "proof of motive, intent, preparation, identity, plan, or knowledge."

Strange said he wanted to clear the way for the testimony of two witnesses whose testimony would be limited to having heard Massey regularly talk about decapitation of girls and sexual acts with girls' bodies after decapitation.

The prosecutor said such talk by the defendant was "extremely relevant" to the case because it showed "plan and a signature kind of act."

Strange also wanted to introduce some writings of the defendant—specifically, one page from his diary that was part of the Dallas hospital medical records—that would show Massey's fantasies about decapitation, sexual mutilation, mutilation of the breast area of a girl, and decapitation of a girl around the same age as Christina Benjamin.

The state also wished to introduce into evidence a certain letter received by a girl named Anita Mendoza of Ennis and the photographs of the bodies of mutilated women that had come with it.

"We wish to introduce only a portion of a letter," Strange told the judge. That section was about two dreams Massey said he'd had about Anita that included her abduction and stabbing with a knife. The same letter also said that the photograph of the mutilated woman was what Anita would look like if Massey ever caught her alone.

"That photograph is one of several in which the woman in the photograph is split, eviscerated, cut down the middle, the way Christina Benjamin was," Strange said.

After hearing testimony of the witnesses the prosecutor wanted to use, and considering the objections made by the defense, Judge Knize ruled that they could testify before the jury. He also ruled the letters to Anita Mendoza and Laura Meadows were admissible. The ones to the Meadows girl had been obtained under a legal search warrant, the judge decided. He said:

"I find the search warrant is valid on its face. Further, there's been no showing that any information contained in the affidavit for the warrant is false.

"Therefore, I overrule any objection to any search . . . at the Vernon State Hospital. Secondly, I overrule objection and any [legal] privilege the defendant thinks he may have had with Laura Meadows. As far as I know, the only privileged statements are between a priest and penitent and husband and wife. I've not been shown they [Massey and Meadows] are married."

He also found the testimony of the two witnesses admissible. "It amounts to a statement 'I want to kill somebody' and then somebody ends up dead. I find it admissible for the purpose of showing motive, purpose, intent, preparation, plans, and identity. Objection is overruled and evidence is admissible."

The stage was set for testimony that would shock the jury and the spectators, which probably was the reason for most of the spectators being there.

* * *

The man entered the courtroom with dignity and sat down in the witness chair. He gave his name as Carlos Mendoza and said he was the father of Anita Mendoza. He spoke with a slight accent as he was questioned by Clay Strange.

He identified an envelope and a letter handed to him by Strange as items received at his house in October 1989. He had opened the letter. He also identified one page as having been part of the letter.

The courtroom stirred as a pretty black-haired young woman took the stand just vacated by her father. She gave her name as Anita Mendoza, twenty years old, now living in Dallas, and previously in Ennis.

Strange: Did you at one time go to school with Jason Massey?

Mendoza: Yes, I did.

Strange: Were you in the same grade with him?

Mendoza: I was in the seventh grade. I'm not sure whether he was in the same grade I was.

Strange: Were you ever friends with Jason Massey?

Mendoza: *No.*

Strange: During the course of going to school with him, did he have an obsession with you?

Mendoza: Yes.

Strange: Did he call you on the phone a lot?

Mendoza: Yes.

She answered that he also wrote her letters, threatened her, and stalked her. She identified state exhibit 154 as one of the letters Massey had sent to her. She identified his signature, with a symbol below, on the last page.

Strange: Miss Mendoza, would you read the portion of the excerpt, please?

She began to read in a quiet, soft voice. The audience was silent, the jury intent on her words, the purported words of the man at the counsel table who stared at the floor.

"Do you remember the last letter I sent? I said I had several dreams about you. I should have told you what they were . . . So here it is. You were sitting on the floor at this house. Then I grabbed your arm and laid you down. Then I said, I have been taking Karate. Then I said, have you ever heard of a floating gun? Then I put my tongue into your mouth. Then you started crying, so I left.

"The other one is better, though.

"This guy I know and I were in a garage looking out the window. We saw your mother leave. When she did we seen your father sitting in a chair in the yard. You were taking trash to the garage. When you came in I put my hand to your mouth and a knife to your throat, kissed you on the side of your face and said goodbye. Started cutting your throat. But my knife would not cut your throat very well. So I pushed it through the back of your skull. Well, I think you can figure out what did or did not happen. By the way, my knife is very sharp. I do love you, Anita. Write me back, please."

The state called Jeff Estein, eighteen, who said he had known Jason Massey for two years and "had gone riding around with him at times."

Strange: Were there ever times that Jason Masssey would make comments about women—unusual, bizarre comments about women?

Estein: Yes, sir. Just that he would like to kill a girl.

Strange: Would he call them girls when he said that?

Estein: No, sir. Bitches.

Strange: Would he say what he wanted to do in regard to them, or say any other things?

Estein: Well, he specifically said how he would kill them.

Strange; Jeff, would you tell us what, in addition to wanting to kill them, he would say?

Estein: Just said first he would like to have sex with them, or kill them first, and then have sex with them. How he would kill them was by cutting off their head and their hands.

Strange: Would you sometimes say, you ever saw an attractive girl, that you would like to go out with that girl?

Estein: Yes, sir.

Strange: What would Jason Massey say, sometimes, in response to you saying that?

Estein: That he would like to kill them.

As the witness testified, Massey glared at him. It was the first time that the defendant had shown any emotion. He had never looked at witnesses as they'd testified before now. Usually he'd stared at a spot about two feet ahead on the floor or written rapidly in his notebook. But now his eyes locked on Estein's face.

Strange: Did he ever say anything to you about having sex with a girl after he killed her and cut off her head?

Estein: Yes, sir.

Strange: Where would he want to have sex with a girl?

Estein: Where her head used to be.

During the cross-examination by Defense Attorney Hartley, the witness admitted that he ran with a group of boys, drank, took dope, and did not have a job. He said, answering one question, that he had earlier made a statement to sheriff's officers in which he had not mentioned any of Massey's comments except that he "would like to kill girls." He had not mentioned Massey's sexual intentions.

Hartley: Isn't it true, Jeff, that once you all drank a lot of beer and smoked a lot of dope, then everybody started talking pretty big?

Estein: Sometimes.

Hartley: This type of comment, wanting to do harm to somebody, Jason Massey wasn't the only one in your group that said something like that, was he?

Estein: He's the main one that brought it up.

Hartley: So the rest of the fellows were talking the same way, weren't they?

Estein: Yes, just joking around.

Hartley: They were joking around, but what you are saying is he was serious?

Estein: Well, looked like to me he was.

On re-direct examination, Strange asked Estein if "Generally when the defendant made these statements he was drunk. Was there sometimes when he would make them when he was not drinking?"

Estein agreed, and Strange then asked "What about when the defendant was actually around girls? Was he nice to them when he was around them?"

"Yes, sir," Estein replied.

Taking the witness chair next was another former buddy of Massey's, sixteen-year-old Ben Byars of Ennis. Byars said he did not attend school; he had dropped out.

Strange: When you were out with Jason Massey during 1993, did he ever make any statements about women you felt were unusual or weird?

Byars: Yes, sir, he did.

Strange: Can you tell the jury what kind of statements about women he would make you thought were unusual?

Byars: He would just, in the middle of everything, you know, we would be sitting there, and he would say something about raping a girl and cutting her head off.

Strange: Would he call her a girl or would he use some other word?

Byars: He said bitch.

Strange: Would he say that only when he had been drinking or other times?

Byars: Not only when he was drinking . . . Just not every time we got together, but just every once in a while, different occasions. Sometimes we would be drinking, sometimes we wouldn't.

Once again Massey honed in on Byars as he testified. An

assistant prosecutor said later, "If looks could kill, Estein and Byars would have been dead."

District attorney's investigator Phillip Martin was the next witness. He testified that he executed a search warrant for the bedroom of Laura Meadows, the day room, and the annex building security areas at the Vernon State Hospital on September 26, 1993.

The prosecutor asked Martin to read from letters he'd confiscated during that search. They were letters from Jason Massey to Laura Meadows.

Martin read parts of letters in which Massey referred to having seen six angels take a girl's spirit up to heaven while he was on a road in the woods; how drinking affected him adversely and made him dangerous; and to the date July 27, 1994, as being one year since "it all happened." The state contended the words "it all happened" referred to the murders of the two teenagers on that date a year earlier.

Jason Massey's letters to Laura Meadows sounded like a Sunday school lesson as compared to his diaries that his mother had found in Dallas, the one which had inspired her to take him to a psychiatrist. The doctor, and investigators who later read them, found the contents of the two notebooks disgusting and depraved and indicative of a potentially dangerous young man.

But Strange noticed that Massey's letters to Laura Meadows were greatly restrained. He kept out the obscenities and violent longings that overflowed his diary entries. But there were hints that his interest lay elsewhere than the thoughts he recorded in his letters.

Knowing that all mail is screened before it leaves the jail, Massey had had sense enough not to write in his usual style. In one letter Massey mentioned that the correspondence might be read by the district attorney or even the jury. One had to wonder why, if he was concerned about monitoring, he wrote anything.

Massey's egotism had probably won out, his desire to brag about himself and how he had been the subject of "a big investigation by the FBI."

The two-way correspondence had started in June and was still intense in September, when Massey went on trial. The state would show that even while he was confined for capital murder, Massey, from his jail cell, was again stalking a sixteen-year-old girl, who could be his next victim if he ever "hit the ground" again.

He was optimistic and expected to go free at the end of his trial. One of the letters among those Phillip Martin had taken from Laura's room gave her the latest rundown on his courtroom proceedings. Dated September 16, 1994, only ten days before Martin's raid on Laura's letter cache, it said:

"My Dearest Laura, I'm writing you again to say I miss you and all. I'm sure that by now you got my letter. Well, I know you should have gotten it Monday or so. I hope I didn't screw up sending those newspaper articles.

"I don't want to give us away. I guess I'll know soon enough. But basically I had a good day at the courthouse. My lawyers really fought hard for me, but I'm a little blue. I'm just ready to go home. I want to see you there. So many things I want to do.

"Mostly I want to come see you. I would feel better if I could see you in person. That way I could look you in the eye and say, 'I missed you' and tell you I love you.

"I would feel so much better to be able to hold you in my arms and tell you I care very much about you. I don't think a pen and paper are the proper instruments for me to use to tell you I love you.

"Love brings about trust, openness, and honesty. Love casts out worry and fear. Love is a wonderful thing. Just talking about it got me off the subject.

"I was telling you my blue day. I've been in here 13 and 1/2 months today, and I have only two weeks to go and I will have done 14 months. I've never done this much time.

I love Laura Meadows. How much time have you done so far. I was going to ask you where do your parents live? Just wondering as I thought I would go visit them when I get out or maybe I should call first. I'm sure they will like me once they get to know me, their son-in-law. I'll bet they will be real surprised.

"Dad wouldn't shoot me down, would he? Yes, I've heard *Have You Ever Danced with the Devil.* By the way, no, I sure haven't. I did walk in him for seven years.

"Sometime we will go to all those places if you want. Do you keep my letters or get rid of them. I had best stop with the questions. I hope you're keeping my letters hidden well from the staff. Not because any reason other than I wish to keep writing, but more so now because my heart is troubled. I wish to talk to you about it.

"I've a personal problem. I don't know if you will have any solution, but I feel better telling you about it sometime. It's just that I have temptations to do things. We all do. However, I don't want to do these things. It's just after being tempted so long I have trouble pushing it out of my mind and I hate it. I tend to think on a temptation that comes to mind, too.

"It's real screwed up. When we meet in the world I will go into detail on it. Well, baby, I probably won't write until I get some stamps and stuff. That will be at latest the 20th. I'm sure my trial will start Sept. 26th. It's real close now. I'm getting excited. I mean, 'I feel' destiny taking its course. I mean, it's odd, but I know who I am, where I'm going, where I come from.

"All things are going as I planned. Within three weeks I will be a free man, free to do according to my will, to roam without restraint. Oh, how I love America. I'll pick you up as soon as I am able. I'll write you before I come to get you, to get it planned and all. Sorry I can't write poems. I'll just have to settle saying you're so special and wonderful to me, and as you are aware I love you.

"You can send me a photo ASP and write when possible. You'll be in the heart of my thoughts, baby. I look to the day that I can show my love instead of saying Laura I do love you. It's just not good enough. That's not for my lady. But it will have to do for now. So I love you, I am,

> Jason Eric Massey."

In another letter, Massey spoke of the murders of Christina Benjamin and Brian King:

"The FBI helped investigate the murders of those two teenagers, and it was a major investigation. So I try not to draw any attention. I don't want them on my tail for the rest of my life . . . So I'll always have to be careful, Laura . . . When I do get out the FBI will be watching me. They may be even monitoring my letters now."

Massey sent her a picture of him taken, he said, after his baptism in December 1993.

"Laura, send me the picture of you in the bikini. Sometimes, Laura, I wonder if I'm this side or that side of the fine line, the one that divides psycho from genius. There's a fine line between insanity and intelligence, so I continue to wonder where do I stand."

Massey waxed paranoid, also.

"How do I know you aren't a spy of some type with the behavioral science unit in Virginia. I mean this could be a setup. I'm stupid for writing you back. Maybe I'm just paranoid, but I'm curious, too."

He decided to tell her about his past:

"I had sex for the first time between 7 and 9 years. I fell down some stairs and cracked my skull at 2 or so. I think. this played a part in my actions later in life. My biological father was never around. He and my mom separated when I was 2.

"You'll laugh at this, but trust you will tell no one. I used to wet the bed until I was 12.

"I have special places. I've places out in the woods in Ennis I like to go by myself. I'll take you there some day when we get out. I'll show you something when we get there. I can't tell you, though. It's a surprise. Don't worry, you'll like it, all of it. I went to those woods very often. I used to do my hunting there. I used to camp there, and I also grew weed.

"It was also there where a demon screamed out at me in that place in those woods. I have many memories."

The state rested after entering excerpts of Massey's letters to the girl in the hospital.

Twenty-eight

The defense had taken some hard licks in the case presented by the state. Now, Hartley and Griffith hoped they could convince the jury to look at some of the evidence differently as they began their side of the story.

Cross-examination had done little to the integrity of the state's case, despite the background of some of the prosecution witnesses. The state's test-tube evidence may have been clouded slightly by Hartley's interjection of some contamination possibilities, but it was still strong.

Massey's letter writing to the teenage patient in a mental hospital had come as an unpleasant surprise to defense lawyers. This testimony hurt their case, coming on the heels of Anita Mendoza's story of the threatening letter from Massey, as did the impact on the jury members and courtroom at large of Massey's quoted depraved remarks about girls, when considered in the light of the autopsy report on Christina Benjamin.

Even though the bizarre comments were reported by questionable witnesses, the words would ring in the ears of the jurors, the defense lawyers realized.

The defense called Nancy James, the heavy-set mother of Jason Massey. The strain was apparent in her face. Her resigned look and words reflected that life had not been easy for this woman.

The courtroom had an air of expectancy. How must this mother of a son accused of such horrendous acts feel as she prepared to testify in his behalf? What could she say that would make much difference?

Her initial testimony focused on a family beset by problems. She and her husband had moved to Canton from Ennis because both were out of jobs and had moved in with his folks. Nancy, who had worked in nursing homes, testified she was planning to pursue a career as a nurse and return to school.

Jason had a "good job" at McDonald's in Ennis that he did not want to give up, so he did not move with them to Canton. He moved out in the country with his dad, she said.

Yes, July 18, 1993, had been a significant date, she replied to a question from Hartley. It was her birthday, and the family had a party for her.

Hartley: Did you see Jason Massey on that day?

James: Yes, sir. He was supposed to come and see me for my birthday. We had a party and he didn't show up that day. He came late that night between 11:30 and 12:30. Well, being when he came late, that was unexpected because I figured he wasn't coming. When he came in he was very nervous and upset, and I was nervous by the time he did come in.

Just before Massey arrived, she received a phone call from a girl asking for Jason to call her and indicating that he was in some kind of danger. (This was the night that Mark Gentry and his friends rammed Massey's car, as related earlier in the trial by Nowlin. Nancy knew nothing about that when she received the call.)

When Massey got home, he had phoned the girl after making a call first to Mark Gentry. Nancy had asked what was the problem, but said Jason did not tell her what it was all about. But he was more nervous after the calls. His mother said he intended to stay at the house because she noticed later he had brought all his clothes.

It wasn't until about 4 A.M. when she stepped out to get the morning paper that she noticed the clothes in his car and that the car had been wrecked on one side, with broken glass everywhere inside.

Hartley: Do you recall the following Monday, July 26?

James: Well, I'm sure of a few things. Jason had come home late that night. I don't know what time it was, and I was upset with him. We had a few words because he was supposed to have come home and take me to the revival at church 'cause I didn't have any gas. And when he came in we had words about it.

Hartley: Do you know if he went to Ennis that day?

James: Uh-huh . . . He was gone all day in Ennis.

Hartley: Do you remember specifically the time he got home?

James: No, sir. It was before midnight is the closest I can say.

Hartley: What sticks out most in your mind is this argument you had with him about not showing up?

James: Yes, sir.

Hartley: Do you remember when he came in whether he had had anything to drink?

James: Yes, sir, he had.

Hartley: Where was he on July 27?

James: He was in Canton, but he went to Ennis that day. He came back.

Hartley: All right, and what happened on July 27 if you can recall?

Hartley now was targeting the date Jason mentioned in his letter to Laura as "it has been one year since it all began."

James: We went to church that night, and he went up when the altar call was made, and he prayed and he cried and he got saved.

Hartley: Was this something unusual? Had this happened before with him?

James: Not since he was a little bitty boy.

Hartley: And you could tell that this experience for him was, in other words, there was something you could observe about his experience there at the church?

James: Yes, sir. He prayed with the preacher a little bit. He prayed. He did good.

Hartley: Do you recall on the next day, the twenty-eighth of July, where he returned to Ennis, or did he stay in Canton?

James: He went back to Ennis.

Hartley: Did he stay in Ennis late that night?

James: He came back Wednesday evening to go to church Wednesday night. My mother [Granny Sue] brought him back in her car. He drove his car to Ennis and had problems with it and couldn't get it home. He went back to Ennis on the twenty-ninth to get his car. And he came home.

Hartley: Do you know why Jason would have wanted to take his car to a car wash?

James: Because it had been wrecked and it had glass all over the front and the back and all over, and I had stayed on his back to clean it up because his little brother wanted to go with him, and I told Jason he couldn't go until he cleaned that car out because he would get cut up, and he finally did.

The defense attorney asked why Jason kept the tools in his car that were found when it was searched. His mother said, "He had linkage that would stick, and he might have to jack his car up. They were my tools and my toolbox and he kept them in the car most of the time." She explained that the roofing ax found in the car was for his new job as a roofer. He had been scheduled to go to work the week he was arrested.

Hartley: I show you a couple of excerpts from letters. This one says, "The last time I had a drink was July 26, '93." Is that your son's signature? Do you know what that symbol down below is?

James: Yes, sir, it's his. It's in Arabic. I taught him how to write his name in Arabic.

Hartley: That July 26 was the last time he drank anything?

James: Yes, sir.

Hartley: And this letter says, "July 27, 1994. It is one year since it all happened." Was that the night of the revival?

James: Yes, sir.

* * *

Clay Strange waited a few seconds before he started his cross-examination of Massey's mother. He needed to firmly establish that July 27, 1994, did not refer to Massey's being saved.

Strange: Mrs. James, do I understand you to say that you feel like the significance of that July 27 was the day your son was saved?

James: Yes, sir.

Strange: Have you ever heard anybody speaking about being saved say, "Since it all began"? Isn't it more typical for somebody to say, "It's been since July 27, 1993, that I became a Christian" or "a born-again Christian" or "I became saved"? Isn't that kind of an odd choice of words, to say, "Since it all began"?

James: No, sir. In our religion when you get saved you are a newborn. It's a new beginning. It's the start of the beginning of a new life.

Strange: In your religion, being saved, would that mean a person wouldn't fantasize about sexual acts with juveniles?

James: I don't know.

Strange: Are you familiar with these letters that your son was writing to Laura Meadows?

James: I've heard about them. I don't know about them.

Strange: Did you know Laura Meadows is sixteen years old?

James: Yes, sir.

Strange: You say the night your son came back from Ennis on July 26 was before midnight?

James: I didn't know it was before midnight. I just had a feeling, it was as close as I could put it.

Strange: Were you having trouble remembering what time things happened back in those days?

James: I don't remember.

Strange: Same way you said to the grand jury last August that he was home at dusk, and now you said that's not true?

James: Well, I've never had anybody in my family, or nobody I know, in capital murder. I was in shock. I couldn't tell you. If it hadn't been my birthday on the eighteenth, I probably wouldn't told you when he came home then. If we hadn't been in revival that week, I wouldn't know which day he got saved.

Strange: The fact is, Mrs. James, for whatever reason, I suspect the one you just said is a pretty good one, your mind was in turmoil?

James: Well, that's so.

Strange: The truth is, it's very difficult even today for you to tell the jury with correct certainty about what times things happened on Monday or Tuesday [July 26 and 27]. Am I right?

James: . . . I don't look at clocks every move I make. I don't know what time it is every time I turn around.

Strange: Now, you said he went to Ennis on Monday, and he went to Ennis on Tuesday and on Wednesday. Considering he didn't live in Ennis anymore, do you find that odd?

James: No.

Strange: Now, I believe at the grand jury you said he had gone back over there to get his toothbrush and some toothpaste on Monday and return some movies to the video place?

James: Uh-huh.

Strange: Do you know why he went back Tuesday?

James: No.

Strange: Do you think it's possible he went back over to hide something he hadn't had time to hide Monday or early Tuesday morning?

James: No, I don't have any idea.

Strange: Mrs. James, you said those tools in the toolbox he used to work on his car. Do you have any idea why there would be blood on those tools?

James: No, I don't.

Strange: Do you have any idea why there would be blood on the driver's side door?

James: Well, his arm got cut in a wreck, and he had blood on his arm. I believe it was his left arm—I'm not sure—when he came in.

Strange: Do you have any idea how he got blood on the steering wheel? Or any idea how there got to be blood in the passenger seat?

James: No.

Strange: Do you have any idea how blood got on the duct tape?

James: No, sir.

Strange: Did your son at any time indicate to you that he did not do this crime?

James: I haven't talked to him about it. He has a lawyer and I didn't ask him.

Strange: Christina Benjamin was butchered, and your son stands accused of that, and you never asked him if he did it? Is that true, Mrs. James?

James: He has a lawyer. I don't have any reason to ask him that.

Strange: But you are his mother, Mrs. James.

James: I leave it in God's hands. God will take care of it. If he told me yes, or if he told me no, what could I do? It's between him and the lawyer, not me.

Strange: But you still think July 27, 1993, is significant to your son because that was the day your son was saved?

James: Yes, sir.

Strange: Did you ask him that?

James: No, I know that.

Strange: But you don't know the other part, do you?

James: Which part is that?

Strange: Whether he admitted it or not?

James: No.

Strange reminded the witness that before the grand jury she had talked about Gentry and three others.

Strange: Is it your thought these fellows are framing your son?

James: I don't have any idea.

Strange: Is it your thought, Mrs. James, that your son has stopped drinking because he was saved?

James: Yes, sir.

Strange: Do you know he told Laura Meadows he didn't drink anymore because it was just too powerful for him and he couldn't handle it and tended to get crazy when he was drunk and dangerous that way?

James: No, sir.

Strange: Mrs. James, do you know your son told Laura Meadows he had seen six angels take a girl to heaven, that he was on a road, he had seen it at night in some woods, and that he'd tell her all about it sometime?

James: Do I know that? No, sir. There's nothing unusual about a dream like that when you become a Christian. There's angels encamped about us at all times.

Strange: Of course, he didn't say he dreamed that. He said he saw it.

James: Well, you see that when you're asleep in your dreams.

Strange: Mrs. James, do you have any idea why he would ask Laura Meadows if she knew how to use an automatic pistol? Would a question like that be in keeping with his being saved?

James: He was interested in guns. I guess it would.

Strange: Would a person who has been saved and had quit drinking, and in your church, would that also mean they would not smoke marijuana?

James: I don't have any idea. Personally, I wouldn't.

Strange: Would it surprise you to learn that your son was still smoking marijuana as late as October 1993 even as he was in the Ellis County Jail?

James: Yes, it would.

Strange: A person who has been saved wouldn't steal, would he?

James: I would hope not.

Strange: Would it surprise you to learn that your son said in one of those letters to Laura Meadows that he was scared to steal, but he would rather just take it at gunpoint?

James: Would it surprise me? Uh-huh.

Strange: Do you know who Bonnie and Clyde were, Mrs. James?

James: Famous bank robbers.

Strange: Would it surprise you for me to say that he said to Laura Meadows in a letter: "It would be exciting to live the life of Bonnie and Clyde"?

James: To some people it might be exciting.

Strange: Would it be to a person who had been saved?

James: Just because a person's saved don't mean they don't dream and have fantasies and thoughts. They're not perfect automatically, they have to work at it. It doesn't happen overnight.

Strange: I understand. But do you suppose a person who would look back on July 27, '93 as being that day it all began would be thinking about living the life of Bonnie and Clyde?

James: It's a dream world and a fantasy.

Strange: Would it surprise you to learn that he said about them that the end of them was such a waste. They were still young. Would that surprise you?

James: What do you mean?

Strange: You notice he didn't say the life they led was a bad one, or one of crime, that they killed people or held up banks or anything, but their death was a waste.

James: I really don't know about that.

Strange: When he tells her he wants to tell her things, true things he's already done, things she can't imagine in her wildest dreams, do you have any idea what he might have been talking about?

James: No.

Strange: It's true, isn't it, that there were newspapers containing coverage about the murders of Christina Benjamin and Brian King in the bedroom where Jason Eric Massey slept?

James: Sure was, and it was mine. It was between my mattress because I hadn't finished reading my papers. It was still in the wrapper when you took it.

Strange: Do you have any idea why your son would own a pair of handcuffs with blood on them?

James: I don't know why they had blood on them, but I know he was going to start a collection of handcuffs.

Strange: A collection of handcuffs?

James: Uh-huh. He wanted to get guns, too, but I couldn't let him have those in the house.

Strange: Did he have other sets of handcuffs?

James: I don't know. He had just started his collection.

Strange: Would it be consistent for a person who viewed July 27 as "the day it all began," meaning his conversion to Christ, who would ask in one sentence, "Will you go to church when you get out?" and then in a sentence only a few paragraphs down say, "When will I get my photo? Now, that's enough. I don't need to be plain, especially if you're serious about playing twenty questions. I'd rather play tie-up or doctor"?

James: I'm sorry, I don't have any idea. I don't have any idea.

Strange: And what about a person who would say to this same sixteen-year-old girl, "Do you like to be eaten? Would you give me head?" Would that be consistent with a person viewing July 27 as a significant day because of his conversion to Christ?

James: I don't know.

Nancy James stepped down and left the courtroom. Some people in the audience or on the jury might have thought the poor soul had been treated too harshly by the prosecutor. Others probably agreed with Strange that there was no way that Jason Massey—when speaking of July 27, 1993 as being a significant day—had reference to his conversion to Christianity.

Within only a few more hours, the jury would be certain that it would not have been consistent with Massey's way of thinking at all—in view of the things he dwelled on since he was barely into puberty and maybe before that. The things he dreamed, thought, planned, and wrote about almost daily—a driving, uncontrollable hunger to rape and kill young girls, have sex with their corpses, decapitate and mutilate them, eviscerate them, cut out their sexual organs, prepare them and eat them, and then, someday, return to their burial spots and glory in their bones.

* * *

Mike Hartley had one more line to run before he rested his case. He had been implying in his cross-examination of the forensic witnesses that there had been inefficiency and bungling in the homicide investigation. Now he wanted to pound home that idea.

He called to the witness stand CID investigator Johnny Cruz, who had been the lead detective in the probe.

Cruz was forthright in his answers and held his own in the onslaught by the defense attorney, a lawyer who, incidentally, Cruz respected and admired.

Hartley asked if Cruz took statements from the victims' parents on the day when he talked to them at their home.

"Not on that particular evening, no," Cruz said quietly.

"Wouldn't you want to gather that information at the earliest possible opportunity in order to try and piece things together?"

"Well, it just depends on the circumstances. Like I say, on that evening we just made contact to advise them what we found out there and it was quite possible the bodies were those of their two missing kids, and they were so broken up after that, I figured it really wouldn't be a good time to sit down and take a statement."

"Did you ever take a statement from Donna Brown?" Hartley asked.

"I don't believe I did."

"And Mr. King's statement was taken on the seventeenth of August. Is that the only statement?"

"To my knowledge, it is, yes, sir."

The grilling continued along that line. Did Cruz interview the younger sister of Christina on what she heard that night when Brian came into their room? No. Did he consider the friends of Massey as suspects at any time? Yes, all of them. Did anyone take hair or blood samples from the other suspects? No.

Hartley bore down. "Detective Cruz, would you agree with me that the most significant development in your investigation was the statement you heard from Chris Nowlin about Jason Massey's comment about Christina Benjamin?"

"Yes, sir," Cruz answered.

"Were you looking for information like that from the other people, the same kind of statement being made?"

"Yes, I was looking for the same information in reference to any possible suspect."

Prosecutor Strange, in his cross-examination, asked, "Investigator Cruz, in that week or two following the finding of the bodies, your office received all kind of information about people that might have been involved in this, all kinds of possible details about this?"

"Yes, sir."

"Did your office and ours check out every one of those?"

"Yes, sir."

"Did you find one shred of evidence that would involve any other person besides Jason Massey in this case?"

"No, sir."

"Was Jason Massey ever not the prime suspect in this case?"

"No, sir."

The defense rested. There was a recess before closing arguments by each side.

On this day, as the guilt-innocence phase of Massey's murder trial wound to a conclusion, Jim Harp was hiking in the dense woods near Ennis—not along any paths or trails, but through the brush and entanglement of tree limbs and vines. He was breathing hard because it was tough work.

But that was what he wanted. He was getting into physical shape, training for the approaching deer season. He had no idea that he would play a momentous role in the outcome of the Jason Massey murder case.

Suddenly, ahead of him in tall brush, but still visible, he spotted an old, rusty red ice cooler. He stooped to remove the lid to see what might be inside.

Twenty-nine

The historic courtroom was jammed, with only standing room left for spectators, when the final arguments in the shocking double murder started. Lawyers not involved in a case often flock to the courtroom when good trial lawyers clash in the final arguments of a complex case.

This was such a trial, and everybody in town was trying to get into the courtroom.

Seated in the row behind Clay Strange and the assistants working with him, District Attorney Joe Grubbs was more than an interested onlooker. He would listen carefully to Strange's summation, alert for any item that might enhance his presentation. He doubted Strange would miss anything.

Clay Strange, not showing it but feeling deep weariness from the pressure and concentration in the hard-fought trial, stepped forward.

He paused in front of the jury box and his glance ran silently over the jurors before he spoke. They had listened careful through the trial.

"May it please the court.

"The death of a child—it is not possible to think of something more serious, something worse than the death of a child. Now, there's been a great deal of talk during the course of this trial about the seriousness of this trial with regard to the defendant, with regard to whether or not the state will prove its case beyond a reasonable doubt that the defendant committed capital murder.

"Obviously, that is very, very serious. But what can be worse and more serious than the death of a child? A murder of two children can be worse. That's what we have here in this case, ladies and gentlemen. Now, those two children that night, the twenty-sixth of July, 1993, made two mistakes.

"The first mistake they made was to sneak out of that house that night. It's a mistake that teenagers make, a thirteen-year-old and a fourteen-year-old, they make mistakes. The second mistake they made was to not recognize, was to not see, the evil that lies within that man [pointing to Massey]. It was hidden from them.

"They could not see it; they were too young."

Massey sat without movement, staring ahead at the floor. His face showed no emotion. During the trial, in the breaks between testimony, Strange and Massey had exchanged hard looks.

The families of the victims sat in the audience. They listened and watched the prosecutor closely. Their hope for justice for the wrenching loss of the girl and boy rested on the success or failure of this man's work.

Strange continued, "They didn't realize the evil trying to get out of that man, they didn't see it. And that mistake cost them their lives, pure and simple. And it is my job, and has been my job now, to make sure that the evil that lies within that man is not missed again.

"Now, we don't know and I can't stand here and tell you exactly what happened that night near Telico, but I can tell you what I believe the evidence shows, what the inferences are that can be drawn from that evidence, and I suggest to you that James Brian King was surprised and shot in the side of the head by that man and then shot again in the face, killing him.

"Once that happened, that man picked him up, probably out of the car, and dumped him off that bridge. You see that his T-shirt is pulled up [indicating the photo of Brian's body]. From that moment on, that night, Christina Benjamin, as she was outside Telico alone with that man with a gun, began a time of terror that none of us really wants to think about very much, because she knew from the second that gun went off and killed her stepbrother what was going to happen to her. There wasn't going to be anything good happening to Christina Benjamin after that moment.

"She knew that she was going to die.

"The only question was what was going to happen to her between then and the time that she died. Of course, you know what happened. Shot in the back, but she wasn't shot in the back straight on. Bam! Was she on her knees? I don't know.

"She could have been on her knees. That man shot her and then what he did to her next, we don't know. We know he hit her. We know he hit her right there. He hit her hard. And from that point on, we don't know.

"We know that later he butchered her. And as a result of that butchering, he has blood on his hands even today. The defendant in this case, the method to commit these murders is not in question. It's that motive—why would he do it?—that has to give rise to some question at some point in this trial.

"You had to ask yourself, why would anyone do such a thing? Why would anyone do it? Was it driven by fear? No. Was it driven by revenge? No. Was it driven for money, theft, robbery? No.

"It was driven by lust. It was driven by desire to commit a sexual homicide, and that's what happened.

"Now, what would make a person do that? I suggest to you that what would make a person do that is evil, the evil that lies within that man, the evil that's in there now, and the evil that's waiting to get out again.

"I want to show you what the state has presented to you in the form of evidence linking Jason Eric Massey and no one else to the death of Christina Benjamin and James Brian King. . . ."

Strange went over the evidence step by step, tying one exhibit to another, summing up the technical forensic testimony and evidence on the blood, hair strands, fibers, and other items that bound Massey to the ghastly murders. The gun seen on his person the day of the murders, the gun he had stolen from a relative, the ammunition for it he'd bought at Wal-Mart, along with the knives, and the handcuffs that were stained with blood.

And Massey's stated goals in life, as shown by his diary copied by the psychiatrist and his letters to Laura Meadows, his depraved remarks on his desires to do sadistic and savage things to young girls, and his cruel torture and killing of numerous cats, dogs, and livestock.

"The handcuffs Massey had owned for eleven days—isn't it interesting and bizarre that in the eleven-day period he managed to get blood on them? Bloody handcuffs, you know what they were used for and how the blood got on them."

The .22-caliber bullets that were fired into the victims were the same type of bullets that Massey had bought five days before the killings, Strange reminded the jury.

"He bought the ammunition the day he bought those handcuffs."

As Strange continued his argument, District Attorney Grubbs's beeper went off. *Who in the world would be paging me right in the middle of the arguments?* Grubbs wondered, not without slight anger over the inopportune disturbance.

He rose and quickly walked from the courtroom. It flashed through Strange's mind fleetingly: *Where in the heck is Joe going right in the middle of this?*

District Attorney Joe Grubbs phoned the number shown on his pager and learned from a sheriff's officer that Jason Massey's long-sought "death diaries" had been found!

Officer Tom Payton, now a member of the Ennis Police Department, had responded to a call to the Ennis dispatcher from a man who said he'd found a cooler with the diaries and animal skulls inside.

Payton drove to the residence of the man, James Harp, who had brought the cooler from the woods. When Payton saw the contents, he notified the Ellis County Sheriff's Department. Johnny Cruz drove to Ennis immediately to pick up the cooler.

Payton had worked on the case when he was an Ellis County deputy and knew that investigators had been searching for a cooler that supposedly held Massey's diaries. One of their biggest frustrations was they couldn't locate the cooler that friends of the murder suspect had described before the trial had started.

Now, Grubbs was faced with a major decision. Strange was about to conclude the state's arguments asking the jury to convict Massey of capital murder. Should he interrupt the final arguments and request the judge reopen the case because of vital new evidence just discovered, or let the case go to the jury and introduce the diaries during the punishment phase?

If the diaries were as explosive as Grubbs thought they would be—judging from Massey's writings in the two volumes that the Dallas psychiatrist had copied—the death penalty for Massey almost would be guaranteed.

But the district attorney believed the state had presented strong evidence to the jury of the defendant's guilt. The judge had already read the charge, the explanation of the law applicable to the verdict.

With this in mind, Grubbs resolved his dilemma by standing pat. When the punishment phase opened tomorrow, the state would be ready.

Grubbs went to the sheriff's department to examine the cooler. The animal skulls were in various stages of decay; the smell that rose from the cooler was nauseating.

Inside two plastic bags were four spiral notebooks, the kind schoolkids use, filled with pages of writing on both sides. The notebooks were slightly damp but intact. And a glance at the handwritten pages revealed they were diary entries written by Jason Massey over four years. On the covers of the notebooks were the hand-printed words "Slayer's Book of Death, Volumes I, II, III and IV."

Witnesses interviewed by investigators had mentioned that Massey kept diaries and stored them in a cooler somewhere in the woods. Searches had failed to find them. To the prosecutors, it seemed to be divine intervention that a random hiker had come upon the cooler in the tall grass and brush within the dense woods.

Now, the D.A. and his staff were faced with reading the diaries and copying them for presentation to the jury. They would have to work late into the night to do it.

In the courtroom, meanwhile, Clay Strange continued his summation, unaware of the bonanza of new evidence that had been uncovered.

Strange reminded the jury that Massey came back to Ennis during the day of July 27, after being there the day and part of the night before.

"It's interesting to think why he came back the twenty-seventh, isn't it? And I think we know. The defendant, Jason Eric Massey, said a lot of things about girls the summer of '93. He says, quote, 'I want to do this to—', he calls them 'bitches.' Kill them, cut off their head and hands, and as Jeff Estein said, 'Have sex where her head used to be.'

"Then Chris Nowlin recalled Jason Massey, the moment after he met Christina Benjamin, said, 'I'd like to kill her. I'd like to cut off her pussy lips and eat them.' And to Laura Meadows, he wrote, 'I've seen six angels take a girl to heaven, her spirit anyway. I was on a road and I seen it at night. I'll tell it all to you in time.'

"These words, ladies and gentlemen of the jury, are the words of a man who killed two children in one terrible night in Telico. He did it on July 27, 1993, because July 27, 1994, was 'one year since it all began.'

"And to think that's the anniversary day of his being saved is outrageous! What kind of man would say things like that? Only one—a killer. It's a terrible and horrible case, ladies and gentlemen.

"But I believe that justice is going to triumph in this case, and it's going to shine as bright as that fiber in that photograph. The family deserves justice, and I'm confident you will give it to them. Thank you."

* * *

Mike Hartley took his place in front of the jury box to begin the defense arguments.

"Now, I told you when we started that this case was tailor made by the State of Texas to convict Jason Eric Massey. And in order to establish that I am going to go back to the beginning, and that is the night the young people were supposed to have disappeared. . . ."

Hartley launched into criticism of the sheriff's department, which, he said, "had decided on the basis of what little investigation they did that my client was guilty and there was no need to look into the facts about the disappearance. . . ."

Hartley dwelled on the "fuzzy-headed" young man James King said he saw in the back seat of the car that came to his house that night. "You were never brought any descriptions by the sheriff's department of a young man we talked about [not Massey] who matches that individual he [James King] saw in the back seat. I would suggest to you at that point in time it was incumbent upon the sheriff's department to flesh out this information if they wanted to prove who killed these children beyond a reasonable doubt."

He said the testimony of Brian King's father indicated there may have been three persons in the car, two in the back seat and a driver.

The attorney suggested the investigators did not want to bring forth any information that would make it less likely to convict Massey. "Either that, or it was just sloppy police work. We had all these indications, but why follow up on them? We had one suspect, that's enough.

"The State of Texas has been tempted to tailor this case to cover up for lack of proof that Jason Massey did commit this crime. There were other people who were just as likely on the basis of the same kind of evidence."

After questioning the job done by investigators, Hartley then chipped away, in minute detail, at the forensic evidence, suggesting that tests had been used that are not considered reliable by some DNA experts. He thought it was possible that the blood samples either had been contaminated when collected or were too poor in DNA quality to give an accurate analysis.

Hartley told the jury Massey had made no effort to conceal the boxes containing the knife and handcuffs he had purchased on July 22, nor had he gone alone to the store. "If Mr. Massey masterminded some horrible, evil crime, those two boxes in his girlfriend's car are no indication that he's any kind of a criminal mastermind. If he purchased these items with the intention of using them to commit a crime, why did he leave the boxes in the girl's car and why didn't he go to the store alone?"

Summing up, Hartley told the jury: "The problem with a circumstantial evidence case is that the state gets to throw the kitchen sink out on the table, everything plus the kitchen sink, and puts Jason Massey in the position where he's almost forced to prove he's not guilty, and that isn't how the process works.

"I am going to ask you to keep an open mind and not to go back there with preconceived notions. Look at each item of evidence in the best and worst light before you draw any conclusions.

"If any one of you believes that the state is not proving the case beyond a reasonable doubt, I am going to ask you to stand on those convictions we talked about. Stand up for what you believe in."

If just one juror stood firm on a belief that guilt beyond reasonable doubt had not been proved, there could not be a verdict and a mistrial would result, which is not good—but better than a conviction, as any defense attorney knows.

Under the law, Strange had the last say.

"The defense's case in this matter can be boiled down basically to this: the police ignored all kinds of evidence, they didn't check their leads, they didn't do this, they didn't do that, sloppy police work, they had all kinds of suspects, they ignored them, the police were incompetent.

"You heard investigator Cruz say the only suspect they had was Jason Massey, in the sense that he was never considered not to be a suspect. Once they got into him, he was the prime suspect. They continued to look at other possibilities. But they found not one shred of evidence that anyone else was involved."

Strange said it was preposterous to think that there was a big conspiracy against Massey by the sheriff's department, witnesses, forensic scientists, the FBI, and the district attorney's office.

Nearing the end of his argument, Strange said quietly, "I represent the dead. The dead have spoken to you in this case through these brilliant people. The dead, Brian and Christina, ask for justice. They only cry for justice. Don't let those cries go unheard.

"When we comfort our children when they are afraid of monsters, we tell them there are no such things as monsters. You don't have to be afraid of a monster. But unfortunately, in America today, that isn't true.

"There are monsters. This man is a monster. He doesn't look like it now. But he did that terrible night outside Telico. That evil that is within him came out that night, and it will come out again and again and again if you don't find him guilty of capital murder."

It was about noon on Thursday, October 6, 1994. The seven-woman, five-man jury began its deliberations. They were back with a verdict in three hours. The courtroom was crowded again as the jury members filed in and took their seats.

Judge Knize asked, "Have you reached a verdict?" The presiding juror replied yes.

"Pass it to the bailiff, please."

The judge silently read the verdict form, then said, "Stand up please, Mr. Massey."

Massey rose and stood with his hands in the pockets of his purple trousers. He was stone-faced, as usual.

"The verdict is the jury finds the defendant guilty as charged in the indictment," Judge Knize said.

Massey showed no reaction. His sister, who was present in the audience, started crying and put her head on her grandmother's shoulder.

Relatives of the victims sought Strange and others of the prosecution team to express their thanks.

Conviction on the capital murder charge meant Massey would get one of two possible sentences: life in prison, or death by lethal injection.

The judge told the jurors he was allowing them to go until tomorrow morning to give the attorneys time to get witnesses together for the punishment phase. He instructed the jurors not to discuss the case with anyone and not to read newspaper accounts or watch TV newscasts on the trial.

Thirty

"Time to get their witnesses together" was putting it mildly, as far as the district attorney's staff was concerned. The lights would burn late in the D.A.'s office. Grubbs and Strange met with the other assistant prosecutors around the table in the conference room.

It was decided immediately not to introduce the cooler and its grisly contents into evidence. The stench was overpowering, and the lawyers knew the district clerk, who had custody of all evidence, would not cherish handling the nasty diary depository.

Grubbs, Strange, Lacy Buckingham, Cindy Hellstern, Bobbi Reilly, Kamala Cromer, Marlena Pendley, and Phillip Martin, the chief investigator, dug into the notebooks. The office had only two copying machines, so it took time.

Everyone got comfortable. Bobbi Reilly ran one copier. Every few minutes she came back into the room where the others were working, exclaiming, "Look at this!" The others were doing the same thing, pointing out pertinent excerpts that would nail Jason Massey.

When the more than 500 pages of the diaries had been copied, they were divided among the lawyers to read and mark the passages that could be passed along to the jury.

They all wore surgical gloves to handle and go through the "scuzzy" notebooks, as they were described by Grubbs.

"They were really foul," the district attorney recalled. "They had been there among the decomposing animal heads for months."

After going through the pages, the attorneys would gather again at the office to plan the next day's strategy.

The district attorney took his share of the reading home. Grubbs said that "it gave you a creepy feeling, sitting there in the semi-dark, reading that stuff." Some pages and parts of others were illegible. "He must have been either drinking or doing dope when he wrote at times," the D.A. said. The writing often was as wild and out of control as the thoughts expressed.

Back at the office, the attorneys discussed their findings, which had been tabbed with labels or markers. All of them had been astonished at the wealth of excellent evidence in the recorded fantasies, desires, and elaborate plans compiled by the accused killer from October 1989 through July 1993.

Although they were the "personal writings" of the defendant, they did not fall under the search warrant clause that had prohibited the searchers of the house in Canton from seeking Massey's diaries or letters, even if they had been there.

The diaries in the woods had been discovered by a citizen, which meant the diaries were "published" (the legal term) or in the public domain and available as evidence. No search warrant was involved.

The spelling was so bad that it was hard to make out the words, combined with the scrawled writing. Other pages were easily readable and though the spelling still was bad, it could be decoded.

One thing struck them all: Massey's writing reflected the desires to kill and mutilate girls and women in ways that had been done to the body of Christina Benjamin—the beheading, the severed hands, the gutted abdomen, the mutilation of the pubic area and inner thighs, the slashing away of the nipples.

The courtroom tomorrow was going to echo with some of the vilest obscenities ever to be spoken in a public gathering. It would be far beyond an R-rated movie's contents.

When Lacy Buckingham finished her part of the diary research, she went home and worked several more hours on the opening statement she would give for the state in the punishment phase.

Ordinarily, there are no opening statements when the punishment part of the trial starts, but Buckingham had asked Judge Knize if she could make an opening statement, since the nature of some of the evidence to be offered by the state was so unusual. The judge had given his permission.

Word had spread fast that the lurid diaries of Jason Massey had been found and would be read to the jury. Massey must have been secretly pleased, even though his neck was on the line. His "works" would be the center of attention. From letters written to Laura Meadows, it was evident he was basking in the limelight of the TV news coverage.

The courtroom was overflowing Friday morning.

Besides the sensational "Book of Death" volumes, the state had a lineup of witnesses to convince the jury that the convicted killer should be put to death. Among them was Anita Mendoza, making her second appearance before the jury.

For the death penalty to be given, the jury would have to be convinced that Massey would commit acts that would be a continuing threat to society. The state believed his diaries would leave no doubt.

Buckingham had graduated from Baylor Law School in 1991 and started work for the D.A.'s office in Waxahachie in 1992. She left for five months to take a job with the Lubbock County Criminal District Attorney's Office but returned to Ellis County as an assistant D.A. in August 1993. She had walked into the biggest homicide case a young assistant ever would be involved in helping to prosecute.

"Call your first witness," Judge Knize said.

Buckingham was startled. This was the time she was supposed to make her opening remarks, before any witnesses were called.

"May we approach the bench, Your Honor?" Strange requested.

State and defense attorneys huddled around the judge's bench, speaking in low tones to keep their remarks from the jury, which was already seated.

Buckingham reminded Knize that he had given permission the day before for her to make an opening statement.

The judge denied that he had.

Buckingham knew that she had heard him right, so she persisted. The judge realized he had *thought* she was asking to make the first part of closing state arguments at the end of the punishment phase testimony.

Hartley remarked that the defense had no objection to Buckingham making the statement she had prepared, adding that the defense did not wish to make one. The judge told her to proceed.

Silence descended as the prosecutor faced the jury box.

She began, "In Mr. Strange's closing statement he talked to you about motive in this case and how motive of Jason Eric Massey to kill Christina Benjamin and James Brian King was not readily apparent. We are about to present to you evidence that will tell you why he did such a thing, and that in this case his motive was lust or sexual excitement and pleasure in killing those two children.

". . . In criminal forensic science, there are classifications of murderers. One of those classifications is a lust murderer. And you'll hear evidence in this trial that Jason Massey fits that profile, that classification, to a T. We are about to bring you evidence that will flesh out that part of the case right now.

"What better evidence of the defendant's character and background could we bring you than the defendant's own writings about his true feelings and desires and wants and yearnings? . . . Not many people get to have that kind of evidence, but in this case, that's one of the things you will be asked to look at and look at closely. . . . In those journals Jason Massey writes about what he wanted to be, and in one journal he writes about being asked the question, 'What do you want to be, what do you want to do with your life?' And his response in the journal in quotes is, 'It is forbidden. It is forbidden.'

"Once you hear this, you'll know that's exactly right. Because over and over again Jason Massey repeats that his goal in life was to be a killer, a murderer, and not just any killer, not just any murderer, not just one time, but that he wants to be a serial murderer just like Henry Lee Lucas, just like the Green River serial killer. He plans and plots.

"All his time from about the fourth grade was spent planning and plotting to become a serial killer. You'll see from his journals that he has planned how many people he would kill a month, how many people he could kill in his lifetime, how to kill them, where to kill them, how to bury them, how to get away from the police.

"What you're about to listen to is the most heinous, the most revolting, there's not even a word to describe what you're about to hear.

"Mr. Strange told you in his opening argument you would come face to face with a kind of evil you have never seen in your life and never will again.

"And you have, in the first part of the case, and I'm here to warn you that now you're about to come even closer, closer than you'll ever want to be to someone, a person disguised as Jason Massey is, a fair-haired young man. The evil inside, as Mr. Strange said, is trying to get out. I want to warn you, even now, that some of this evidence we plan to bring you, some of this evidence is distasteful in both its appearance and its smell."

She said the offensive evidence was necessary because the state was asking the jury to give Jason Massey the maximum penalty—death.

The state called James Harp of Ennis.

Harp testified that he was walking in the woods about a half mile behind his house when he noticed a rusty-looking ice cooler. "It was just sitting in the weeds. I opened it up. As soon as I opened it up, I smelled the smell. I knew something wasn't right. There was a plastic bag sitting on top. I raised the bag up and there was skulls under it.

"Right off, I knew it had something to do with Jason Massey. He lived right next door to me at one time. I had heard before about a cooler [from news stories on the case]."

Lacy Buckingham walked to the witness stand and handed Harp several color photographs. He identified them as pictures of the spot where the cooler sat—". . . That dark spot in the grass, that's where it was sitting."

Indicating another photo, Harp said, "That's the cooler and the books that was inside it."

He also identified a photograph of the skulls from the cooler. "They were underneath the plastic bag on top."

Buckingham turned, walked to a table nearby, and picked up a large plastic bag. The contents were obviously heavy. She carried it to a table near the witness and undid the plastic bag. Inside she could see hordes of ants crawling around and over the cooler.

She had donned a pair of surgical-type gloves before she lifted out the cooler and placed it on the table. When she opened the lid, a terrible stench became evident to the jury and others near the exhibit.

The jurors stared in fixed apprehension at the cooler.

The attorney withdrew an animal skull, thought to be a dog skull because of its size.

"Is this one of the skulls you found in there?"

"Yes."

She pulled out more skulls, nine in all.

"And there's some more jaw bones, some more teeth, down in here?"

"A bunch of jaw bones."

Buckingham replaced the skulls and closed the lid.

Buckingham removed the Latex gloves, put them on the exhibit table, and sat down. She happened to glance down and what she saw sent a tremor of disgust through her body.

She was covered with fine dust—on her suit's skirt, its sleeves, even on her panty hose. For a moment she was filled with panic as she realized what the grayish dust must be.

Oh, my gosh, I've got that dog dust from those heads all over me! And I'm going to have to sit here all day long with dog dust, this horrible dust from those skeletons and skulls, on my suit, she thought. She wasn't even aware of anything else going on in the courtroom, which had been completely silent as she had withdrawn each skull and showed it to the witness.

As she tried to compose herself and think what to do, the judge called a brief recess. She rose and hurried to the women's rest room. There, as she examined the dust more closely, it struck her what the dust actually was.

It was only talcum powder from the box from which she had taken the gloves. She heaved a big sigh of relief. A relative of one of the young victims, the grandmother of Brian King, helped her clean off her clothing. It was a relieved assistant prosecutor who returned to the courtroom.

Clay Strange thought it was the funniest thing he had ever heard of happening at a murder trial. But he compensated for his amusement by telling the young assistant she had done a good job with the opening statement and introducing the gruesome exhibit, "dog dust" and all.

During a brief recess, as she watched Jason Massey being led from the courtroom by a deputy, Lacy Buckingham's thoughts went back to the first time she had ever seen the neatly dressed young man now on trial. Several months before the slayings, the assistant prosecutor had stood within three or four feet of the then disheveled, long-haired blond kid who'd come to court to plead guilty to a driving-while-under-the-influence charge growing out of his arrest by Ennis police. Buckingham at the time was the misdemeanor prosecutor in the D.A.'s office.

As she later said, "You would think that anybody who had spent their entire life—every moment of their life, every minute part of their being—thinking and planning and plotting to become a serial murderer, that you would somehow get some sense of evil from that person, or some sense that he was bad. And that's not true. I never felt that way.

"And all I thought then was, here's this blond kid who obviously has a big alcohol problem."

Since it was a first-time offense, Massey had been placed on two years' probation.

Thirty-one

Some things in a murder trial have to have a "sponsor." In legal circles this means a witness through whom evidence can be introduced by his positively identifying it for what it is. In this particular case, the sponsor needed was a witness who could testify that the death diaries of Jason Massey in the four notebooks indeed had been written by him.

The state had a sponsor in a young man who'd come forward early in the investigation and admitted that he not only knew Jason Massey in Dallas and had roomed with him for a while, but he had also joined Massey in killing animals, planning to rape and kill girls, doing dope, and pulling the armed robbery of a chicken restaurant where Massey had formerly worked.

His name was Paul Anthony Demomio, the next witness called by the state. He was the "mystery witness" who had initially phoned District Attorney Grubbs anonymously to say Jason Massey should be investigated in the murders of the two teenagers.

Later, he gave his identity, plus a full statement about his past relationship with the accused slayer.

Demomio had a background as bad as some of the other witnesses the state had brought before the jury. But the crucial difference was that this witness had cleaned himself up and was leading a new and admirable lifestyle. He was now a student at a Dallas college, was receiving psychiatric counseling, and had involved himself in a spiritual life.

Demomio was the former friend that Massey once dreamed

would be his partner in Massey's planned rampage of girl and women murders, "like Otis Toole was with Henry Lee Lucas."

But Massey decided Demomio always would be an incurable slave to a drug habit that kept his mind "fried" most of the time and made him a "stupid shit." Even with that, Massey once wrote, he would always think of Paul as a brother.

Now, on the stand, Paul was about to betray him. Strange conducted the direct examination.

Strange: What was it made you become friends with Jason Massey?

Demomio: Similar interests: music, just death and similar dreams, similar interests, and so on.

Strange: Was one of the things you had in common with Jason Massey—were you interested in killing?

Demomio: Correct.

Strange: An interest in drugs?

Demomio: Yes.

Strange: Did you ever witness him kill animals?

Demomio said he had on several occasions, and had taken part in the killings, too.

Strange: Did Massey ever express to you why he wanted to do things like that?

Demomio: For the adrenaline rush, a high, a turn-on, a love to mutilate.

Demomio never had seen Jason Massey "kill by moonlight," as the prosecutor asked, but Massey "told me personally that he had killed a cat and sliced its neck, with blood on the blade, and it was a roulette knife, and it was a full moon, and he put it directly in the moonlight and watched some of the blood drip down, and that's the honest truth of what he told me."

He told of the robbery of a Popeye's restaurant they'd pulled together in Dallas. He said he had been promised immunity from prosecution for the Dallas robbery. "But not from perjury if I don't tell the truth here."

The witness identified the "Slayer's Book of Death" notebooks as being written in Massey's handwriting. "I had read some of them when I was seeing him and hanging out with him."

The state had its evidence identified for introduction.

Strange: Did he ever say anything to you unusual about what he would like to do to girls?

Demomio: One phrase that I haven't ever forgotten that he would say frequently when I knew him is he would like to cut a girl's head off and drill a hole in her head and fuck her brains out, literally.

In cross-examination, defense attorney Mike Griffith tried to turn the witness to some benefit for his side.

Demomio said he had been drug-free for two and a half years.

Griffith asked, "To what do you attribute your success in pulling out of that kind of life?"

"Mainly, to my brother-in-law, my sisters, mother, and many friends and family who convinced me during that period that Jason was not a good person and I needed to get away from him. Also, that I should start college, get on with my life, and get away from sick people and sick thoughts, and that's mainly what I attribute it to—basically, maturing and growing up."

Dr. Kenneth Dekleva, the psychiatrist who'd examined Massey in Dallas in 1991 after he was brought in by his mother, took the witness stand.

Strange asked, "Would you tell the things you found in the diary written by Jason Massey that you found significant?"

"On the first pages of the diary, dated in January 1991, Mr. Massey spoke of the desire to begin his career as a serial killer, to begin his 'sacred journey.' And he, on the very first page, listed the names of several girls who he planned to kill, and that included Tessie, Anita, and a Jolene. He speaks in the diary of wanting to reap immense sorrow and suffering for the families of the victims, to lash out at society.

"In a later portion of the diary in March, he speaks of wanting to, every time he sees a girl that he likes he's going to get her.

And if I remember correctly, rape her, fuck her violently, and drink their blood from their necks. . . .

"He describes the many years of fantasies that he had, violent and sadistic fantasies, and he speaks of having carried out violent acts toward animals."

The psychiatrist said that as he read the diaries back then, "the most alarming things to me were the shift from fantasy to more specific, deliberate planning and the purchasing of weapons. . . . And the specificity of the fantasies in so far as they were the names of specific people he knew.

"I was very concerned about the implications and the dangerousness of this person at that time to society, and I know that was approximately two years before the murders occurred."

He testified that Massey would be a continuing threat to society and not a good candidate for rehabilitation.

A witness who testified earlier in the guilt-innocence phase of the trial, Anita Mendoza, was recalled to the stand. She related in detail how Massey had phoned her, written threatening and obscene letters, sent obscene pictures of mutilated women, and stalked her from 1989 "until he was arrested" in 1993.

Asked by Strange about the telephone threats, she said, "He would go into that big spiel about how he would like to be my boyfriend. But I would say there wasn't a chance of it, and he would get real mad. He said he would get me one way or another. And eventually he would say over the phone that he was going to kill me."

He stalked her at times when she didn't know he was around.

One of the letters Jason wrote her, entered as evidence, said, "When you were at the movies, did you know I was sitting behind you. I remember you were wearing red fingernail polish."

Referring to another girl who was with her, he wrote, "I remember when the two of you walked in I could smell your blood.

It smelled sweet. I would love to spill your blood and sip it like a fine wine."

To introduce Massey's diaries and also the letters he had written to Laura Meadows, the D.A.'s investigator, Phillip Martin, returned to the stand. Directed by the questions of Lacy Buckingham, Martin read on and on the diary entries by Massey about his strange longings and plans for killing "countless young women" and becoming the serial murderer who had slain more victims than any other in America's history.

At times, the jury appeared semi-dazed from listening to the mass of the defendant's morbid and sleazy writings. They seemed shocked and revolted by some of Massey's phraseology, his mental graffiti that peppered the pages of the diaries. More four-lettered expletives were uttered in court than at a Hell's Angels' reunion. The young housewives or single women and others in the jury seats alternately turned red with embarrassment or pale with disgust.

Massey displayed almost no reaction throughout the trial except to turn bright red in the face as one diary excerpt was read in which he deplored that he could not have sex with any living girl without a condom since he had been given herpes by Rita. He also blushed scarlet when it was disclosed in a letter that he was a bedwetter until he was twelve.

In another entry read by Martin, Jason Massey wrote:

"If I'm caught, I'll become a Christian and turn myself around. But my chances of getting caught are very slim."

Dr. Clay Griffith, a Dallas psychiatrist, who said he had testified as a forensic psychiatrist more than 2,500 times throughout the United States, told the jury he had read the diaries and letters of Massey and formed a conclusion.

"My opinion is that without a question this man would be a tremendous danger to society in the future."

Asked if Massey would "be a candidate for rehabilitation," Griffith replied, "Not in the least."

Defense attorney Mike Griffith asked the psychiatrist about the extent of his research on Massey. The witness admitted he had not interviewed anyone, either Massey or any of his family.

Griffith asked, "So you assume what's in those diaries would be more true than what you would get from actual people who participated in that background?"

"No, what I got from the diaries and the letters was sufficient evidence for me. It comes from him."

"You didn't want to find out whether he had been physically abused as a child?"

"It really wouldn't make any difference with somebody with a personality like he has."

"Would anything have made a difference to you, doctor?"

"No, not with the information that I have."

The psychiatrist explained why he was so emphatic in his diagnosis: "I base it on the fact that this syndrome has been known and described since in 1911, which was done by Dr. Ambroso. He used a different name at that time. He called the person a moral imbecile.

"Over the years the symptoms have not changed. The label or diagnosis has changed three or four times until now we call it sociopathic or antisocial behavior. There's been a lot of work done in the research area to try to find some way to treat these people.

"There are not very many of these particular kind of people that have personality disorders this severe. There has been nothing found despite all our advances in medication and different kinds of treatment.

"It doesn't make any difference. There just is nothing. There's no treatment. These people do not learn from experience.

"It's very rare to see anything this severe. There are only a very few people in the United States that are this severe, thank goodness."

The state rested.

* * *

With Mike Griffith conducting the examination for the defense, Phillip Martin was called to read excerpts from Massey's diaries, entries that reflected his harsh life. Phrases ran throughout the entries such as "I'm so confused . . . I seen for the first time a man die . . . I can't trust my own fuckin' mom . . . I don't know who my dad is."

Griffith had Martin read an entry dated September 29, 1992: "I just remembered something. My mom told me one time when we were going over I-45, and she said I might marry her some day. Man, that makes me feel so good, I can't even explain it. It's a very nice fantasy, but that's all it is. Well, maybe not."

The investigator read on, from the entry of Tuesday, October 13, 1992: "I watched a documentary entitled 'The Mind of a Serial Killer.' The narrator and others said a lot of things that pertain to me on almost everything except the physical abuse by a parent. Well, not really. When I was 2, momma said dad whooped me excessively, plus I remember when I was in kindergarten and a guy mom had baby sit me sucked me and I hit him.

"I went to school without a shirt one time. I remember how stupid I felt. I guess no incident caused me my personality. Just many combinations. Funny thing is I somewhat understand why I'm like I am."

Another entry: "It seems like everyone wants something from me. I'm tired of giving and not getting. Tired of everyone. It seems the only one who cares for me is me. Fuck all of 'em. There's no place for friends in my life. Can't trust anyone anymore. I don't even know who my fuckin' dad is. . . ."

The defense's next witness was Massey's sister, Johanna Nicole Massey, a quiet, pretty young woman. She told of the hard life that she and her brother had endured as children, including spankings by their mother with a wooden paddle or a belt that their granny eventually threw in the lake, failure of their mother to help them get ready for school or cook meals for them when they were small, and their mother asleep all day in her bedroom with all the food stored there.

She usually threw "screaming fits" if the children entered to get food and woke her up, the witness said.

She related how her mother had once pulled her out of school to babysit their little brother by telling school authorities they were "moving to California." The witness recalled she and Jason were left alone at night while their mother went out to bars.

Buckingham came back on cross-examination with the question, "Would you say, given the environment you grew up in, that you've turned out to be what appears to me a nice young woman with plans for a future?"

"Yes, ma'am."

Jane Peters, a woman friend who had run around with Massey's mother when both of them were young, before and after Jason was born, told of the two staying out until early morning, drinking and running around.

She remembered how Massey, as a baby, would be carried around in the back of their car while they continued the night life. She said the children were neglected badly, left by themselves, left without food at times.

The defense rested its case following one more witness, who also testified about what she termed the "neglectful life" of Massey. She and her husband had taken him into their home for two weeks at the request of Massey's grandmother, who was a close friend. Massey seemed to be doing well, but then his mother moved with him to Dallas, according to the witness.

Strange called as a rebuttal witness Allen Brantley, a supervisor special agent with the FBI and a member of the behavioral science unit of that agency. Brantley and his colleagues specialize in profiling murderers of all kinds, especially serial and lust killers.

Brantley testified he had reviewed Massey's diaries and letters, the crime-scene photos, and other evidence in the case. Asked if such a person as Massey would be a threat to commit continuing acts of violence against society, the FBI agent said:

"I would say, based on what you told me and the information I've reviewed in all of the case files and all the documents that have been written, medical examiner reports, school reports, etc., without a doubt in my mind that this person is extremely dangerous and will continue to be so."

"Is it possible to rehabilitate this type of person?" Strange asked.

"There are no known examples of that, that I'm familiar with."

"Could a person become that way because his parents neglected him?"

"Absolutely not."

The state closed, as did the defense.

Thirty-two

On Wednesday, October 12, 1993, when Clay Strange took his place before the jury box to begin the state's closing arguments in the matter of punishment, he was about to do something he had never done before.

He was going to ask a jury to put to death a human being. That was pressing hard on his mind as he began to speak.

"On July 29, 1993, when Kenneth Jones was driving that motor grader on Telico Cutoff Road, he saw something that he knew wasn't good . . . and when the smell hit his nose he knew a terrible thing had happened near Telico.

"But Kenneth Jones, no more than you or I, could possibly have known what we know now, what we know by having read Slayer's Book of Death I, II, III, and IV. We now know that there was a terror, there was a suffering, there was a torture that we can't imagine.

"I told you at the beginning of this trial that you would encounter an evil the likes of which you've never seen and hopefully never [will] see again. I suggest to you that's just exactly what you've encountered in this case, and even more, you've encountered an evil in the person of that man right there that is worse than any nightmare that you could have.

"And he has set right there in that courtroom with you. No one could have predicted, no one could have known it, not Kenneth Jones, not you, not me.

"There have been times when I stood where I stand now, and I've called people like that an animal. I've stood here and called people like that a predator. But you know, that's not true in this case. Animals or predators do not kill for reasons that man kills. Animals and predators kill so that they can survive in God's plan. That man is not a part of God's plan or anybody else's plan, except his plan—his plan to kill again and again and again."

Strange paused a few seconds to let that soak in. If anything ran like a theme throughout this trial, it was the plan and plotting of Jason Massey to rape, torture, kill, and mutilate.

Continuing, he said, "A trial of this length, a trial of this complexity, I've got to tell you that I've gone over this a million times in my mind, but there's no one particular part of this trial that I have not really been able to think about except one, and that's the one I'm about to do right now.

"I stand before you for the first time in my life, before a jury, and ask that you return a verdict that will result in the death of a human being.

"And you know that I've had to ask myself, can I do that? Do I have the courage to do that? I've got to tell you, in some cases I wonder. But you said you believed in the death penalty in certain cases, and you could return the death penalty in a proper case where the death penalty is assessed.

"Well, I'm here to tell you that I can stand right here in a proper case and ask you to return a verdict of death. It's exactly what I'm doing, and I'm here to also tell you that you people have the courage to do the same thing. You people have the courage to do what you know must be done.

"If there's to be justice in this case, there can be no other result in this case but death. Not the gift of life, but death.

"And what can mitigate, what could lessen the moral blame for what this man did?

"Hartley said he wanted to look at . . . the personal moral culpability of the defendant, his background, his character. We sure do agree on one thing: we would like you to take a good, long look at character here.

"We know that as early as the fourth grade he began to think about the murder of girls. In 1989 he began keeping a journal, 'Slayer Book of Death,' he called it, a journal that he continued to keep until April of '93. We know that he wrote about things that are barely imaginable. Fantasies, he called them.

"We all know they just weren't fantasies. In 1989 those fantasies took life. He began a terror campaign against a little girl, a seventh-grader at Ennis Junior High School, Anita Mendoza."

Strange pointed out that the Book of Death diaries became "more and more sophisticated, more and more diabolic, more and more terrifying in what he thought about doing.

"On July 27, 1993, he commited the capital murder on these two children that brought us into this courtroom.

"That evil, that darkness, that murder, that mutilation that brought us into this courtroom. And I told you the light of justice could lead us out.

"Three experts said he was a continuing threat to society and could not be cured.

"We knew he did these murders, but what we didn't know is how much he enjoyed doing that, why he did this. We didn't realize he did it for lust, for his sexual pleasure. He wrote about it and he did it.

"He has changed. He's learned the Ted Bundy secret. Isn't that wonderful? Having Ted Bundy as a hero. He's trying to beat Ted Bundy.

" 'I love you, Laura.' Where have we heard that before? The next sentence he says is, 'I'd like to kill you.' He'd do the same thing to Laura."

Strange told the jury that Massey's being "neglected" was not mitigation for his actions.

"Read some of his diaries."

The defense attorneys felt they had been broadsided by a dynamite truck when Jason Massey's nightmarish diaries were found in the woods. In his own words, the state had Massey telling the jury what he wanted to do to girls, his goals, his plans to become the nation's greatest serial killer.

Not spur-of-the-moment thoughts, but the stuff repeated over and over, a growing obsession for murder and mutilation. The defense team knew the diaries were solid evidence that would be difficult if not impossible to overcome.

The jury had already convicted him of capital murder in the teenagers' deaths. The only thing the defense could hope for now was that the jury might show mercy and render a verdict of life imprisonment instead of death.

Mike Griffith made a valiant attempt to gain life instead of death for Massey. He had an example to show the jury, one of the state's own witnesses, Paul Demomio. "This young man, Jason's age, called by the state, looked you in the eye and said: 'I had the same desires. I had the same wishes. I wanted to do these same things.' And he did some of these same things with Jason Massey.

"He told you that he turned to his family and his friends, and they got him help. You saw the FBI agent come up here for the state and testify with his textbook that he uses in teaching a class that things we showed you that happened in Jason's background 'correlate,' but they don't cause this kind of stuff.

"They correlate. Being raped as a kindergartner is a correlation. It's not a cause. Being beaten with a board by your mother—and you heard his sister say 'and I didn't know if she would stop'—correlates and is not a cause.

"Jason didn't have anybody to cry out to.

"Through these diaries you've heard of his fantasies and his delusions and you've heard about his background and you've heard about his family, and the delusion I hope you all don't overlook is when Jason wrote, 'All of my misfortunes are my own doing.'

"Jason Massey did not choose to be raped as a kindergartner. Jason Massey did not choose to be dragged around as an infant in the back seat of a car while his mom was drinking and looking for men. Jason Massey didn't ask his mom to beat him until he didn't know if she would stop.

"Jason Massey didn't ask to have to sneak into his mom's bedroom if he was hungry with the fear of getting beaten. Jason Massey didn't ask everybody that was put in front of him as his dad to call him a bastard.

"Mr. Strange wants you to believe that a sexual attack on a kindergartner is not severe abuse. I couldn't look a kindergartner in the eye and tell him that was just a bad incident. Jason Massey was not born a capital murderer. He was a baby. He wanted a dad. He wanted love. Instead he got rejection and he got hit.

"If you want to believe what the state told you, there's correlation but not a connection, then that's your right. But in voir dire you also heard that you have a right to disagree with those experts.

"And if you believe that the FBI agent could look a kindergartner in the eye after being sexually assaulted and tell him that's not severe—it's just a bad instance that happened to you; that doesn't hurt where your mom hit you—that's just a bad instance that happened to you; that's not bad if you're hungry and have to sneak into your mom's room for food—that's just a bad instance that happened to you; that's not important that your dad calls you a bastard—that's just an instance that happened. That's your right, if you want to believe that.

"And as Mr. Strange said, it happens to millions of people. Thank God, there are people around, some of those people like Paul Demomio had when he cries out for someone to help him. Jason Massey cried out in those same [diary] pages."

Griffith said that the only time Massey shed tears during the trial was when the woman who told of how she and her husband helped him for two weeks cried on the stand.

"He cried through all of the scars you saw in his diaries. She reached through all those scars, and evidence will show that in a twenty-one-year life there was a two-week period when someone loved him.

"But his mom pulled him out and took him to Dallas, where he lived in a house with shit on the floor."

Griffith closed by reminding the jury that when Jesus Christ died on the cross 2,000 years ago, he looked down and said, "Forgive them, Father . . . they know not what they do."

"If the evidence in this second part of the trial showed you anything, it's Jason Massey does not know what he did. Nobody was there when he cried out."

Under law, the state always has the last word. In closing remarks now, Strange said that he disagreed with Griffith's implication that the jury members had the power to forgive.

"That's not something you can do. Maybe if you were the parent or the brother or the sister of one of these victims, or God, you might. But that's not one of the things you can do, forgive that man for what he did.

"Now, mercy is what we are talking about here. Mercy is what he wants. He gave none. He gave pain and he gave torture, and he has the audacity through his lawyer to ask for mercy.

"He didn't ask to be abused. He didn't ask, he didn't ask, he didn't ask. Christina Benjamim didn't ask to have those things done to her, either. Mercy, ladies and gentlemen, is nothing more than receiving less punishment than you deserve. Justice is nothing more than getting exactly what you deserve.

"As long as this man, that man right there, is breathing the breath of life, he is dangerous. He is a threat to do it again and again. There are no guarantees save one: he will do it again. As long as he is alive, all of us are at risk.

"You know and I know it is open season on women by that man. Women age ten to forty. When the murder is done for lust, when the murder is done to satisfy his sexual satisfaction, how can that be mitigated?

"What could be worse than the death of a child? What could be worse than this kind of a death of a child? What could be worse than the dismemberment of a child? This is as bad as it gets.

"I said he is evil, and he is. He is the personification of evil. He is a butcher, the butcher of human beings.

"Ladies and gentlemen, the light of justice has shone in this case, and it has shone by finding those diaries. It has enabled that light of justice to shine on that man and show what he is and what he is not. For he is not a Christian, as he would claim.

"He said in his diary that he will carry on until he's finished. He's not finished. You must finish him."

When the arguments ended, Mike Hartley walked to the back of the courtroom, where his wife had been a spectator. He was surprised to find her crying. She said it was just the thought of their own children who might fall prey to such a killer.

With his wife's reaction to the emotion generated by the arguments and especially the diary contents, Hartley knew then the defense didn't have a chance.

The jury was out less than fifteen minutes. They returned a verdict mandating the death penalty for Jason Massey. One woman juror said the jurors didn't even discuss the case when they entered the jury room, but immediately took a vote.

"The journals really spoke for themselves," said another juror. "They showed there was no hope for rehabilitation, and we just didn't want the possibility of him being out again."

Another woman juror told a reporter, "I couldn't get over how he killed her, and then played with her body like a new toy. If he got a chance, he would have done it again. I know he would."

Massey didn't reveal his feelings in his expression or actions. He didn't answer the questions of reporters as he was taken from the courthouse.

His relatives began to cry, especially his sister, who was com-

forted by her grandmother. Massey's family left the courtroom
without a comment.

Later, the victims' families released a written statement, saying, "Unfortunately, it took the senseless murder of Brian and
Christina to stop this brutal butcher. This is a price much too
dear to pay."

Defense attorney Hartley told a Dallas reporter, "I don't know
that there was anything that could have diminished the effect
that his own writings had. That was unexpected, to say the least."

Massey was back in the courtroom on Thursday afternoon for
formal sentencing by Judge Knize. As the prisoner stood before
the bench, the judge pronounced the death sentence. His next
words left no uncertainty of how he felt toward the defendant.

His face stern, Judge Knize said:

"Mr. Massey, I suppose the only injustice in this case is that
you will be permitted a more humane method of death than you
gave your victims."

The victims' families and friends in the courtroom applauded
and cheered at the judge's words.

Massey did not reply, but in one of his letters to Laura, he
had referred to the judge as "a jerk," which had brought one of
the few laughs in the somber trial. The judge himself had chuck-
led.

Later, as Massey, wearing handcuffs and ankle shackles, was
led to a patrol car to be returned to the detention center, a woman
in the crowd suddenly rushed forward, pinned the startled prisoner against the patrol car, and began hitting him. Officers
pulled the woman away.

Massey's attorney said Massey did not wish to press charges
against his attacker, but the district attorney's office filed a Class
C misdemeanor charge of simple assault. She was fined $210
by the city judge.

Grubbs explained to a local reporter, "We couldn't live with
the precedent of having somebody attack a prisoner. I think we

were very fortunate the prisoner was not hurt. I spoke with the woman and told her I understood what she did and why she did it. But I couldn't live with the precedent of nothing happening to her after she did it. She understood that."

Massey would be confined on Death Row at Huntsville while the death verdict was automatically appealed to the Texas Court of Criminal Appeals. Officials said the appeals process could take several years.

Sue Wickliffe of Ennis, Jason's grandmother, said that Jason's life was not "anything like what they're trying to portray it. They chose to take a route to prove that Jason had a bad childhood, that his mother was some kind of beast, thinking that maybe the jury might have mercy on him, is what they did.

"So there were a lot of lies. A lot of stuff wasn't true. They were poor, they didn't have money, but they had a good life. I've seen a lot of kids who had a lot worse life."

Clay Strange moved to another job several months after the trial. He now is unit director, Criminal Prosecution Division, DNA Legal Assistance Unit, American Prosecutors Research Institute of the National District Attorneys Association in Alexandria, Virginia.

Quiet returned to Courthouse Square in Waxahachie. It is said that everything changes.

But not the devilish faces that still look down from the courthouse's exterior walls. They have not changed since they were placed there a century ago by a rejected suitor of a pretty local belle.

Thirty-three

Darkness still lay over Waxahachie when Capt. John Knight, administrator of the Ellis County Detention Center, got out of bed. This was the day that convicted child killer Jason Massey would be taken to Texas's Death Row Unit at Huntsville, a two-and-a-half-hour drive away. It was being done at an early hour to avoid any crowds, a time when security would be easier.

Knight, with twenty-one years of experience as a lawman, had more on his mind than transporting the murderer safely to the cell where he would await execution by chemical injection. He had had a restless night. The hours had passed slowly. He wondered if he could do what he wanted to do. He had prayed about it. He believed Massey was ripe for what he had in mind.

As the father of two daughters aged thirteen and fifteen, he was appalled by the murders of Christina Benjamin and Brian King. He couldn't even imagine what that girl had gone through, what heartbreak it had been to her folks. He couldn't stand to think about something like that happening to his own daughters, and he wondered how anybody keeps from breaking when it does.

But as he had grown accustomed to doing during his years in law enforcement, especially in his role as a jail supervisor, Knight concentrated on keeping his professional life and his home life separate, determined that one would not have any interfering effect on the other. It was hard to do sometimes.

From the beginning, he had steered clear of the murder investigation and subsequent trial of Jason Massey. It made it easier to go about his day-to-day contact with the cold-eyed young killer. He didn't want to know much about the case of Massey, or, for that matter, any of the inmates under his supervision. It was good business not to become personally involved in their cases and lives.

In his opinion, Massey was without a doubt the most cold-blooded antisocial-type murderer he'd ever known, a killer who should never be back on the streets.

He could have made life in jail unpleasant for Massey. But aside from his role as jailer, in which he believed unbiased professionalism should always be his guide, Knight was a Christian, too. As such, he tried to "walk the talk," as his fellow Baptists like to put it.

"I pray just to get out of bed in the morning," he once said with a grin.

He had prayed about the mission uppermost in his mind this morning as he'd moved quietly about his home to keep from waking his wife and daughters.

He dressed in his full uniform, then drove to the fortress-like Ellis County Detention Center on Jackson Street, two blocks off the town square where the historic old courthouse stood, where the fate of the accused killer had been decided. The detention center was a modern corrections facility, sharing space with the sheriff's office. The center had replaced the old jail.

It didn't take long to get Massey ready and escort him, handcuffed with waist restraints and in leg shackles, to the transport car. The prisoner, sullen and silent, was helped into the barred rear section, "the cage," and Knight and a young transport officer climbed into the front seat. Knight took the wheel.

The sun still hadn't given its first pale hint in the east when the jail captain pulled out.

There was no conversation after Massey and his overseers exchanged greetings. The silence in the car prevailed as the sheriff's unit moved along the highway to Ennis, Texas, from where they would head south on interstate 45 to Huntsville, north of Houston.

As the car sped along the road with little morning traffic, Knight made a couple of calls on the phone to his jail staff to lay out the day. His own boss called the car to ascertain the Death Row trip was safely under way.

Entering Ennis, Knight turned into the takeout drive of McDonald's, the only place open this time of morning.

"I'm getting a cup of coffee," he said to the other two men, and asked if they wanted anything.

"I haven't had a Coke from McDonald's in a long time," Massey said. "Yes, sir, I'd take a Coke."

It was the first time the prisoner had said anything since departing the jail. In his silence, Massey must have been full of memories as they drove into the quiet town, Knight thought to himself. He knew that Massey had spent years of his life here, had once lived only a short distance from McDonald's. Memories especially of the woods several hundred feet behind McDonald's. Once, Massey had scribbled in his journal, a demon had talked to him out there. Always the woods seemed to have special meaning to the dark side of Jason Massey.

When they were moving again on the freeway, Massey asked, "How come you're making this trip, captain? In uniform, too. Isn't it kind of unusual?"

Knight normally did not escort convicted inmates to the state prison or regularly wear a uniform.

He hesitated, then spoke with obvious feeling.

"Jason, I want you to tell me what you did with that little girl's head and hands. Her people need to know this for any peace of mind at all, if they ever have any."

Knight had observed the relatives of Christina Benjamin during the course of the trial, had felt an affinity for their concern and hurt that not all of the girl's body had been found. It was something he would want cleared up if it were his child. It was something that would haunt the rest of their lives. It was in the hopes of finding out, of learning the truth from the killer, that the jail administrator had decided to make this trip himself.

He had watched Massey change since his arrest in August

1993. On the night he entered the jail, he was a cocky, grubby-looking suspect. He had the look of what Knight called the "mega-death bunch," the long hair on the sides and back, almost a flat top on top, wearing drab clothes, an antisocial look.

The jail supervisor remembered the metamorphosis that Massey went through. The next morning after his arrival, Massey was visited by a lawyer and the boy's looks underwent a drastic change. Within an hour after the attorney left, a barber was shearing Massey.

Now the suspect had a short haircut and a change of clothes for those times in public when he needed to wear something other than jail garb. He had the Mr. Nice Guy look lawyers want for their clients.

The jailer had watched other outward transformations. Massey met with preachers at every opportunity. He took part in jail church services. He was baptized. But he still gave off an undercurrent of stress. It built noticeably as his trial neared. When the trial was over and the sentence was in, Knight saw the tension go out of Massey. To Knight's way of thinking, Massey's letdown in tension might open the door to his talking about some things in the case.

It raised Knight's hopes that he might find out about the missing body parts. But the answer that came now to the captain's question about the missing head and hands deflated these hopes.

"I wish I could help you, but I can't," Massey said.

"What do you mean you can't? You're the only one that knows." Knight's voice rose a little in his disappointment.

"I don't know, captain. I put her head and her hands in a pillowcase and dropped them off a bridge into the Trinity River." He said he didn't know the location along the river that winds its way through Ellis County, not too far from the Chambers Creek bridge where the killings happened.

Knight did not believe this for a minute, but he held his tongue.

It didn't fit the pattern at all, Massey getting rid of body parts he had severed. He had kept all of the cat and dog heads in the past, treasured them as his "trophies," bragging to friends about them, stowing several of them in that ice cooler with his diary volumes.

It went against everything Massey had written in his notebooks about what he wanted to do with the heads and other body parts of the girls he planned to kill, how he dreamed of having his own graveyard for his girls and their varied remains.

Knight, like the officers working the investigation, believed that the killer had kept the head and hands so he could return to them later, probably burying them somewhere in the deep woods.

But though he talked freely about the killing of the two youths as the sheriff's car drove through the early morning light, past farms far off the road and sections of heavy woods, Massey was adamant about having tossed the head and hands into the river.

Yet it *was* the first time Massey had admitted it was he who'd killed the kids. There was no talk this time about what a "third party" might have done, as on the night of his arrest in Canton.

Confessing to the murders, he still remained silent regarding other details of what had happened to Christina Benjamin.

"I did what I did," he said slowly. "But the girl never suffered. I did what I did to her after she was already dead."

Knight knew that this statement, too, was in total disagreement with the fantasies and obsessions of lust murder, sexual deviance, and mutilation that Massey had committed over and over to his diaries, describing in gory and perverted detail everything he planned to do with the girl victims both while they were alive and after they were dead.

As the murder trial brought out, Massey dwelled repeatedly on the desire he had to see his victims in pain and tears, to bask in their suffering from the tortures and unspeakable indignities he would inflict.

Massey related some of the events that happened on lonely Cutoff Road that July night in 1993. He, Christina, and Brian were the only ones present, he said. He had told Christina and Brian when he'd picked them up that they were driving out to this location to meet Chris Nowlin and Mark Gentry. It was Nowlin who had introduced Massey to Christina back on July 16.

He said he stopped on the road close to Smith Creek, from where he and Brian walked toward the bridge. Christina had stayed in the car. Massey said that as they walked down the narrow road with dark woods on both sides, he "popped" the boy in the back of the head with a gunshot.

"He didn't suffer at all—he never knew what hit him," Massey said. He didn't make clear whether he tossed the youth off the unenclosed bridge or he fell to the creek bed below when shot.

Returning to the car, he was asked by Christina, "What was that noise?"

He replied he thought it was fireworks. But apparently she was suddenly afraid and jumped from the Subaru to run. Massey said he shot her, probably in the back. Then, as she twisted around and started to fall, he shot her again in the head.

He had carried her over the barbed-wire fence into the woods, down a corridor through the trees to a spot where bright moonlight penetrated the blackness of the thick woods and dense undergrowth. He put her on the ground, then walked back to the car for a knife to make his long-harbored fantasies bloody reality.

He told the jail captain that as he turned from the car to return to the the the girl's body, he saw an amazing sight. Massey said, "You wouldn't believe it! I saw three angels rising upward in a circle. I knew then she had died."

He said again she had not suffered when he "did what I did."

He did not tell what he did after the shootings, except that he had put the girl's head and hands and all of her clothing in a pillowcase and later dropped them off into the Trinity River from a bridge—where, he wasn't sure.

At the Death Row Unit, no longer located within the red brick walls of the old prison in downtown Huntsville, but in a separate facility just outside of town, the officers with their prisoner were met by the host of guards who turn out to receive a condemned inmate. He was taken to a room and strip-searched and moved to another section for processing.

Knight and the other officer with him sat on a bench drinking coffee while the prison personnel completed the necessary paperwork. Massey had been seated on a bench, too. When the Ellis County officers rose to leave, he shook hands with them and thanked Knight for the Coke and the trip.

Driving back to Waxahachie, Knight thought about Jason Massey and his professed conversion to Christianity. He wished he could believe it was sincere faith, but he didn't think so. Maybe that would change.

Knight always held out hope in his own Christian beliefs that "anyone can find God in their heart and their soul, that there always would be the opportunity for true faith for a truly repentant sinner, however bad the sin."

But in his opinion after long association with jailhouse conversions, Knight thought "the young man was saying what he thought we wanted to hear."

He knew Massey was lying about what he'd done with the little girl's head and hands, too, but he realized the truth might never be known.

Author's Note

Jason Massey started keeping a diary in 1989. He continued to do so up until his arrest in 1993. He titled the notebooks *Slayer's Book of Death, Volumes I, II, III, and IV.* The entries were written in spiral notebooks, the kind kids use in school. Numerous misspelled words have been corrected in the reproduced diary entries to improve clarity. Many pages in the diary are illegible, the wild scribbling done while he was "tripping on acid" or intoxicated on alcohol. Some pages were carefully written and the words correctly spelled. Massey's thinking from day to day, his up and down moods, his fantasies and obsessions are reflected in the entries.

Names have been changed to protect the identities of innocently involved people. His fantasies of rape, torture, violent death, cannibalism, and necrophilism climaxed in a frenzy of murder in July 1993. The diaries, wrapped in plastic bags inside a rusty cooler, were found in the woods by a man out walking during Massey's murder trial. Sentences in italics are Massey's fantasies that investigators said were at least partly carried out in the murder of thirteen-year-old Christina Benjamin.

Slayer's
Book of Death

Volumes I, II,
III, and IV

Volume I

Friday, Oct. 13, 1989

Time to start a diary again, because I can't keep all inside, especially after what I found out today. I found out this guy who was only 21 shot himself. I really didn't know him that well, but it really hurts inside.

I think I have just realized what God wants me to do. Defend the weak, help the misfortuned, comfort the old and the small children, and promote God's word.

Friday, Jan. 26, 1990

It looks like everything is going as planned with the exception of my mother. Yeh, she's been ripping parts of my history out again. That's how she reacts in any situation. She childish. It really is fucked. Now my thoughts aren't private.

April 20, 1990

I just got back from Ennis, and, yes, I done it again. I found out where my baby lives; she tried to move.

She changed her number, then I got it and called her, so she changed it. Now I *know* where she lives. I even know where her bedroom is! She had better realize two things. She can't ever hide from me, and two, I will have her soul, as she fears.

Tuesday, May 1, 1990

I was just counting how many animals I've killed, at least 18 cats, more likely 20 or so, 18 for sure that I can remember; 9 dogs and 6 cows. What a fuckin' trip.

Sunday, May 20, 1990

I believe Sally is her name and ah! shit, is she fine! She so, I can't describe her, but she's got long, black curly hair so beautiful and she looks so helpless. I swear, here and now before God, the Earth and all of creation that if I ever get any time alone, I will come upon her like the mighty blast of a whirlwind and with orgasmic delight spit upon the frozen blood inside her, then fuck, all night, day long.

Thursday, May 23, 1990

What to say? I don't know if I just write how I'm going to do this and that it probably will never get done. Then I end up being like —, a big bullshit talker who has nor ever will do anything.

Me being a human has desires & fantasies and that's natural. But if I don't fulfill my desires then they're nothing but fantasies. I don't think I have ever opened up in this little book.

I'm 17 years old, a dropout dope head with almost glich to look forward to. If a man don't do what he says he'll do, then he's nothing. When I took Tommy to the park the other day, the children's parents looked at me like I was going to snatch up their kids and fuck 'em or something!

Every since grade 4, children and old alike have despised me, laughed at me, whispered behind my back, made stories of "sick" Jason Massey.

I heard people say they heard I fuck my own sister! They have babies! . . . me as a devil worshiper, chased me down and beat the hell out of me and there are probably more lies that haven't surfaced yet. They have betrayed me, spit in my face and upon my name. Those so-called "friends" are the seeds of these lies. Just tonight, Joe was saying how bad he'd kick my ass after I told him what I'd do to his car after he insulted me and my father.

When I'm in public and see a beautiful woman, I look at her and smile. Then by the expression on her face I know she's saying that little pimple-face punk actually has the nerve to look at me. Then I frown and disgust fills that once beautiful face! Most girls in school, too. Anita actually told me and I quote: "You're just a piece of shit that only picks on girls."

Well, she'll see different as will all. If I choose to pick on girls then I will. It looks like a lot of people hate me. Yes, it hurts, but oh well, I hate more people than hate me. If there is to be any revenge on my part, then I'm going to have to change a lot of things about me, physically and mentally as well:

1. Stand up for myself or no one else will. 2. I must be bold and speak what I feel, as long as I don't get myself into some real troubles. 3. Trust no one. 4. Learn to know when and when not to speak.

If I don't kill those who I have chosen, then I'm nothing more than a goddamn chicken shit. Anita, Ellen, Rosalyn, Jackie, and Frances, all of them will die by my hands. I shall spread death, destruction as no man has ever done. I shall choke to death this nation with fear. I shall sit upon the heights of hell and feast upon the flesh-blood of living and dead alike.

Sunday, August 5, 1990

Yesterday I went to Ennis. But anyway I was left in Ennis and Hal came and picked me up & took me to Anita's. I sat out in front of what I thought was her house & went to her window and knocked a couple of times and no one answered & it isn't a room at all. So I went next door and got a bag of trash and found out where she really lives.

I also went up to her back porch & grabbed a dog by the throat & strangled it, then beat its head against the concrete.

Then I took it and wrote "Anita's dead" in blood on the back of a car in her yard. I don't know if she seen it or anyone else because it rained about 5 or 6 P.M. So the rain probably washed it off. If anyone does know about it, I should find out pretty soon.

I forgot to write about my .380. I got it about the 3rd or 4th of this month, August.

August 22, 1990

Shit, life is fucked. My whole family too, especially my mother. I hate my life, but I want to live. I have never had three sq's [squares] a day except when I was in jail and at Marie's [she once gave him foster care] and that was every other day. She says she loves me. She probably does but it not focused where I need it. For example, 1 week ago she promised 3 or 4 times to get me a new pair of shoes. I am still wearing my shoes I have had since last year.

I believe the most powerful rules of life are self reliance, and just simply stay away from those who aren't.

Thursday, October 18, 1990

Shit's so fucked up it ain't even funny. Well, it is a little. Today this dude said he thinks my next door neighbor, Tessie, likes me, but the two things about it is I realized its probably true because she kept getting close to me. I don't believe this shit—she's only *10!* I swear, every time I go to Flagpole Hill some goddam fag tries to pick me up. But I have a hard time trying to get pussy. Decent pussy is all I want. Not 10 years old or some damn fag.

Tuesday, November 13, 1990

The past few days have been tripped out. First I tripped my 3rd acid trip the 9th of this month.

Paul and I was really fried. I also had about 35% of her [Tessie's] trust, but I accidently burned her with my cigarette on her top lip today. I think I'll be forgiven in 2 to 3 days, tops. Oh yeh, the 9th I also seen Fred and his whore. He is trying to be a good boy. He thinks he has power over me. He have even confronted me with his Christian dogma.

He said to me, "You know why I'm here," and I said, "Yes, and you know why I'm here," and he said yes. Fred is a fool. I shall reap his soul for the Master. There is, however, one small set back in that his wife, she changed him from what I have created. She destroyed him, now I shall destroy her. I will mold him into the Master's image. My task is to separate them and set up my kingdom once again and through hate and many other tales *I SHALL DO JUST THAT.*

[This entry was followed by a sketch of a star-shaped face with slanted eyes]

Sunday, November 25, 1990

I have been thinking about some shit. Like Thursday I woke up at 3 A.M. I heard a voice calling my name again. It said "Jason" 3 times, and the 3rd time I said "What?" It was weird. It whispered my name so I whispered "What?" or "Why?" back and it stopped. I think it's the same demon that called for me in Ennis. That was after I was home when I ran away the last time.

Damm, I don't have my guns anymore. My mom stole them from me. She has had them Sept. 6, 1990 'til today. I am getting tired of her. She really thinks she's smart.

Shit, I can't leave without my guns. I will get them. When I do I'm going to take her gun and $96 she owes me for the time I had to get my gun out of the pawn shop. It's time for me to go & think of my master plan.

Wednesday, Dec. 5, 1990

Shit's starting to fuck up. Last night I got drunk and accidentally let Arlene's cat out. My mom thinks I killed it. She's starting to piss me off. Last night I heard her say I can forget my guns.

She's wrong. I won't forget, they're mine. I paid for them, and by god, if she don't get them I'll get her.. She took it away for a year, then I had to get it out of pawn. Sept. 6, 1990 she took it again. If she wants to go to war, I'll take her.

But for now I'm going to do whatever it take to get my shit and get the fuck out of Dodge . . . Tessie was playing with me. I think she likes me. She pulled down my pants. I hope she'll let me fuck her. I think she might.

December 27, 1990

A revelation: I at this very moment realized all these girls are mine. They have been chosen for me . . . I don't like to look at it this way but through me loving them, through Lucifer,

I can keep them forever and ever. I need to do this, and then I say focus all these things into one master plan and I'll have my goal.

Paul has not really been with it for a while. So I give him 2 weeks, and that is all for today.

All my girls! When can I and WHERE?

[An undated entry]

I know she [a relative] feels sorry for me because she thinks I'm doomed. Uncle Phillip, I love and admire you more than almost anyone in our whole family but even you have said, "You'll be dead or in the pen in the next 5 years. "and that's long range." Enough of this shit. I bet everyone sees me only as doomed. Fred, you wrote me a letter one time saying you'll be my "friend till the end" even when I'm in the state pen.

I say fuck you, fuck you all. I'll never go to the pen. I know the odds are against me, but Anita, you are the only reason I care to live. And Tessie. My time is short & I have all these girls to get. Hell, Lucas killed over 260 people and he started in 1960. Shit, I should be able to do at least that many. Maybe not. It's all up to the Master. .

Hell, as long as I am as careful as I can be & think about what & how I'm going to do my mission, I'll be cool. I may end up killing till I'm dead . . . I don't care as long as I get my chosen girls. I'll get away with it all. Murder is my love.

There's not much more I can say but I'll *never* ever rest until I've got them all. There's something in me that won't let em go till they're dead, mutilated and mine. If I let them live then they've escaped. If I kill all of them that's the only way I'll keep them FOREVER!!!

Volume II and III

Thursday, January 10, 1991

Well, here I am ready to do it again. I know I can do it, but I just hope to see her out the right time. This could be the beginning or the end. It's basically up to me & how I perform. This could very well be my start or finish. Hell, I know I can do it and get away with it. Lucas killed 200 or more people. All I want is 1 right now.

If this is the end of me and this book, I'd like to say a couple of things. First, I had no choice. Lord Satan as a sign of our pact. Two, I love her too, plus I get off on it sexually, mentally and in my spirit.

He told me my soul will gain wisdom, power and most important his love. He smiles upon my actions. If it's the beginning, it's just that. He has already given me a "knowledge" or should I say a "knowing" or understanding. If it's the beginning the world will live in shame an sorrow. No one has never seen such horror or brutality before. The stench of blood and sorrow will fill the air as plague. I have asked the master to release his wrath in me, upon those he has chosen. If this is the beginning, woe to the people for none are unreachable!

January 19, 1991, Saturday

Friday morning I went to try to kill my girl friend but I couldn't break the window. I threw 2 rocks and the bitch wouldn't break. I am going to kill her if it kills me. I'm tired of feeling like shit for not being able to kill. I will keep trying to kill her until I do or something major stops me, but right now I'll just lay back and get a plan going. I'm going to kill her as soon as I can. Damn, I love her. I have to kill her, too. I hope I get her before the people next door move in. I can't let anything stop me. I'll kill as many as I can. For now I'll get an unbelievably master plan going and kill.

I am going to kill Tessie. I hope I am caught. If not I won't be able to stop and I know there will be so many more. I love them all, too, but Tessie will be my first. I want to see her face when I cut her throat and drink her blood. Tessie, I love you and I want to kill you & drink your blood.

Sunday, January 20, 1991

I will always remember two things Tessie said. The first thing is she asks me if I will kill her soul. Two, she just told me I was evil. Yes, maybe I am, but little girl I'll kill your soul, too, and yes, I'm evil. You're not the only one I love and I'll kill.

January 22, 1991 Tuesday

Here it goes, this is the first time to use this new book. I don't really have much to say, but what I do have to say is very important to me. Today or technically tomorrow, I am going to embark on a sacred journey. A journey to a new beginning for me. I am about to start my career as a serial killer. Yes, I'm about to start my campaign of mass murder.

I will be the best at what I'm to do. Out of all of the killers before me surely I'll be in the ranks, the ranks of the most high. If not, then I wish to end it here. If I'm caught this first time, there will be no more suffering for me or for the people close to those I've chosen to kill.

There is 2 things that scare me. One is getting caught and going to the pen and being criticized by people who don't understand me or my love. They don't matter, nothing matters anymore. But who has the right to justify my love?

Two is what scares me the most: I don't know if I'll ever be able to stop. I have only planned to kill Anita, Tessie, Ellen, Rosalyn, Jackie and Frances, and Dale Holt. [Holt is police chief at Ennis.] Those are the ones I have to kill.

They are the only ones I've planned to kill, but I *know* there will be more, especially in the Pacific N.W. Even if I kill only Tessie, my campaign has only began.

Sunday, January 27, 1991

The 25th Friday I went to her place to kill Tessie. I would have, too, but she caught me off guard. She was walking too fast for me to get her. Not really too late but it wasn't good. I could have gotten her, but I wasn't ready. That's gonna change. I have a new plan as to how to get her. First, I've gotta rob a place, get a van and then I'll be ready. I should be getting my Colt .45 soon, too. then I'll start my career. I will get them, my girls, in this order: Tessie, Dale Holt, Paul Fisher, Anita, Ellen, Rosalyn and the rest who aren't so important. They are all very important to me, but they all have their time, place and order in which I'll make love to them. But Tessie, she's special. She is my little baby. Too bad she rejected me. I really love you, girl. There isn't a day I don't think of you, all of you. I wish you all could understand how much I love & care for you all. If you all knew, if all you really knew how determined I was, you'd all give in and submit your selfs because I'll never give up. Especially on Tessie. She's so young, innocent, fragile and beautifully fine. I just fell in love with her, with the thought of how much sorrow I'll create from her disappearance and reappearance . . . She so young and weak, that one of the the reasons I'm attracted to her.

Plus I get off on knowing how much I can hurt her and her family. There's only one thing that can separate us, "my girls," and that's Heaven & Hell.

Sunday, February 9, 1991

I tripped my 13th time Wednesday and also went to see Tessie. She's playing some bullshit shy game. When I went over there the other day, she peeped out the door and went inside like I just asked her to fuck, just playing the game. *WHY?* I know she likes me, maybe not enough to sex me but I know she likes me, but mom and probably her mom and others told her I am on drugs & shit, and I can just imagine the thoughts she has about me. She probably thinks I'm some wild crazy beast who will rape her and kill her.

Once she told me I was evil; she thinks I'm crazy I bet, too. She's scared of what I might do to her. I have gut feeling that she likes me but she is scared because she's got a stereotype on druggies. Everyone seems to me to know what I am, and I haven't even yet began to start my campaign. That's my campaign of DEATH and my life.

Tuesday, February 12, 1991

I'm getting tired of my mom. She's starting to piss me off. Every day she's always got some smart-ass remarks to make about me. She literally makes me sick. I can't stand to even think of her . . . Let's cut the bullshit. She hates me & I hate her . . . I'm just sick of her, period. The faster I get to B.C. [British Columbia] the better. The longer I stay the worse shit gets.

The thing about the whole deal is it seems as everyone including mom & I know what's up but to say anything would be "a dirty word." It's all just too much stress for me; not knowing if I'm making any progress towards B.C. and living here day-to-day is bull. I'm making marks on the calendar, making marks that seem to be the best day to kill Anita, Tessie and the others. I think they'll be the only ones that I'll kill; I'll get Dale, too, and Paul if he don't give me my gun by 3-15-91. My main worries are, of course, my girls. I think the main thing in a person's life is leaving their names to be remembered.

My granny told me, "What ever you do you better make your

mark." That's just what I intend to do, engrave my name, face and my actions on the face of society and possibly history, to change it. I want to grab society by the throat and shock 'em with terror until they're awake and realize what's up. So they'll remember who I am when & why I came their way. I'm only passing through this world and I intend to make my mark.

I believe the only innocence in our world is in small children. I also believe Satan has his eyes on me, too. If I align my self with him, he'll give me the wisdom to do so. Some times he'll give me a "knowing." Like if I killed a cat I'll get the knowing that someone's coming & I'll not be caught. He'll smooth my path to do his & my bidding.

All I want is the murdering of countless young women.

I wish to reap sorrow for the families so people may feel it in the air. Mainly I want my girls . . . If I'm not where I should be by 6-1-91 I'll kill Tessie and go from there and that's a promise.

Sunday, February 23, 1991

I tripped for my 15th time on acid Friday. I was really fried. I was hallucinating bad, too. Anyway, I have been thinking a lot about Anita, Ellen and Tessie. I've also been thinking about Canada and the Pacific N.W. a lot, too. And how long I've been waiting for all of the things I've just said. It's been 7 years for Anita and over 5 years for Canada.

It all really started 8 years ago in the middle of the 4th grade. It almost don't matter how much time has passed because I'm still here. I'm tired or getting tired of Paul because he thinks we have all the time in the world. I'd say it now. I'll try by all means at my disposal for it to work for me & him, but if we're not where we need to be by May 6-10, 1991, then it's all over.

I will kill Tessie, Anita, and the other girls by going up to the high school in Ennis & there I, probably more than 3 or 4, will die. I like to do it like that for the publicity and the shock & memories that will be engraved in that town. But I hope it don't come to that. I'd rather get it all done the way I've been planning it for the past 5 years.

Like killing all the girls as I've chosen & plus in the Pacific N.W. and when my time has come to be caught, I'd wish to be an ultimate symbol of evil. Because those few, very few, who really now think I am. I believe I'm able to speak to Satan & him to me. Lucifer has invoked his wrath in my thoughts. Lucifer is the one that let me have the "knowing" of who must die. He's given me 10 names special who I'm to kill. If shit fucks up, oh well, because this year is the only chance I'll have to get all the "main" girls in one attack.

March 13, 1991 Wednesday

The number of girls I've decided to get getting higher. It's just when I see one I know I have to get her, and I just fall in love with her and thoughts of killing, torturing, and mutilating them. Especially between a sexy woman's legs next to her beautiful cunt. I would love to cut their tits and their throats, to drink these beautiful girls of their blood.

I must say I'm not very interested in 10-year-olds but Tessie is special. After her I will only go for 17 and well it (age) really don't matter because when I see the one I'll know it's the one.

Anyway I think I'm going to make history . . . It seems to me that I need to try to stop getting so many girls to get. Besides the 12 girls on page 33 is a little to many in Texas and in a area as small as between Dallas to Ennis and so far as E. Texas.

Well, actually I won't be able to go to Florida for a while. I think that one day after all the robbing an killing and shit that Paul & I do that this will be turned into a book & then maybe a movie. But I do know now that I will lead a murder machine that will leave nothing but sorrow, tears, and wonder. Wonder of how so many are dead. Wondering of parents and people that have or know someone who is missing. Do they share the same fate as all the others. It will be revealed in time.

Monday, March 18, 1991

How fuckin' hard can it be? I'm pissed, I'm tired of all people. I just want my gun so I can 'jack McDonalds and get the hell out of Dallas. I know if I'm not able to reach my goals soon, then am going to slip. And when I do all hell is going to break loose. I almost don't care anymore, and if I don't get my goals met, then I'm sure I'll go on a rampage and if that day comes then I will be prepared to Die! But I don't want that. All I want is to kill a couple of my girls, rob Mc. and go to Canada. This is it, if Paul and I are not where we need to be by Sept., then that's it. I'll go to Ennis the 13th and end it all.

I know God's coming soon, so I must hurry if I'm to get my girls. Not only that but it's been 5 years. I have waited long enough and it's time to get to it. Paul Fisher, he's dead if he don't give me my gun, and that's it, no excuses.

No, I am mad because I've a feelin' & Granny said it too, but I feel good, trying to tell me to change my life or God's going to kill me. I think God feels I'm a threat to, well, almost every one in humanity. How can a loving God kill me? I have also more to ask & say, but I don't want to write all night. I just might go on my rampage by 5-13-91 if things get any worse or I don't get a gun.

I want people to feel what I have felt since I was about 10. I want the mothers to feel my hate, love, sorrow,, and I wish all that their nor my tears or my name will be forgotten, for if it is all the thing I've done will be repeated. So I ask you to awake and ask "if our children care?" People, what is going on in our world.

Thursday, March 21, 1991

On Tuesday, March 18, 1991, at 5:30 P.M. I seen for the first time a man die. He was shot in the back. I have only seen him 10 times or so in my life, but when you see a man die it not like T.V.; it really dead serious. I don't want to get into it all, but I don't know, how or why, God would allow it. I have been so, well, many things, but mostly scared because I feel in my heart that if I don't begin to serve God he'll take my life.

That's something that I don't understand and it make me mad because of all the others that kill over and over and who are worst than me, but he allows it to go on. The young and weak are destroyed, but he wants me killed because I don't worship him.

All I want to do is get a gun, rob Mc, then go on and kill all the people on page 33 and go to the Pacific N.W. and Canada and kill around 50-100 more people in Wash., Canada & etc., in the woods, the campers and just live in the mountains. I'm tired of God. I wish he'd let me do what I've said, then I'll be more than willing to turn my life around because I sure don't want to be in hell.

Saturday, March 30, 1991

I've been thinking a lot about raping Tessie lately. I think I'm in love with her, as strange as it may seem. Sometimes I wish I could talk to a shrink and see if I have a problem. Sometimes I think I do because I come up with ideas, good ones on how I can rape her, kill her and shit like that. They just "pop" inside my head and I don't even have to try hard at all to come up with them.

I think I might be demon-possessed because I get those ideas and sometimes I just "know" something that I couldn't known, without the demons. Any way I just wrote because I'm falling for Tessie more each day. I think of her hair and eyes and her stomach. I really love her in my own way. I just wish Tessie could fully understand my feeling for her. If she truly could, then I believe she would go with me.

But unfortunately for her, her mom and I think that she couldn't. But I will give her one chance and by no force will I convince her to do so. Realistically, I'm afraid I will end up putting her 6 ft. under. I know that if I don't strike by May 15, then I've lost her for all eternity. So April is going to be a very busy time for me & Paul because I will have to get one gun at least, but I do believe I can come up with a .38 and a .22, both pistols. Plus Mc. and Tessie and selling & buying weed. Yeh, it's a lot of shit but someone's gotta do it.

Monday, April 8, 1991

I just remembered that when we lived in Sulphur Springs when I was between 7 and 10 I climbed up on that old shed I used to use for a club and pull my pants down and try for some reason to sun-tan my dick. Crazy, but I just wanted to write it down before I forgot. I also played with a dead dog, too.

Tuesday, April 30, 1991

It's been a hell of a week! It's all been so wild and unexpected. First, I met Rita & got high. Then later she ask if I like her tits and she told me she likes when her husband comes home & eats her pussy. But the best of all is that I got me a gun, a 9 mm model. I think it's so fuckin' bad ass. I can't believe it's true. I still haven't shot it. I guess that's why I felt disbelief, it was too easy. It might be broke.

I think I might have got a new girl friend named Barbara. She's 12 but she's mature for her age. Anyhow her mom [Rita] told me she started her PMS when she was 11. If I'm to get her, too [sex] then it will be thru manipulation and understanding her. I can. I won't kill this one. I have too much on my mind anyway. Like Tessie.

Wednesday, May 8, 1991
THE CHASE HAS BEGAN!

I've been thinking a lot about Tessie. I think of her daily. I remember her face & that little mole above her top lip where I burned her. I know I'll never rest until I do get her. I don't understand why I want her so bad. I guess it's because I love her. I love her body, her face, hair and her child-like innocence. I still remember the time she pulled my pants down. And when she said I'm evil and the time she asked me if I'm going to kill her soul.

Monday, May 13, 1991

I don't know about Paul anymore, he's so far into drugs. For me it's just something I do if I've the money or I need some guts to rob something. I will drink 4 beers or so, but I'm tired of having to depend on his stupid ass to get shit together so we'll go to B.C. I want to do something, then goddamn I want it done. Fuck Paul on all his party bullshit. Sometimes I think he believes life is party.

When I die I want the people on page 23 to be there. Mom, if you're reading this please, as a last request, comply with it.

It would have meant a lot to me. If I live past the 15th, then I and only I alone will make the biggest change in my life. If I'm still here after the 15th then I'll take it that the Lord isn't going to kill me. If I'm alive by then I will take it that God is going to let me live and thusly I will truly began the chase and live out my "fantasies."

Tomorrow I'm going to go see if Tessie still lives in the apts. where we lived. If so she's dead by next day.

Tuesday, May 14, 1991

Here we go, I'm at it again. I went to Tessie's and she's still there. So tomorrow I go for it. Will I regret it years later? I will if I don't. I don't know if I'm going to be able to fuck her. I don't think I should get that close to her. I'll decide when it's time. But now I just wish she hadn't rejected me. I'd have liked to spend some time with her. If I'm caught I just hope the pigs just kill me. I'm not scared to do it. I think I'll do it, but I won't know till I'm there. That is when I'll chicken out. I might never read or write in here again. I shouldn't even write now. I'm going to go hide this.

Wednesday, May 15, 1991

I am alive. and as I've been thinking it's time to began the chase, summer of hate or what ever one may call it. I've thought if God don't kill me by 5-15-91, then I'd do what I've been waiting to do.

Let it be known this day. I won't kill without warning is my Slay back-patch, and my eyes & and face, that's the only warning or signs. I'm not going to Rita any more for a while, to see Barbara. I'm going to my same deal of fascination with Death & Sex and power & as a whole. All rage so to speak. Wrath runs wild as does my spirit of hate. I'm not going on a total trip as where I forget what I know and have seen. I can forget going & I'm not shielding a mortal. I won't fear none any more. I'll carry on until I'm dead or I've finished. The chase has begun!!!

Tuesday, May 21, 1991

Tomorrow is Tessie's 11th birthday. I believe it's sometime this month. I wish you could read this. I've so much to say. I've put off killing you because *I want to fuck you violently, kill you and drink your blood from your neck.*

Thursday, 5-23-91

I'm going to kill Tessie. I haven't taken off this bracelet that Tessie gave me or made for me while we sat on my porch. I am going to take this bracelet off as a vow. A vow that am going to kill her and that I have finally started my campaign. I need to get Tessie anyway so I can concentrate on Anita and getting a job. Then after I've a job I can slowly manipulate, rape if necessary. I'll rape her and get the fuck out of town to Ennis, get Anita, dig a hole and go to Pacific N.W.

I've said the chase has began. It hasn't. Not yet, not until I've taken off my bracelet.

Action always speaks louder. I'm going to give all I have for my campaign, and soon I will bury this and part of me too, memories and feeling mostly. I starting this book over again, so I can write better.

Saturday, June 1, 1991

I'm sad, I've not gotten Tessie. I've no job, money, car, girl-friend. I do have memories. I should have graduated from high school yesterday. I should have done a lot of things I haven't. It's done now. It's been a year to the day when I was caught for killing her [his sister's] cat. I hurting so bad I just want to be remembered by all the girls who I can remember. The special ones, not every girl I meet. I feel like a fuckin' coward since I've not killed Tessie yet, but I think I'm starting to get a con-science. I'd feel bad for taking out that little girl. I will feel bad if I don't also. I am in a bad mood. Right now I still wonder what happen to me. I guess I changed after I seen Doug Vinson die, but I'm not as violent or evil as I once was.

What am I good at? I've no high school. I don't want to go and live with a wife, kids and a dog named spot. I want to kill. I want to travel and kill and go to Canada & kill.

I don't know why I still depend on Paul to get me to B.C. or any where else. I've been waiting for the right time to kill my girls . . .

June 24, 1991

I haven't been writing lately because I don't want mom to go through my books again reading them. Well, I'm feeling de-pressed and sorry for myself, thinking of the past & future. It pisses me off that I can't write what I want just 'cause a nosy woman can't mind her own business.

I'm especially tired of the police. I feel like I've been raped after the mother fuckers took my "g" [gun?] and put me in jail. I hate security guards too. I've been arrested by two twice and I'm going to get revenge. All the time I've spent trying to get my girls. Five years. I have to go do it all in a hurry. I should not have wrote their names. I am going to get them and go where I've planned. I am doing for several reasons: #1 I love them #2 I want to show people who I am #3 I want vengeance.

Thursday, June 27, 1991

Another day. I got drunk yesterday. I am starting to get a little closer to [named marked out]. She's getting closer. She letting me touch her and last night she asked me to come in her room and watch T.V. I think she likes me a little, but she's like me, shy. I told Jimmy Rita's been coming on to me. I told so I can gain his trust. So stupid she don't even question it. I have her better than I could have if I tried. I think they still want me to move in. I think I will to.

I have to do something. July is almost here. Figure in 2 or 3 months [word marked out] will let me know she likes me.

[Paul] won't be going with me to the Pacific N.W. or Canada. He's into drugs *too much* anymore, I believe. I know he's frying his brain with all the crack and shit he's doing. I think all he does is try to get or do drugs. I don't know about him anymore. He will still always be a special friend, like a brother. I feel sorry for him because he thinks he needs drugs to help get through shit. Hell, maybe he does.

I thought for a while we'd be like Henry & Otis O'tool [serial killer Henry Lee Lucas and his sidekick, Otis Toole]. I should've knew better. I probably won't ever have a Otis O'tool. I guess I don't need one. He'd just get in my way. I can't speak any more of why I'm here. A man, he asked me, "Jason, what do you plan to do with your life? What do you want to be?" I reply, "It is forbidden." And it is, only my Father and I will know my *true* intentions.

Monday, September 16, 1991

I told Rita about all the dogs & cats & cows and she believed me. I've not told her my biggest secret & I won't. I can't. The only one I've ever told is Paul, and he's not my destiny—as much as I wish it were it's not. I want to think I'll have another, but I'll probably end up just being solo. Sometimes I feel God'll kill me because he knows what I wish to do with my life.

Jason, can you count the years that all this B.S. started, 4th grade. I've never killed anyone. I've had 1 good chance & 2 in all. I go now to "try" & kill a girl. Be prepared.

Monday, September 23, 1991.

I'm so' sick of people. I trust them with all my thoughts and people are to be distrusted. I want to trust 'em but I can't.

Rita hit me in the mouth for no reason last night and I won't ever forget it and I want revenge. Stupid bitch, she said thanks for not killing me. I'd like to put a butcher knife in your chest. I would probably chicken out in the end. Boy, Jay, what a great serial killer you'd make. Winter is coming. Jay, are you able to do what you planned to do? .

Monday, October 7, 1991

In 3 months I'll be 19. I was just counting all the cats and dogs I've killed and I think I've over-estimated, so I'll write all the ones I can exactly remember. At least 25 cats, and at least 19 dogs, so I'd say between 25-32 cats & 19-21 dogs. Oh well, I don't even care about 'em as much as I do other things. When I'm off probation is when I'll do what I planned from the start.

Tuesday, November 5, 1991

Mom had one chance to help me. "The system" had one chance, too. So what can I say? It's not my fault. After reading all the shit in those two books they had a reason to get a court order to get me some help.

But now, I have chance to beat them. I have the mind and I know what I have to do; but for me it's just a matter of doing it.

Almost always in the past I have gotten in a hurry to get on with it, getting on the road and heading up north to the mountains. Now I'm on probation for 3 years and why not take these 3 years of probation and turn them into something positive?

November 11, 1991 Monday

It was the 8th of this month I told Barbara some things that hurt her. She started crying. But after this day I can't speak of Death any more. The sooner I stop it then the more likely it will go farther into the back of her mind; providing me a little leeway. Be smart and stay off the dope & shit. Exercise and eat right & I will be ready to go before I know it.

Just told Barbara a lot of real deep shit. It will, and must be, the last time for quite a while. Until she comes to me, crying, asking me to stop and what's to do to prevent from any more sorrow. I can do it in 3 years. NEVER SPEAK YOUR *TRUE NATURE!* The least *friends* you have the better. You use to not speak your nature to anyone. But now everyone and the police have copies of names and my twisted and sadistic "lust" for Anita on them.

Sunday, November 17, 1991

I've always wanted to be recognized, muscle-bound, fast, powerful and loved by the one I love.

I want to be a killer. As odd as it may seem I want to be a killer who's very strong & handsome.

Jay, it's only the beginning for you. Do you want people to one day say "Lucas, Bundy, Manson, boy, that was the good ol' days. Now we got this Massey feller."

November 24, 1991

I feel so stupid for leaving this out for Rita to find. Now she knows everything. She read my book. Barbara hates me. I feel like shit because I always snap at them. I'll never change. I don't know if I should move or stay.

Friday, December 6, 1991

There is so much I want to change about myself. My bad habits, but there's some things I can't change, my feelings for Barbara, or anything else for that matter. I've decided to kill her. I love her and I want to fuck her even worse. I know how I'm going to do it. I just don't know when. If she would love me or have sex, it would be cool, but she doesn't have feeling and I can't change that. I must be crazy for writing this shit. It's just that I'd like to look back on this in a couple of years or remember it. I guess this book isn't finished, not until it comes reality.

Monday, Dec. 9, 1991

I have decided that after today I will not use drugs. I am real scared I'm going to die soon. If so, I want my beloved little brother to know I love him more than any one in the world. I would even die for him. I believe I love him more than my own life. I so high on crack it's not funny.

I feel like I'm going crazy. I'm so confused I don't know what to do. God help, please.

Volume IV

Wednesday, Dec. 25, 1991

Well, here's a new book with a new beginning. This book IV will last up to the point of "it" and further. This book will see 3 yrs. of me & me changing & growing. In that time can't I keep all of "it" hidden? I must change myself for the better. I don't need to write "it" down, I know what I must do.

December 26, 1991

All of this effort I'm to put forth is for Tessie, them and myself. From the dream I had I know I really do love her because she was on top, fuckin', and when it went in her she was tight and we both were surprised, so had to pull it out slowly. See, in my dream I was concerned that I might have hurt her. I do love her.

December 27, 1991

Last night I dreamed I attacked Tessie with a pitch fork in the throat. I guess I really do want to kill her, if I dreamed it.

December 31, 1991

It's 11 p.m. now & one hour from '92 and remember last year what I was doing at this same time. Planning for my future as serial killer. Last year at this time I had no idea I'd be where I am. I do know I want Barbara more than the rest & Anita is an obligation.

January 2, 1992

My 19th birthday is 5 days away. I've got a long way to go before my work here is complete. Can I, during that much time, day after day, resist playing the sucking game?

To touch her beautiful skin, to wish for her to spread her legs, to run my tongue between her legs, up to her cunt. The smell of beautiful hair, to wish for her to love me. It's only a dream for sure.

She laughs at my love. Loving never works. Even one I love never loves me. It was not meant for me . . . I will do what I must. Then I will get on the road & spend time in the mountains.. I'll be 21 . . . 22 when time for "it" is ready. If I'm to make "it" then I must stop playing with her. If not, then surely in 3 yrs I will be known, Rita's suspicious. She believes I've come here only to kill her beautiful daughter Barbara, something I'd never bring myself to even think, much less do.

Friday, January 10, 1992

Well, needless to say I'm 19 now & this birthday is one I'll never forget. I went mad. I spilt my guts to the cops. They put me on a card downtown & have probably read my plans I had in my wallet. Rita found & read my attack plans so now I must be even more cold & calculating than before.

January 16, 1992

I've went to AA Tuesday & I'll go some more. I see it has a lot of wisdom in it.

When I went to detox, Scott told me most satanists are in it for personal power.

I am but not the "power" most are, but the power of *wisdom*. Wisdom is *one* of my rewards. To have a sound, calculating mind is what Power I seek. For in her [wisdom] is power. I know now I must stop using because drugs destroy *my* power. So if I'm to win I've no choice but to stop using.

I've come, I've vowed, & now I've work to do to reach *all* those goals, for they're my desires. He'll give me the WISDOM to do my task. People know not of my violent thoughts. If they did they'd kill me *to prevent my, our, work from being done.*

Wednesday, January 22, 1992

I started keeping a journal back in October of '89. About 1 or 2 years later I made some vows, 7 to be exact. Now, here today I make my 8th. It is to stop using drugs, all of them for good. They weaken me, & will destroy me if I don't stop. They take away my power. Jay, don't fuck your *life* up with drugs.

Friday, Feb. 14, 1992

It seems, as the more time I stay here, the deeper I fall in love with her. She's become my life and my hope. She is what keeps me going. She is what I look forward to. I look to the future because she'll be there, with me I hope. I just wish that some day she will love me as much as I do her. I really can't expect her to after all the hell I have put her through.

Think back Jay. Nov. 8, 1991, the cat heads, dog heads, killing her dog, Sugar, and talkin' trashy sex every day. She did like you until you "betray" her.

Thursday, February 20, 1992.

Today is a sunny day. Nice, it reminds me of Barbara. I don't know what to do. I don't want to kill her but she don't love me.

She rejected me. She laughed & sneered at me. All I ever wanted to do was love her. She never even gave me 1 chance. Now I have finally made my choice. She must die. It will be done soon as we have gotten her glamor shots back. I just want to have a last & most current picture of her, just for memory. It makes me sad now just thinking of her being dead, not growing into a fine woman. I would've been a king, to have her bear my child. It's fantasy, unless I keep her in the woods for 10 months. It isn't worth it, the child might die before or after birth. I can't forget that idea. She'd scream & shit & alert someone eventually . . . I knew I'd have to do her but I just didn't know it would be so soon . . . I am the Slayer. For the love and memory of Barbara.

Saturday, March 1, 1992

Well, Barbara, this as always for you, just & only because I love U. Of course, as I always have. But now I'm in Ennis. If only you would've listened to me telling how much I love U. You had to be bitchie. You have defied me.

I can't explain my love without saying: All I ever wanted to do is for me & U to do it and have a son, a baby, to be married. I can't say any more. I LOVE BARBARA.

[The following are undated entries.]

No woman has ever loved me as much as Rita, but I guess there's things I will never understand and change about myself. I do mean my emotions, my "strange" love, some would say my "lust" for killing, blood, power and creating death. I still have the urge to kill. It's my life, DEATH.

. . . But for now I just want Barbara to love me. I don't know if she will. I know I'll always love her. Because she's special, she'll be my first. I just want to hurt her and see her cry. I want to drink her blood. I want her to say, "Jay, I'm sorry. Please don't hurt me. I love you." Then I'm going to ask her to go north with me and marry me.

Wednesday, April 29, 1992

I'm still killing. I've got 29 dogs and 37 cats, now 66 in all. I know no man's promised tomorrow. So I must make all I can out of the day. I must be a lot more self-reliant. I can't expect any favors from anyone. I've said it before, I have no "friends" in Ennis. None. All of 'em will probably sell out. I will get my gun the 4th. I have $100 saved for my gun.

Tuesday, May 10, 1992

Today I got a letter from Rita with a picture of my beloved Barbara.

I just wish I could be with her and make love to her. I wish we, Barb and I, could have married and had babies with one another. I guess all that's gone now. She never did like me. So now I must do it all alone. I should have planned it that way from day 1.

I guess I will still carry it out the way I planned it . . . there are a couple of things I must do first:1. get a gun 2. get my probation straightened out 3. get a new job, then a car and finally a license . . .

So far just thinking of killing a lot of young girls makes me happy, but it's at a point where it's going to be reality. I've read a lot about serial killers, criminal investigation and the likes. I'm ready to begin... I'm ready to dedicate my life to death, sorrow and violence as well as chaos. I will be another face who hides what's really underneath. I will stalk in Texas for over two years. I bet I can get 48 in that amount of time. We'll see, huh J?. I guess it's going to be hardest to do the first ones, harder to get away with anyway..

Barbara, I still love her. Maybe some day she will be my bride-in-heaven. She is my love. Just think, she'll never get to finish school, nor bear children, or be 14 years old. I loved her. I guess that's why I want to do her.

Jay, be careful, the devil might just be trying to trick you. Remember those urges where you feel you needed help, they felt evil. It passes. A trick to send you to prison!

Saturday, June 6, 1992

I just set here, listening to the songs I've heard a long time before and thinking of the same thoughts: Murder. It's always on my mind.

I think of killing young women and fucking them before and after it. I think of my "trophies" and that time when I reveal my graveyard. I got some other special ones. I know what I need to do. Jay, remember Tessie was 10 and 1/2 when you seen her last. She's 12 now, developed and needs to be fucked violently and killed.

Saturday, June 6, 1992

I guess the sorrow for the killing will always be there. Barbara, the sorrow. Your love, I missed. Jay, you know it is time. You know it is real.

I'm a little more sober now. It seems so hard to think what I must do, and it looks like you'll have to do it, cold and calculatingly. It's just having to think I won't see her for so long. What if she meets other men and what if she begins to talk? People will be after me. It's been 7 years since I began my chase with Anita. I can't wait 7 months, much less 7 years. I've been thinking about doing them in now. I don't know if I can do it anymore I mean, I love 'em. Just hope I don't lose Barbara before I get her.

Wednesday, June 10, 1992

All the analyzing and shit. I know myself and my "problems." The professionals would say I feel inadequate with myself. True.

They would say he feels inadequate with women. Sometimes. I understand all of this, as I read, study and learn. I don't feel inadequate with myself, my capabilities, no.

But I do about my small frame. I can and will change that by proper dieting and exercising. If I, as a serial killer, are to be successful, then I must: Be in as best physical health as possible, worry free; basically, condition my mind into a further state of confidence by a lasting study of criminal investigation, the B.S.U. and other serial killers, their mistakes, their M.O. and their successful careers. Then apply it all to what I've learned since Jan. 1991.

I guess I've unconsciously, at first, wanted to be a serial killer at age 14; that is, I was planning on killing many at that age. I remember my first thoughts of human murder was age 9 or 10. I was in grade 4. It was Eunice whom I first desired to kill. I actually tried it at age 13 on a known girl. I tried, unsuccessfully, to poison her. I guess her drink tasted strange? She didn't drink it.

Thursday, June 18, 1992

I sit here tonight while most sleep and I think, when I begin killing, how will I deal with my driving lust for murder, blood and sex with corpses. Just looking at these pictures, it seems hard to wait 6 months. I can wait. I've had to for months for Barbara . . . I think as soon as I have wheels I do #1, then Barbara.

I've gotten the master plan figured out for AK 470329ER9ER, so not to worry. The best killer is one who's unseen! I like the idea of going all over Texas and Oklahoma. Besides, I like having 3 or 4 days in a row off.

That gives me enough time to go to Springfield, Mo. and back in that time. Plus on my short days I can go to East Texas and, like Springfield, check into a motel and then go explore.This is the time to be cold, calculating, relentless and get my body built up so I can attract for the slaughters of hustling women in bars, on highways and in cities across the nation.

Monday, June 22, 1992

I can't trust my own mom. She denied me food, she turned me in for . . . my uncle cusses me. My "dad" told me I'm not his. There's no more time for B.S. I must do it this time because she won't wait for me after November, and if I'm not ready by then I've lost my Barbara. I am pretty sure that I can get a license, stun-gun, a .22 and everything I'll need for November.

But I guess when it comes down to it the hardest part is the actual killing. Can I? Yeh, I have to. I guess after I get my license and ride around I can find a spot I feel comfortable with. I guess the worst part is being a suspect and being scared of that fact.

Missing: 4 people. Yeh, the police will press this case hard. I've never killed anyone. There's only 3 reasons I'm going to kill Barbara.

Because she'll never accept me or my love. I want to have sex with her. And I don't want her to be with anyone else. This also is a reason: I want to kill girls. *Just sex, dead girls all naked, dead, bleeding turn me on.*

I've gotten it all thought through. I will probably give Barbara pills. I bet if I give her pills she'll sleep at least a good 5 hours. Plenty of time for me to take her where I can tie her up and fuck her for 2 days, out behind the old barn by the pond. I guess that's where I'll bury her, too. Oh well, it will take time and I might go out there soon to check it out.

Well for now I'll just have to fanaticize about her as well as the others. Be glad when I am finished with "it" and begin on the new ones. Here in Ennis and one in Dallas, too. All over the county, then on to others in East Texas, etc.

There's a pale corpse, so dead in the moonlight. She lays in my arms, silent but she's beautiful. She's dead, she's mine.

Wednesday, July 8, 1992

I have memories, too, lots, like the shit I got from Rita the whore. It will be with me for the rest of my life. So will the memory of Barbara, and the way she'd try to "relate" to me, like putting her head in my lap, etc. If it wasn't for Rita I'd have Barbara instead of herpies. For that Rita will pay with her life. I want a fucking car so bad it's unreal.

I want to get drunk, drive, pick up a fine female victim, rape her, kill her, then make love to her once again. It seems my desires for the death of untold numbers is growing. I want to kill just to have sex and now that I've herpies that desire of sex with the corpses of beautiful young girls grows.

Because of my feelings of unconfidence when I have sex with women, plus I don't want to have a girl come back to me and say you gave me herpies or telling everyone I've got them. Rubbers, NA!

So I will just kill her before sex. Plus I just have this picture in my mind of this dead girl lying on back, eyes and mouth open, naked, the moonlight shining down through the trees and how so romantic it would be to climb on top of her lifeless, naked, pale, cold, clammy corpse and make love to her throughout the night. And then after sex to drink wine and look at her beauty; wish I'd drank her blood while making love to a living, willing, human being.

Yes, I can differentiate human and object. I do know good and evil, right and wrong. My mother taught me these things. She's not at fault where my upbringing is concerned. She's done every thing and more a loving mother should. My personality is just me. I was killing [animals] before I listened to Slayer, before I knew what death and sex was.

Age 9 was the first time I killed anything of essence, a cat. In that time it has progressed to as many as 38 cats, 30 dogs.

And in time I'm sure my "sickness" desires, as I choose to call 'em, will progress as well as my murder of living victims. Criminal investigations, police procedures and murdering without getting caught or until I choose to reveal myself.

Who will be first? Last? How many?

How long will it be when I spend free days on the road, traveling, looking . . . for the next unsuspecting victim? .

I will win. I will have Barbara. I'll probably end up killing just her. I can see her crying already. I know what I'm going to do to her. I've even figured out about where I'll bury her. And hopefully all the hurt she's put me through, I am going to hurt her. I want her to cry, beg and tell me she loves me.

Tuesday, July 28, 1992

Well, I've been here in Ennis for four months the first of August. Seems a lot longer. Even when I'm not bored I still think of two things more than anything else. Raping and killing beautiful women [10-40 years]. And two, driving my car around. I guess it would be best to drive around for a good while, or until I feel completely relaxed and confident in my driving.

Thursday, July 30, 1992

Today I mostly got high. I went to find a special place for Barbara. Did nothing but have another day to remember. Hell, I went to her room two days ago and lifted her shorts and got my fingers about 2 inches from her pussy hole.

I guess I'll stun her and drug her and carry her out in the yard. Take her to my ALTAR OF SACRIFICE, rape her, kill her. I will tie her up, eat her and suck her tits and eat her 'til she comes. Then fuck her in cunt, but I'll eat her 'til I can't no more. Then finally I'll hog tie her and fuck her in the ass . . . can see her face in agony . . .

Saturday, August 29, 1992

Well, the act itself occurred around 12:30 A.M. It's about 6 a.m. Saturday morning. Well, Jay this is a day to remember. This is what I did.

I smoked some stones for a while, then I drank about a 12-pack. Anyway, I went into Barbara's room to get to myself. Before long I began to imagine and more realistically plan a "rape."

She came into her room and I was caught. Then a while later I drank a beer or two, then I went into her room. Before I knew what I did, I just put the knife to her throat. She kinda thought, well I guess she thought I was B.S.

When I put the knife to her throat I told her not to move or I would kill her. She was very scared . . . I fucked with her mind for a while. Before long I had her so scared she began to cry. And I put my knife to her throat and told her "If you scream I'll kill you."

Anyway while I fucked with her head talking shit it got her believing I was going to kill her.

Anyhow, I told Barbara to pull her pants down and I had my dick in my hand . . and cut her pants off and was about to fuck her . . . I almost raped Barbara . . .

Tuesday, September 1, 1992

It has been 4 days since I attempted to rape Barbara. Everything is normal again. Man, I can't believe I did what I did. I remember it well.

I remember putting the knife to her throat, hearing her gasp, telling her not to move, climbing on to her, terrorizing her for so long, then making her take off her pants, and then I cut off her panties, pulled off mine and then Rita comes home as I was seconds away from raping her. God, I came so close I don't know what would have happened if I did of raped her. God, I love her so much. It hurts me to think I probably won't ever win her love. It hurts to think of her with her friends in the mall, laughing, smiling and having a lot of fun without me, forgetting me and growing up without me. She's so fine, so beautiful. I don't know what I'll do about staying here with Rita and them. I know I'll be able to do "it" sooner if I live here. But I'm afraid Barbara's going to talk. She told Rita about it, all but the attempted rape, I think. It's going to be a sad time after I leave and even sadder when I have to kill her. But if I can't have her, no one will. Her neck, hair, throat, inner thighs and her eyes are so fine. Even her smile gives me great pleasure.

Thursday, September 10, 1992

I left Rita again; for good, too. Shit was really crazy there at the end. I hit her in the eye, and last night she pulled my hair. And before I knew it I had her on the ground by the throat strangling her. Came within literally seconds of raping Barbara, and during all of it I was drunk.

I just get uncontrollable when I drink.

This morning Rita said she wanted me to leave. I played her so I would not have to stay out of the house. She suspected me and Barbara of fucking. Barbara, Jan and all of 'em are out of my life now. I can't say for good because I plan on getting Barbara.

Sunday, September 20, 1992

Tessie, damn I still want that little girl. Well, she isn't little no more. Hell, she'd be 13 in mid-May, the 22nd? If she still lives there by the time I'm able to get her, I'll do just that, rape her, kill her, bury her and the others. See, the thing is when I start it's going to be hell to not do it every time I get the urge. If I do there'll be so many missing girls someone's bound to connect it all.

I have a feeling that in 1993 I will kill two people. Barbara is one, Tessie #2. I don't know. I just have a feeling once I get started my confidence will overwhelm me. Then I'll begin to kill regularly. Maybe uncontrollably!

My lust to kill women and have sex with the dead consumes me and my thoughts daily. When I see a woman on TV being strangled, it excites me sexually.

I continually think of naked, helpless girls who moan while I fuck 'em. I dream of asses in the air with me putting my dick in 'em. I think of the time when I travel in my car to other towns to lure and kill many young girls.

Every fine girl I see I think how nice it would be hurt her, make her cry, cut her, drink her blood from her wrist as we make love and then doggie style in the ass, more pain, tears, pleas and then cutting the neck, drinking blood, then sex. Then rigor mortis when the body stiffens up, put her in a position for more sex. Before rigor mortis, holding her, telling her I love U, then gentle sex, all beautiful.

Tuesday, September 22, 1992

As I sit here, I look at photos of me and I ask myself what happened? I look at myself at age 5, 8 and 1/2, and I just wonder what made me the way I am. The fall at age 2, the incident at 5, 9? I don't know. The drugs, porn, the devil or a combination of all. I guess it don't matter what went so wrong. I am the way I am.

I look at these photos of Barbara and I think, man, she would have grown up and done things with her friends. Remember how she always wanted to be a doctor? I will remember it all. Even when I go down the highway, I'll look over and say that's where my girl is.

There'll be times when I stop in the rain to see her grave site. Other times I'll just pass on by without a tear. Even if I don't get her, I'll always say that's where I was going to bury her.

I guess in a heart so full of evil murder, sorrow and destruction is one's only lust. It makes me happy to think of all the hurt I can cause. My life, it will be one as never seen. I don't think there has ever been a serial killer who ever planned concisely to be one at age 17.

Study criminal investigation, at 18. Someone wrote, "Compared to what's ahead, Henry Lee Lucas will look like the good old days. "

He is right. I'm here.

Friday, September 25, 1992

Today I went to the woods. I symbolically buried Barb. I felt like what it's going to be like after Barbara's been gone a while. I can feel my future turning around . . .

Well, I dreamt I went into a church and seen a young girl with long hair. She was 10 or, yeh, 11 years old. I forced her into a bathroom where I strangled her to death, then fucked her. I guess those things are all I think of, sex and death. It kinda scares me and makes me sad to think of what I'm capable of inflicting on humanity. It scared me to think that when I get my D.L. and drive, a killing will be all I can think of. I can see me already in the cold seasons driving with a smiling, unsuspecting girl.

One whom I've no connection with. I don't know it might be weather. It's this way toward the end of each year. After the murder, I guess in time I won't feel nothing for taking folks out. They'll be like another dog.

I know if I do drink beer and get a little drunk I feel no emotion and I could kill a girl with little or no second thought, but I want to be sober so I can feel all the emotion.

Saturday, Sept. 26, 1992

I'll have to do is go to another city and get drunk. And I'm sure when I see a happy, beautiful young girl, I can see her smiling and laughing. One who is self-assured in her drunkeness. Maybe when I start filling out after my exercising and after I turn 21, I can go to bars and play a personality with a chick and get her to call me and shit a boy does. I guess there is unlimited ways for a mind to find new ways when he spends most thoughts on the subject. Well, I believe when most 'teens were wanting their D.L.s and girl friends, etc., etc., I was learning from the Master.

My, it's been 1 month and 1 and 1/2 hours since I almost raped Barb. I can still remember it pretty well.

I remember the power I felt as I got on top of her. I remember it felt like I had done it a hundred times before. I remember how she cried and how I felt on her right tit as I went down on her neck, up her face and the taste of that tear. I remember how she took off her pants so fast, almost in anger.

But most of all I remember how it all began with her putting her head in my lap. I'll always remember the things she did, said, liked and didn't like.

But more than anything I'll remember the pain and the pleas for her life. Too bad she didn't listen to my pleas. I'll remember how she died the most.

I'm still having trouble deciding where to bury her. I want it to be close enough so I can visit her but far enough as to where the police suspect me of murder they won't find her. I guess it won't matter much as long as it's a deep hole . . . I guess Barb and Tessie are the only ones I know how I'll kill. No more love kills, only lust kills, that's "J" law.

The next Book of Death will be entitled 6: The Beginning: My Life As a Serial Killer, by Jason Massey. I've even had thoughts of writing a book to publish. Some type of Satanist Book. Hell, I've a lot planned but it's time to act, not dream.

Thursday, October 15, 1992

I've been devouring everything I can about serial killers, police and murder investigation in general. I devour all information on police, the FBI and their operations, especially on serial murder. I watch every cop show. I just wish I could go kill, rape and hurt. Man, I've got to get some whores out of the way.

Saturday, October 17, 1992

I've often looked toward the day that I can say I am a murderer. It is that day now. I've been one since age 9. A cat, yes, but never-the-less a life of some value. In the eyes of God I am one. But to me there's a difference in human and animal. I've committed sexual murders of 5 cows. I, from what I've learned, have almost all capabilities of a "to be" serial killer.

I just yesterday got the idea to mess with a gas gauge, drain the tank, then follow until it's empty. If I know 'em, it's an easy kill.

I'll be the first serial killer in Ennis. But there's so much killing I want to do now. It's hard to wait . . . When I turn 21 I'll probably be able to kill regularly. With the "bar" scene open to me [at 21] . . . when I'm off probation and able to roam at will . . .

Oh, my dear people of the world. Prepare for the greatest slaughter and carnage wrought upon the earth by a lone man. In time it will all be mine. I want to kill a lot of girls. Who knows the number of the dead? Who shall be spared? Not one . . .

October 25, 1992

I've seen so many fine chicks at Wal Mart today. They all would be nice to follow. First as practice, then for real. Probably won't be writing much. I want this book to last until June.

I just want to kill a girl so bad I can't think of anything else. When I see one, fine, in public I look at her ass and think of pulling off her shorts, fucking them in the ass, turning her over, tying her up, spreading her legs, eating her pussy, then biting her inner thighs, fucking her pussy, and biting her nipples off and chewing them up and eating them, then cut her inner thighs and put salt and acid in them while fucking her in the ass, cutting her ass, then stab her in her pussy and the thighs.

My life: It's been about chasing girls, finding the one to rape and kill. Rape is not enough. I must have a body for the next day or two, to hold, talk to and make love. Bones to talk with. Burial sites to remember, towns in fear.

A fear that one can feel in the air. The body would keep me satisfied for a small season. The bones will cry to me from the earth. Their sorrow is my joy. Their tears my fountain of youth. Society's children's blood is mine. To all the girls and women who have crossed my eyes, may we cross paths in time. Those who know me, feel privileged. Those who mock and defy me, be warned . . .

I would like to kill some one, anyone, almost. I'd just love to beat someone's fuckin' brains out of their fuckin' skull. Women, bitches of the earth. All these fuckin' whores from hell with the damning curses. I hate them. They are all responsible for the death of countless.

Rita, a fuckin' whore, she gave me herpies. Fat, noisy women bitches, I hate them. They must die as well as the daughters. It's written in Esekiel 16:35. They're the ones who curse me, the ones who don't acknowledge me, those who laugh at me, those who play shy games. I'll kill as many as I can.

Mostly I just want a truck or car and women to stalk, women to murder, mutilate and have sex with. I've found out there are few "good" girls anymore. Most girls over 18 have had multiple sex partners. Whores deserve to die.

Saturday, November 21, 1992

I remember the time I was going to kill Tessie . . . I blame myself for not doing it. She just didn't walk by at the right time or I would have grabbed her and stabbed her. I'm glad I didn't, or that gray car would have seen me. That's been near two years ago.

Now it's Barbara's turn. I remember how she said "ohhh" when I bought her the little rabbit. I remember how she fed it with a bottle, and I just wish she would reconsider. She gave me a chance but Rita fucked it up real good, forever. I'll ask Barbara to run off with me when I get her. Rita will be the lucky one if she don't end up dead. I'll kill her, too. Murder, it's hard to be patient for a victim.

November 25, 1992

Tomorrow is Thanksgiving. Almost all my family will be there. It's going to be nice to see everyone. I would like to see Dad thanksgiving.

But I'm sure "they" all have their own little deal so I won't interfere. I guess I just love the holiday seasons. The winter, too, all in one. I don't know if it's the air that in winter I get a deja vue feeling and my urges to get sexy women, murder and rape grows. I know my chances to ever marry Barbara is almost nil, a better chance of killing her.

Thanksgiving, Thursday, November 26, 1992

I asked my "Dad" to come out tonight. He said no. It pisses me off. I love him, and he, too, seems to push me away. Fuck him! I'll give him one more chance, then to hell with him. I might as well forget buying dad's truck.

. . . I clearly see myself emerging into a serial killer. Life on the road? I don't know. I know I want to kill over and over again. Right now I'd be happy to just be able to go creepin'. really, I need to stay to myself. At work, on the streets, all the way around. Just save my money and keep on moving ahead.

Monday, November 30, 1992

Last night I dreamt I raped a 14-year-old at knife-point. I think it was Maurine. I forgot to write about the dream where I shot Ashly in the head with a Uzi. My dreams speak of my desires. December is a day off. The time for conquest is approaching.

Wednesday, December 2, 1992

Here's something not to forget. Women are fighting back against attack. So I must choose very carefully.

I'd imagine, those found in bars or in town, wherever that might be, those seen drunk or drinking would be good choice. Lack of self-respect badly indicates somewhat of a carefree type. Always be extremely careful when attacking. The best choices would be those who are confident that they can take care of themselves, those who are drunk. Maybe not the best choices but easiest to get in my car. I guess I'd be safe to choose one and follow home and learn everything about. But for now Barb is my true love. Mildred? My first kill? I hope.

I'd like to fuck her, I'll have to fuck her dead because I'll have to kill her her as soon as I knock her out and 'cuff her. I might have to with Barb, depending on how long the stun [gun] works. As long as I'm able to inject her, I'll be able to bring her here.

If I'm cool enough, I'll inject Mildred, too. That's what I really need to do so I can see how many hours a stun and 4 Phenobarbital will produce.

This will work, *I'll be having a lot of fun with her in the woods. First take off her top, then pants and panties. Then fuck her (when she awakes, fuck her more), then bite off her nipples. Then bite her pussy, thighs, clit, then fuck her, then strangle 'til passes out, then when awake fuck her in the ass, before coming cut her throat.*

Thursday, December 3, 1992

I had another murderous dream. I killed a lady's two boys and herself, Sex and death with girls is what I want.

I had a dream I killed Lois and cut her throat viciously in a bath tub. I did it so hard it cut myself.

These younger girls? It's their vibes they give off of a care-free, laughing, fun, outgoing, life's-a-party, cheer leader type with long, dark hair, a lot of laughs and smiles that attract me, innocents. There are so many I have on my list. It's sex and destruction of young girls. I want one NOW! I hate wait-ing. If I had a chance I'd do one now. Being this desperate is dangerous.

I've noticed something when I kill cats and dogs. I believe the same is true of people. Some will fight like hell. Most just fight a little good bit. But a few hardly fight at all. They just accept death and go on to the other side. Some won't accept it until life is completely gone.

Basically, even though I do know whom I might be killing, I don't know how they'll fight. So before the attempt, security and death for them must be certain.

Sunday, January 3, 1993

I worry about killing a girl before sometime I shouldn't because within the next year or 5 months I will do Barb. As much as I think of murder, I will end up doing it. Right now I'm just beginning to form as a serial killer. Who knows, I might end up killing one today or next week. Who's to say? One thing certain, I know what I must do. . .

Something's happening to me. I think the Holy Spirit is working on me. It kinda offends me. I believe I'm very demon-possessed.

The only reason Satan has not killed me is his demons rest in me. Powerful ones . . . I feel like I'm losing my mind. I want to die and I want to live to kill. Barbara is fuckin' up my life. She's driving me crazy. If I don't kill her, I'll just fuckin' lose it. Whatever it takes. It don't matter any more. She hates me. If I can go with Plan A, great. If not I'll just catch her walking home and blow her fuckin' brains out. I can't give up. It's just hard for me to have a relationship with any woman.

It just seems a lot easier and appealing to pull a gun on her, tie her up, rape her, drink blood and all the other things I want to do than to have a relationship. I'd rather have it this way, too.

I don't know. Maybe she really likes me. I think my drinking is what, in part, made me lose Barbara. Damn, this little bitch has really done a number on me . . . I'll have a car in April, just in time. I never want to grow old and fall into the endless circle of society. and I don't want to be poor all my life neither. I'll go the Army when I turn 24. Before it, I'll have some fun creeping. Summer of '95 is what's going to be hell on the women in N.E.

Texas. One day far into the future people will say I knew Jason, I worked with him, he lived by me at so and so. People will be astonished by the sheer numbers that are dead. The media, film, I'll have it all. I can't explain it all here. Will just have to live it, day-to-day.

Thursday, January 14, 1993
The Final Solution
This morning I have come up with the master plan. It is truly the final solution. I don't recall a plan so devious and ingenious, too, I've ever made. I'm sure it will work.

It's hard to realistically visualize murdering her sometimes. *I can see it, my making her put on the perfume, taking off her clothes, making love under the covers and stars above. I love thinking of her crying, tasting her tears once again, feeling her breath, her breast. Before I bury her I'm going to strangle her, then fuck her again, fuck her brains out literally. I'm going to eat some of her brain, heart, cut out her pussy to fuck later, then after preparation eat it and her ovaries, stab her inner thighs, breast, butt. I'm going to go ahead and live out my fantasy, this one last time with her. While she lives I'll do this all. I'll show her just how I love her so and how sick old Jay is.*

I see Doris crying, wondering . . . why? Saying I don't understand. If I could only tell her it's O.K. She nor anyone understood how I love her. I see the kids asking, "Mama, when is Barb coming home?"

"I don't know . . . Mama just don't know, babe."

Then she'll begin to cry. Tears not comparable to Barbara's. Nor to mine, for I'll always love her and miss her dearly. Same question asked by Barbara: "Why are you doing this, Jay? Why?"

Well, it's a good question, one many will ask. Why? Why so many? Why so much pain? Why my daughter? Why, Jason, why?

January 16, 1993

I went to the woods today to put my trophies out there. Also I want to plant my tree in a high place. It's a lookout, a place of rest and of retreat, a place to think. It's another special place of mine, all my own . . .

I guess I really need to write my feeling in this book more than my plans, so someday someone might understand.

[Undated entry:]

Kissed her 'bye at 8:13. Anyhow, I really like her a lot [new girlfriend named Marti]. She's got fine legs, a fine ass, very fine. Nice size tits, too. I don't know when we'll be able to do anything. I need to budget, I really do, girlfriend or not. I really get off thinking of [Marti] putting on the blood-soaked gloves I use to skin "Baldy." Dog #31. Any way, it just goes to show. *No* one really knows Jason Massey. [Marti] also told me her mother never lets boys in her room. I'm privileged, I guess. I just hope we're together for a while, at least 3 months. I believe we'll have sex in that time. If not, I'll continue to date her for social reasons. I need to keep a good, damn good, rep and at the same time, some way people must know when J. M. says something, don't fuckin' question him.

Sunday, January 24, 1993

I went to church this morning. Anyhow, I went to [Marti's] at 3 P.M.. We went to the lake.

She was talking shit on what I said Friday. I love you. Won't say it no more. We did a lot of French kissin' today. She made my dick hard. I played with her hair and shit. I held her for a while. It was good.

I got invited for supper. I thanked her. After she said that shit at the lake I began to wonder, will I ever be able to have a normal relationship with a woman or anyone. Will I ever lose the desires to roam and kill. I don't understand it. I guess it will always be there like my drinking problem. . . .

If [Marti] doesn't give up her pussy by one week after her return from Kentucky, I'm finished with her. I'll never be able to fuck her without a rubber, or any other living girl.

Tuesday, January 26, 1993

I had a O.K. day at work today. I'm working 38 hours this week. That's good. I went to [Marti's] again today. We made out. She began to talk about marriage, kids, the whole bit. I'm not ready. I want to get a car, go to the Army and finish it, then go to getting things going, setting myself up for life. I think she really likes me. I think she was also hinting at marriage. She says she give "it" 'til the first or end of summer. I think she means marriage. I don't want to until the Army, but I don't want to lose her. But my career is more important. I love her though, but Barb must be done. I've got so much to do I haven't time to write. I guess things will be easier in July.

Wednesday, January 27, 1993

I really like [Marti]. I don't want her to think I don't. I don't think I'll ever be able to marry, have a sexual relationship with a woman. My path I've chosen, I'll just have to walk different. Sober. It's the only way. [Marti] and I don't know where we're going. She likes me. She thinks I'm going to ask her to marry me. I'm not. Not ready.

Things are going good for me now. But there is still Barb. I'm not sure I'll be ready in June. I might do it, I have much work to do yet. Though I've accomplished much there is yet more progress to be made. My reputation is being "healed." Me paying Granny back there did a lot. She didn't think I'd pay her back. I'll do more, too, this spring. I'll mow her yard, wax her car and go to church.

I'm in good with everyone except me, Jesus, I guess. But he

knows my heart and I've asked forgiveness and for steps G.H.
E.G. is proud of me, too; ma, too. Hell, I'm proud of myself.

Monday, February 8, 1993

*I went today and seen the place where 34th and Chambers
Creek meet . . . There's a car wash in Avalon and Italy . . .* I've
found out that I can go into any small town, join a church as
soon as possible. I believe there are many things I need to do,
first stay straight. There are so many things I want, too. I want
a car, I want to go to the Army, but I'm scared I'll be called to
go into war. Because Jesus Christ will come and all hell will
literally break loose.

I guess if I do I'll work on getting a medal. I'm working on
a good Ted [Bundy] image. It's going to take time . . .

Wednesday, February 17, 1993.

I went to see my P.O. Everything is O.K... No U.A. [urinaly-
sis]. Thank God in heaven. Anyway, I've found my car. *It's a
1976 Toyato. It is also 4-speed.*

Thursday, February 18, 1993

I wish I could just do her and get it over so I can get on with
my life. It's all about my career. I just want to drive and never
stop, just keep moving when and where I want.

If I'm persistent in my efforts, I'll be able to start my career
with Barb. After her I'll just save, travel here in Ellis County.
I'm sure "they" will watch for a while, 6 months I'd say. I think
the killings have almost begun. I can feel it. Who knows how
many or for how long? I just know I'll get Barbara. *But when I
get my car in April, I'll see if I can't do some out of town, this
summer.* I don't need to drink to kill. I think my drinking is
definitely over. I pray to God for it to be.

I don't know exactly when or where but I know in my heart, I will abduct, rape, torture and kill Barbara. Then stay with her corpse the night and make love to her, then sleep 'til noon or so, play with her body for more sex; before sundown sex once more, then I must dismember her for eating, then behead her. Finally disembowel her before burying her, and of course, sexually fantasy.

I don't know if I'll ever be able to carry on a relationship after or during my killing. But I'll keep on going because I have to walk through the pain. I'm sure others will be easy. For one I won't know or love them as I do Barbara.

Wednesday, March 10, 1993

I've been reading *The Stranger Beside Me* [book on killer Ted Bundy by Ann Rule]. It's inspiring. But I worry about becoming disorganized and rampant as Ted was in his last days. It's certainly something to consider. But now I just look forward to getting a car, freedom and a feeling of manhood should engulf me. [Marti] is a problem maybe for the best, who knows. Beside I don't need to travel as soon as I get my car. If I do it will be in Dallas to watch Barbara.

This book is over now. It's been a year since I left Rita. I have a job, a girl, D.L, glasses and a car. So now I'm kinda starting a new campaign. This one is not only for just Barbara. There's some things to be done first. My car fixed up good. I need to get insurance and to play my Ted image really well.

Later this month, I go bury this. It's all for Barbara. In Bk 5 I won't mention her name. This is where everything's coming together. I'll just be glad when I get to rape Barb and kill her and get it over with. I hope I'm ready in August. I still have much to do. I've changed a lot since I wrote in here the first time. I've learned a lot.

I'll continue to study criminal investigations and serial murder and all. If I keep clean by the time Bk 6 is over with I'll be getting off probation. My appearance is on a upswing. May it all come to pass. I want to kill over and over again and years of it, hundreds of victims.

I believe Bk 5 will see many things. My car, Barbara's death and a start of the wandering period. The murder will begin. Next summer will be worse on them than this one and the summer of '95 will be the worst year for Ennis, Texas ever!

March 15, 1993

I'm really changing. I have more love than I've had in a long time. I'm still scared God's going to take me home before I am ready. If so what can I do but pray. It seems God will return soon. I've really been shining my shoes lately. I'm fitting into the personality I chose. I still think of sex and death. My fantasies grow violent. I followed some one for the first time today. Did damn good, even though I lost 'em.

I don't know if I really do love anyone or if I've become accustomed to mimicking those feelings. It's a great disguise.

Killing girls, for sex and death, is what I live for. I just love to think of it. I guess the thought of getting away with it is what excites me.

Plus the violent fantasies of cutting throats in intercourse.

The face, gasping for air. Then death, more sex, cuddling. How romantic to drink wine in the moon light with a candle, watching her turn pale, blue, cold, sleeping all cuddled up with her.

I might get lucky April 30-May 18th. Polka fest [local festival] will produce many drunks. Hopefully girls whom I might get into my car, who I might kill. The same when school's out. *Summer of '93, yep, made for me.*

Wednesday, March 24, 1993

Three more weeks and I have a car. If I stop hanging with the guys, I've been spending like stupid shit with them.

Well, this book is really getting short. When I get my car, *the first day I will go to bury these books* and get a new one. I'll do it all Friday, I guess.

Wednesday, April 8, 1993

I do have a car. It's in my name, too. I owe $100. I have the title. It needs some work, but I'll get it going. I already fucked it up. Some shit in the gears. I need to get some money in the bank first, then I'll save to get it fixed. I'm happy. I'll be ready for Barbara by the time it's fixed, so no need to worry. I know it's going to take some time and patience.

Saturday, April 10, 1993

I went to church last night and told Buck a lot of me. I said no names. I told him about my attempted rape. All the Satanism or worship in this case.

Anyway, I love the Lord. To hell with Satan and his army. The same with drugs. I will not alter my conscience with that shit. Any of it. I've been saved. I still want Barbara. I want to marry her. If it ever happens, it will be of God. I still want to kill. Maybe just Barbara.

Tuesday, April 13, 1993

I have my car fixed and running. I got it fixed the 9th. [Marti] and I had a big talk yesterday. About me never seeing her. Her mom's pissed. She was talking shit. She has a right to be mad. I've been fucking up with her myself, too. My money, and fucking with drugs a little. . . .

Acknowledgments

I want to thank law enforcement officers, officials, and others in Ellis County, TX., and the towns of Ennis and Waxahachie, who helped me during my research there on this book. As well as all of the friendly people in the Waxahachie library, and in restaurants, drugstores, and motels on the square and throughout the town.

The authorities included Lt. Royce Gothard, commander of the Criminal Investigation Division of the Ellis County Sheriff's Department at Waxahachie, whose tireless work on the case landed him in the hospital; criminal investigator Johnny Cruz, a youthful detective who was the lead investigator in the slayings; investigator Brian Thompson, evidence technician; and others on the able staff of Ellis County Sheriff John Gage.

The sheriff's homicide crew and prosecutors paid tribute to the important forensic work of Dr. Sheila Spotswood, pathologist in the Dallas County Medical Examiner's Office; Charles Lynch, evidence technician with the Southwest Institute of Forensic Science in Dallas; Michelle Skidmore, a forensic serologist with SIFS; Jan Resnizek, a DNA expert with the Institute; Mike DeGuglielmo, a DNA expert in Greensboro, N.C.; and a noted forensic entomologist, Dr. Neal H. Haskell of Purdue University, as well as agents of the FBI's Behavioral Science Investigation Support Unit at Quantico, Va.

The officers and prosecutors were grateful for the assistance of Dr. Kenneth Dekleva, a Dallas psychiatrist.

Also, my thanks to Joe Grubbs, the 40th Judicial District Attorney and his excellent staff—notably Clay Strange, the assistant district attorney who spearheaded the prosecution of Jason Massey. Strange supplied me with detailed background information, especially about the DNA evidence in the trial. He now is Unit Director, Criminal Prosecution Division, DNA Legal Assistance Unit of the American Prosecutors Research Unit, National District Attorneys Association at Alexandria, Va.

Also, my appreciation for the excellent help of Assistant DAs Lacy Buckingham, Cindy Hellstern, Kamala Cromer, Bobbi Reilly and investigator Phillip Martin of the district attorney's staff, who took time and showed patience with this writer.

My admiration for the work of Massey's competent defense attorneys appointed by the court, Mike Hartley and Mike Griffith of Waxahachie, who fought hard for their client against great evidentiary odds.

Thanks also to District Clerk Billie A. Fuller and her fine staff, who through their expert help made my long research hours in the old Waxahachie Courthouse pleasant.

Also, to John Knight, a former captain and administrator of the Ellis County Detention Center, who confirmed that Massey admitted to the slayings on his trip to the Texas Death Row when Knight was doing his best to find out what happened to the missing remains of the girl victim, hoping to put at ease somewhat the members of the girl's family.

A salute goes also to Police Chief Dale Holt and Detective Ron Roark of the Ennis Police Department, who helped provide information to the Ellis County sheriff's investigators.

Also thanks to Jeane Bellows of Adams, NY, Christina's grandmother, who provided me insight into the beautiful and warm nature of Christina Benjamin as a baby, a little girl and a teenager.

And to Sue Wickliffe of Ennis, Jason's devoted grandmother who, while beset by grievous circumstances and personal heartbreak, recalled for me her grandson as a kid who had a hard time but never was the "monster" so many made him out to be, and who is convinced that Massey now is a sincere repentant Christian.

I'd like to thank Mike Moore of Amarillo, expert computer technician who made my word processor regurgitate 39 pages of manuscript that it gobbled up one dismal day.

I am grateful for the work of Editor in Chief Paul Dinas and Consulting Editor Karen Haas on this book.

And, finally but certainly not least, I want to express my deep appreciation for the help of my wife Nina, who found the book's subject matter abhorrent but still provided me the accurate copy reading talents of her newspaper city editor days. Not to mention her patience and endurance to withstand the stress from my writing temperament.

—Bill Cox